EMILY HILDA YOUNG

(1880–1946) was born in Northumberland, the daughter of a ship-broker. She was educated at Gateshead High School and Penrhos College, Colwyn Bay, Wales. In 1902, after her marriage to a solicitor, J. A. H. Daniell, she went to live in Bristol, which was to become the setting of most of her novels. Her first, *A Corn of Wheat*, was published in 1910, followed by *Yonder* (1912), and *Moor Fires* (1916).

During the First World War Emily Young worked in a munitions factory, and as a groom in a local stables. However, after her husband's death at Ypres in 1917 she left Bristol for London, going to live with a married man, Ralph Henderson, Head Master of Alleyn's School in Dulwich. She continued to write. *The Misses Mallett*, published originally as *The Bridge Dividing*, appeared in 1922, preceding her most successful novel, *William* (1925). Then came *The Vicar's Daughter* (1928), *Miss Mole* (1930) – winning the James Tait Black Memorial Prize, *Jenny Wren* (1932), *The Curate's Wife* (1934) and *Celia* (1937). She lived with the Henderson's in South London until Ralph Henderson's retirement at the time of the Second World War when he and E. H. Young went, alone, to live in Bradford-on-Avon, Wiltshire. Here Emily Young wrote two children's books, *Caravan Island* (1940) and *River Holiday* (1942), and one further novel, *Chatterton Square*, published in 1947, two years before her death from lung cancer at the age of sixty-nine.

Virago publish *The Misses Mallett*, *William*, *The Vicar's Daughter*, *Miss Mole*, *Jenny Wren*, *The Curate's Wife*, *Celia* and *Chatterton Square*.

VIRAGO
MODERN
CLASSIC

NUMBER

375

E. H. Young

THE VICAR'S DAUGHTER

Published by VIRAGO PRESS Limited 1992
20–23 Mandela Street, Camden Town, London NW1 0HQ

First published in Great Britain by Jonathan Cape Ltd. 1928
Copyright © E. H. Young 1928

A CIP catalogue record for this book is available from the British Library

Printed in Great Britain by Cox & Wyman Ltd, Reading, Berks.

Contents

Chapter 1: *Maurice*

THE REVEREND MAURICE ROPER had been for a long walk and he was tired, but it was not fatigue which made him walk so slowly along the broad asphalt pavement which edged New Framling beach; and a person sensitive to beauty would not willingly have lingered near the ugly line of boarding-houses and hotels on his right hand, the penny-in-the-slot machines, the iron seats, the litter on the fine sand, never reached by the sea, and the deserted, exhausted appearance of a place which had lately been thronged with holiday-makers.

It was an evening in late September and the sun, setting brilliantly, seemed to be finding a malicious pleasure in illuminating these sordid sights, in shining on the Reverend Maurice's eye-glasses and making him blink, so that, if he would, he could not see the derisive beauty in the sky or the little village of Old Framling, huddled under its white cliffs, towards which he was making his way. He was not troubled, however, by the ugliness near him or by his inability to watch the gorgeous departure of the sun: he was merely postponing his return to Old Framling Vicarage. He walked with his head bent, his feet turned out, his hands clasped behind him, and now and then the sun struck a spark from the narrow watch-chain and pendant cross on his somewhat rounded waistcoat. He was thinking with distaste of another solitary evening. He had been living in the Vicarage for nearly two months and daily the pressure of his loneliness had increased; yet when he remembered that it was almost over and to-morrow he would see his cousins, he was filled with a more painful apprehension. He wished he had arranged to go before

7

they came back. He had arrived to take over the care of the parish on the first day of their summer holiday. They had started early in the morning and he had reached Old Framling at night, entering a house in which their invisible presences seemed to linger, and when they failed to materialize he felt both disappointment and relief. He had not lost that consciousness of their neighbourhood as the days passed and his feelings remained complex: desire mingled with dread, affection with resentment, happy memories with bitter: it was one of his misfortunes that he seldom had a simple emotion: his pleasure was nearly always marred by nervousness, his happiness streaked with more disturbing hope, and his stay in Old Framling had not fulfilled its peaceful promise.

He stood still and dabbed his forehead with his handkerchief. He was not strong and the air was hot. He had walked too far, driven by restlessness. There was nothing to do in the parish and he could not be easy in the house where he constantly expected to hear a laugh or a footfall, not those of the two servants who treated him with a distant courtesy, but those of the ghosts who would not materialize. He was made to feel an alien in the house. He had been disappointed in the behaviour of the servants, for, as the Vicar's cousin, he was entitled to a certain friendliness, and it had been refused: they did their duty without a fault, but his advances had been evaded and he knew they were comparing him unfavourably with Edward; he saw, too late, that his propitiatory and slightly playful manner had been a mistake.

He sighed and walked on slowly. He was always making mistakes of that kind. In his own parish, it was different: there he had his recognised position and it gave him confidence; but here he seemed to move in a shadow cast by Edward, who was popular, vigorous, natural, everything that Maurice himself was not. Edward was certainly natural, he thought bitterly, unless

8

he was much changed, and Margaret, whom he had not seen for twenty years, what was she? She had been gay then, and very beautiful in his eyes, and now she was middle-aged and he supposed her charm had gone. For his own sake he hoped it had, but here again his feelings were confused: he did not want to lose a precious cause of enmity for Edward, while it was uncomfortable and improper to look covetously at the wife of another man. Yes, he wished he could vanish as he had come, without a sight of these people who had always so much occupied his thoughts. Of Margaret, indeed, he had thought dutifully little since her marriage, and he had found it easier than it was pleasant to confess; but to live in her house, to find traces of her personality everywhere and, at the same time, to find fresh reasons for disapproval of Edward, had been to revive the memory of the only girl he had ever wished to marry. The remembered fervency of that wish varied with his moods, and when he learnt that she was far from active in her husband's parish, he decided that the Hand of God had dealt lightly with him in this matter, after all; and as he looked round the house he became sure of what he had always feared: she was frivolous, she was luxurious and she was lazy; she was no fit wife for a hard-working parish priest. That, perhaps, was Edward's fault. Maurice was glad to blame Edward as often as possible, yet when he thought of Margaret's mouth and eyes, he doubted whether any man could have changed her, or wished her changed: he knew that he would have found it impossible himself, and it enraged him to think he had cared for a woman who only looked at him to laugh.

It was the elderly widow who looked after him at first, while the servants were having their holiday, who betrayed Margaret's indifference to parish affairs, and of her he made tactful inquiries about Edward also, and the widow, unlike the servants, was ready to talk. Mr. Stack, it appeared, was considered a satisfactory vicar, and though the widow was not equal to explaining his doctrinal position, Maurice could make a guess at that. He had seen the books in Edward's study. He had not read them, for he did not flirt with heresy, but he had heard of them, and their authors and their presence proved the correctness of his suspicions: Edward was lax in his beliefs and, while nothing divulged by the widow showed any laxity of conduct, Maurice nodded his head wisely and his eye-glasses wobbled: he knew what came of intellectual doubt. He wondered if John Blunt had seen those books. John Blunt, who lived in the gaunt house on the other side of the road, was the Vicar's churchwarden, and about him Maurice was to develop almost as much curiosity as about Edward. John Blunt was reputed to be rich, though of frugal habits, and very regular in his attendance at church, and that was all the information the widow offered. She was less well informed than Maurice could have wished, but he missed her when she went. She was what he called a pleasant, body and she had been interested in his health, not with the cheerful heartlessness of the strong, but with a real concern and a curiosity for details.

It was Maurice's ill-health which had brought him to Old Framling. He and Edward seldom met, but a funeral or a wedding sometimes brought them together, and it was at one of these family gatherings that Maurice mentioned his recent illness and received, at once, the offer of the charge of Old Framling during August and September. It would be practically a holiday, Edward said, and the sea-air would do him good, and Maurice, touched by this kindness, had accepted gladly and promised to prolong his stay until the Stacks' return. Kindness from Edward had always pleased him more than anything else in the world since the day when, a thin-legged, spectacled little orphan, he had arrived to spend his holidays in the Stacks' home. He had spent all the succeeding holidays of his childhood and young manhood there and Edward had been his hero from the first. Maurice would have died for him, if he could have done it without physical pain, and Edward had no suspicion of this devotion, still less of the bitter grief and resentment of the small boy he ignored or teased or snubbed, with the careless cruelty of a child, or took into a temporary favour which Maurice believed was to last for ever.

All this could have been forgiven, though Maurice would still have remembered every single hurt, every tear he dropped in secret, and sorrow he concealed, if Edward's offences had passed with boyhood; but when Maurice was no longer teased and buffeted, he was still repulsed, good-naturedly, yet with the determination of an adolescent who would frankly discuss anything under the sun, physical or mental, with his peers, but shrank from Maurice's delicate approaches and his sudden embarrassing confidences under slight encouragement. Maurice was bewildered, and he remained resentful: it became a habit to set down all his disadvantages to Edward's count. It was Edward who had shaken his faith in himself at the most impressionable time of his life; Edward was the one friend he had wanted and Margaret the one woman, and Edward had offered him a kindly, tolerant cousinship and Margaret had married Edward. Yet it was impossible to kill that early admiration, for it was an actual part of his cherished bitterness: it was ready to spring up, full-blooded, if it had a chance, and, with his usual hopefulness, Maurice had seen the chance in this visit to Old Framling. And, as usual, circumstances had been against him.

Maurice sat down on the last seat and looked mournfully at the sea. Quite smooth, like a dark mirror, it held the sunset colours dimly, and when Maurice glanced up he saw that the sun had gone. He rose reluctantly and took a diagonal path which cut across a narrow common and led to Old Framling bridge. Under the bridge ran the tidal river, on the other side was Old Framling village with its rising cobbled street, and just beyond the rise was the Vicarage. What Maurice saw as he went towards the bridge was the white cliff protecting the haven and a dark mass of cottages all plumed with smoke. These, inhabited by the fishermen, were built round the bay and on the ground which sloped up to the street, but between the street and them were bigger houses facing the Vicarage, and neater, larger cottages near the bridge. The walls of all these houses were flush with the pavement: the gardens lay behind and, in the case of the Vicarage, on each side of the house – too fine a house and too large a garden for a country vicar, in Maurice's opinion, and he thought of his own drab dwelling in a noisy street and took an unwarranted credit for it. He had to admit that Edward did not choose the Vicarage, but Margaret had certainly chosen the furniture. He was not deceived by its austerity: he knew that this was only a refinement of luxury and, if he had not known it, the chairs, the sofas and his bed were of a comfort which must have undeceived him: the colours of the cushions and the hangings had occupied the thought which should have been given to higher things. She was a worldly woman and she had been placed in the house which exactly suited her, a spacious house of a period antagonistic to all his feelings. He had a leaning towards the ecclesiastic in architecture, and he missed the beauty of this broad, low front in mellow brick, the wide door flanked by flat pillars and the square-paned windows in which some of the old glass remained, but he owned that the interior had its charm. It shocked him as Margaret had often done; it was, in fact, like the woman herself and it gave him the same uneasiness, compounded of pleasure and distrust.

Yet, he thought, as he crossed the bridge, walking faster, so that the flesh of his cheeks shook a little, becoming more alert and ready to expand his nervous smile for anyone who seemed to want it, who else but Margaret would have put that little nosegay on his dressing-table? She must have picked the flowers before she left that morning. She had found time to fill a little bowl with purple pansies – heart's-ease, some people called them – and she might have put them there in mockery, so little heart's ease had he known since his arrival. Margaret was quick enough to mock, but even she would hardly find amusement in what had chiefly troubled him, and he liked to think the flowers had been put there in welcome. And to-morrow he would see her. To-morrow the people he met on the stairs and in the rooms would be made of flesh and blood as well as memories: the laughter and the footsteps and the voices would be real, and he did not know whether he more longed or dreaded to hear them.

He paused in front of the Vicarage door and cast a hasty glance across the road before he turned the handle and stepped into the house.

Chapter 2: *Hilary*

HE did not advance. He had expected to find the hall as silent as it had always been, save for the ticking of the grandfather clock and the discreetly muffled sounds from the kitchen, to see the lamplight shining on nothing more than the rich but soberly hued rug, the polished table, the chair with the curved legs, and he was prepared to utter the little warning cough with which, half consciously, he marked his entrances before he walked stealthily up the stairs of this house in which he was a stranger and made himself tidy for the meal which Alice, with her professional aloofness, turned into a ceremony, but he stood on the threshold, astonished by the sight of a young girl playing with a young dog on the disordered rug.

A nervous tremor ran over his whole body and surreptitiously he wiped his hands against his trousers. This must be Margaret's daughter! He knew, of course, of the existence of a child, but he had never properly realized it, or wished to do so, and his surprise at seeing her in the flesh was overwhelmed by his annoyance that the Stacks had not given him notice of their earlier arrival. He braced himself for this sudden meeting with Margaret and Edward, as the girl rose and came forward, smiling gravely, and trying with one hand to restrain the bounding dog while she held out the other,

'I'm Hilary Stack,' she said.

'Hilary? Of course, of course!' He glanced towards the shadowy corners of the hall. 'But I thought – I understood that you were not coming till to-morrow.' He made an effort and smiled widely. 'A delightful surprise!' he exclaimed, while all his attention was for the sound of approaching footsteps.

Hilary interpreted his manner with disconcerting readiness. 'I've come alone,' she said, and Maurice felt the slackening of his tightened muscles.

'Alone?' he repeated, breathing a little quickly.

She nodded. 'Because of the dog. I couldn't take him to Aunt Agatha's. Father and Mother have gone there for the night. She wouldn't have liked the dog. She has a lot of cats and she would have been in such a fuss. Mother said it would do her good, but I wasn't going to risk having him locked into a coal-cellar.'

'He certainly seems rather a restless animal,' Maurice said, looking down and wagging his head.

'He is, but he's young. Oh, mind your eye-glasses!' she cried.

He felt them. 'What's the matter?'

'I thought they were going to fall off,' she explained. 'I thought they looked rather wobbly, but then,' she said comfortingly, 'this light is rather bad.'

It was good enough, however, to reveal her as a very attractive young person with fair, shining hair, a large mouth rather like her mother's and a delicately tilted nose. There was something, too, faintly reminiscent of Margaret in the way she fondled and, at the same time, controlled the dog; but Margaret had never had this look of virginal innocence, which Maurice, influenced by the slightly impudent little nose, immediately suspected, as he had always suspected Margaret's amused look of wisdom.

'You see,' Hilary was saying, 'we go every summer to see Aunt Agatha, and she always says it will be the last time, so she'll be dreadfully offended with me, but it would have been worse if I'd taken the dog. I'm sorry to disappoint her, because she likes saying good-bye to people; in fact, that and the cats are her only pleasures; but I can do it specially well, next summer, to make up. Mother said I was to give her love to you and say she is looking forward to seeing you, and she hopes you have been comfortable.'

'Indeed I have,' Maurice answered, referring to his physical welfare only, for his mental distresses had been acute. 'No, no, get down. Good dog, good doggy!'

'I'm afraid you're not very fond of dogs, either,' Hilary said sadly.

'No, I'm – I'm not very fond of them.'

'He was given to me by a shepherd,' she said, 'an old man who knew Mother when she was a girl. There are such a lot of people who knew her when she was a girl – you did, too, didn't you? – but nobody else has ever rewarded me like this. I'll try to keep him in order, but he's so new that I don't like to be hard on him.'

'It would be better to begin at once,' Maurice said, in his pulpit voice, and he was gratified to see that it made some impression on Hilary. She had lowered her eyelids and seemed to be listening attentively, and even the dog, recognizing the tone of authority, remained quite still for a moment and studied the stranger. Then, with a calculated yawn, he displayed the red recesses of his mouth, gave his ears a shake and playfully began to worry Hilary's slippers.

'It would be wiser, certainly,' she said.

'And isn't that the same thing?' he asked and, murmuring something about preparing himself for dinner, he went towards the stairs. He had not expected an answer to his question, and it was with some irritation that he heard Hilary taking up what he had intended as a statement and not a suggestion.

'I don't know,' she said. 'Not always. It sounds right, but I wonder if it is.'

He turned then and looked down at her. Standing half in the light and half in the shade, she seemed to be a person divided into two parts, just as those last words had separated her from the girl who had been talking with so much simplicity about the dog.

She smiled up at him. 'You can tell me while we're having dinner.'

He thought he detected a hint of mockery in those

16

words. They were like an echo of one of Margaret's remarks, uttered so quietly and in so sweet a voice that a man was betrayed into confidences before he saw the subdued mirth in her eyes; but Hilary's eyes, though blue like Margaret's, were lighter, clearer, with no mischief in them, the eyes of a trustful child. And perhaps she was really trustful: he must not read too much of her mother into her, and he smiled back playfully.

'Perhaps, perhaps,' he said, and stepped upward, but again he paused. 'And your father? Did he send any message, any instructions connected with the parish?'

Hilary laughed and shook her head. 'I don't believe he's thought once about the parish since we went away. Anyhow, he hasn't mentioned it. If he did that, Mother would soon stop him. She doesn't like this place, you know; she doesn't like the sea,' she said gravely. 'But she loves the house. Don't you think it's a beautiful house?'

'Yes,' Maurice said, 'I suppose it is.'

He went slowly to his room. He was agitated by this encounter, by his few seconds of nervous anticipation and the succeeding disappointment. His intense effort had left him shaky and it had been wasted: it would have to be made again to-morrow and, dismayed, he sat down on his bed in the dark. It was inconsiderate of the Stacks not to have warned him, and he was not sure that it was proper to send Hilary in advance like this. And how was he to entertain her, to behave towards her during the next twenty-four hours? He knew nothing about young girls, he was afraid of them, and this one had the unembarrassed manners of her generation. She was a pretty girl, slim and straight, like a young tree, and with the frankness of a boy, but he would have preferred a little bashfulness and the necessity to put her at her ease would have ensured his own. Then, impatiently, he reminded himself of his forty-five years and of her youth: it would be strange if a man of his experience could not deal with a girl like that, and he began to hum, tonelessly, while he lit his candle.

By its light, he saw a face that startled him. He had not looked at it with another person's eyes for twenty years, and now he saw it with Hilary's – a plump face, with an appearance of health and happiness which, unfortunately, was false, a wide, thin-lipped mouth, a fold of flesh under the chin, scanty fair hair, and rather pale blue eyes behind the eye-glasses which, truly enough, always slanted at a dangerous angle. There was no doubt about his middle-age and he could be no object of interest to Hilary – or to Margaret. He sighed. Perhaps he had been wrong in thinking the eye-glasses gave him dignity, and he changed them for his spectacles. These widened his face, made him look more benevolent, almost jolly, he thought, and they were more comfortable, but he took them off. He could not allow Hilary to think her words had influenced him: on the other hand, he would never again feel happy about his eye-glasses. He wondered how many other people had shared her apprehension and, in the panic of the super-sensitive, he saw all his past efforts nullified by an absurd effect of which he had been unconscious. In future he must wear his spectacles. He would put them in his pocket this evening, and make the change carelessly, as though he were accustomed to varying these tiresome aids to his defective eyesight, and gradually the red marks on the sides of his nose would disappear: perhaps they would hardly show by this time to-morrow evening.

This decision cheered him, and the sound of Hilary running up the stairs, the dog scampering after her, brought a slight smile to his lips. It was long since he had lived in a house where such sounds were possible and this was a pleasant change from the loneliness of his late evenings. Outside his own Vicarage, children and dogs played in the street, but not since his youth had he experienced that family life which he so earnestly recommended in his sermons. It was not his fault. He had a great capacity for affection, though he knew he did not inspire it, and as he stood, with a clean collar in his hand, he had another of his hopeful moments. How charming it would be if he and Hilary could establish a pretty friendship, like that of an uncle and a favourite niece! It would be delightful to have someone to spoil, some one who would humour him and make the best of him: it would be compensation for all he had suffered at the hands of her father and in the loss of her mother. Then he groaned aloud, as was his habit in distress. He no sooner saw a chance of happiness than it was taken from him, and thus it had always been, for how would Hilary look upon the man whose duty might force him to inflict misery on her parents? But was it duty or was it inclination? He stared at the reflection of a bewildered clergyman who could not answer. Was God showing him the path he ought to take or putting temptation in his way? These were the questions which had been torturing him for weeks. His prayers for guidance had not been answered and, believing as he did that no honest prayer was ignored by God, he felt he was in the shadow of His displeasure. But why? Was it because he hesitated to do the difficult thing, or because, while he dreaded responsibility, he wished to do it, in revenge for all the slights he had endured and the jealousy he had known? And still he could not answer. He rejoiced in his possession of power and longed to be innocently rid of it: he knew that duty could not uphold him under kindness and that his inclination was liable to change, and when he went downstairs, it was in the hope that Hilary would tell him nothing which could soften his heart for Edward, so that duty could still be done with a clear conscience or mercy vouchsafed with credit to himself.

Chapter 3: *Maurice and Hilary*

HILARY was already in the drawing-room, sitting with her head bent over a book. The shaded light of a lamp on a table near her gave the room an air of charmed stillness; the flames of a small wood fire whispered to each other and made the buckles of her slippers glisten; her smooth hair shone in the lamplight. The rest of the room was in shadow, and in that shadow Maurice stood for a moment, looking at the girl and remembering how, long ago, he had watched her mother reading in a garden, with her dark head bent like Hilary's fair one, her eyelashes black against a pale cheek.

Hilary's eyelashes were a mixture of gold and brown and when she looked up her smile was welcoming. 'I've put the dog in the study,' she said. 'Oh, you've changed your trousers. I'm afraid he made the others rather hairy. Father won't mind the hairs because he'll never notice them!'

'But,' Maurice said awkwardly, and he wondered if those clear eyes missed anything, 'I don't mind them so very much either.'

'Besides, Mother said I wasn't to let him break the furniture, and he can't do any harm in the study unless he takes to chewing the books.'

'And that,' Maurice said, and he took off his eye-glasses, 'would not be a very serious matter.'

'Don't you like books?' she asked.

'I like the right kind,' he replied severely, and he took his spectacles from their case and adjusted them calmly. Pleased with the success of this little manœuvre, for Hilary was looking at the fire, soothed, without knowing it, by the charm of the room and her company, he began to walk, flat-footed, felt-slippered, to and fro behind her chair, making the half-hissing, half-humming noise of his more confident moments.

Across this strange sound Hilary's voice came clearly. 'But which is the right kind of book?' she inquired.

He controlled a sigh. It was evident that this young creature had a thirst for knowledge. 'Come, come,' he said, 'this isn't one of my weekly meetings for young men. You must let me have a holiday.'

'I don't want to worry you,' she said gravely. 'I thought you would be able to tell me straight off, without thinking.'

He had seen just such a look as hers on the face of the bad boy of a Sunday School class and he shook his head at her. She must not think she could deceive him, nor must he let her see that he was annoyed.

'Now why,' he asked gently, 'should you assume that I would speak without thinking?'

'I didn't mean that. I meant that you would know the answer.'

'I haven't ready-made answers for all the questions that are put to me.' He smiled. 'I'm not like the Catechism.'

'I've never read the Catechism,' Hilary said, 'except what is your name and who gave it to you. Not,' she hastened to assure him, 'because I wasn't allowed to. I've always been allowed to read anything I liked ever since I could read at all – even the Bible.'

Maurice sat down in the chair on the other side of the hearth, rested his elbows on the arms, his chin on his hands, and stared sombrely at Hilary. With her head lifted, her lips slightly parted, she was smiling at him as though she expected him to share her triumph in the broad-mindedness of her parents. 'Even the Bible,' he said.

'Yes, even the Old Testament. There's nothing in the New Testament that could hurt anybody, but I like the Old one much better, don't you? I like the poetry, and then, when you think of it, you think of hills and rocks and water and the cedars of Lebanon and wild asses and unicorns and eagles and snorting horses. But the New Testament makes me think of sand and aching feet, and that's absurd, because it's about the same country, I suppose; but it just shows what a good writer can do.'

'Did your mother or your father tell you all that?' he asked.

She frowned a little, not in anger, but in the endeavour to answer honestly. 'I don't know. I feel as if it was all my own idea, but one never knows how much one picks up from other people.'

'Germs,' Maurice suggested.

'Yes,' Hilary agreed pleasantly; 'and then they grow up and you imagine they were yours from the beginning.'

'I was thinking of bad germs, dangerous ones,' Maurice said.

'Yes, good and bad,' she agreed again.

He could not be sure whether she were wilful or merely stupid. She refused to take his hints in the way he meant them and, dropping this mode of attack, he asked boldly, without disguising his disapproval: 'And do I understand that you have not been confirmed?'

'Yes. But don't look so serious, Cousin Maurice! I can't see that it matters in the least.'

'I'm surprised,' Maurice said, gloomily. 'I'm surprised.' But his surprise was more for Edward's neglect of the conventions than for his indifference to them.

'Mother hasn't been,' Hilary told him, 'and great-uncle Alec, the one who brought her up, was a parson, too. And perhaps he wouldn't be confirmed now, if he could choose, or Father either.'

'I think you ought to be very careful what you say,' Maurice warned her, while he hoped she would say more.

'But not to you!' Hilary cried. 'Of course I shouldn't

be indiscreet to just anybody, but you are one of the family!'

He could not resist this compliment. He blinked, his mouth quivered, as he asked: 'Is that how you have been taught to think of me?'

She nodded. 'One of the germs! One of the good germs!' she said. 'And dinner's ready at last.'

'Then you must take my arm,' he said, with a clumsy, playful gallantry.

She took it, as she had talked, with complete natural-ness, and here they were, walking down the passage to the ʰ.ll whence the dining-room opened, like the uncle and the favourite niece. She had been taught to think of him as a member of the family, and though, it was evident, she had also been taught many things of which he disapproved, he was not proof against this sign of loyalty. He was glad that Alice should see them arm-in-arm and he hoped she would realize her under-estimation of his importance. He had a pride in the possession of this young cousin, and his own loyalty to the elders who had properly instructed her in one matter, at least, took pleasant control of him.

Smiling, his spectacles glinting in the candle-light, he sat in the chair opposite to hers, and he was hesitating in his choice among several appropriate remarks when he heard her say, with the manner of a hostess intro-ducing a subject sure to interest him, 'I am so sorry the Blunts have been in trouble.'

He looked up with a start. Now, who could have told her that, he asked himself, and what else did she know? No doubt the servants, who had kept him so rigidly in his place, and been ready enough with gossip for Hilary. He had not reckoned on that, and even in his anxiety he wondered what they had told her about himself.

'Oh, the Blunts?' he said. 'Yes, yes – very unfor-tunate.'

'I knew at once that something had happened,' Hilary continued, 'because their curtains have been washed. I suppose their new housekeeper has done that.'

'I suppose so,' Maurice said impatiently.

'And you found her for them, didn't you?'

Maurice made no reply. He did not willingly lie, nor could he deny the fact when Hilary's informant was handing him potatoes, but he had no intention of encouraging the subject and he felt that his wishes were being defied when Hilary gave a little laugh.

'If she is a clean person, she will find plenty to do. Sarah is a nice old thing, but dirty. I should think she must feel uncomfortable in a clean place like the hospital. Do you think she does?'

'I don't know,' Maurice said with reserve.

'I suppose you haven't been to see her often,' Hilary said. 'It's a long way to New Framling.'

'I went as often as I thought I was wanted,' he replied, with a betraying sharpness. 'I confess I found her – unresponsive.'

'She's old,' Hilary said soothingly. 'Old people don't like new faces. And I shouldn't think the Blunts would like having a new housekeeper. Do you think they do?'

'Really,' Maurice said impatiently, 'I know very little about them.'

'Then they haven't been doing their duty,' Hilary said. 'Mother left them special instructions to look after you.'

'That was kind of her. They have done all that was necessary. What time do you think your father and mother will arrive to-morrow?'

'She didn't mean just supporting you at church. She meant being neighbourly. Oh, they'll come when I did. There's only one train they can get. We knew they would do the church part properly. John is Father's churchwarden and never misses a service, but Mother thought you might be lonely in the evenings.'

'That was kind of her,' Maurice repeated, 'but I don't

24

know that I find myself in much sympathy with the Blunts.'

'They're rather odd, but we're very fond of them,' Hilary said. 'Fonder of John than of James.'

Maurice had some difficulty in swallowing his food. There had been nothing but pain for him in his visit to Old Framling. The Blunts had duly called on him; he had been active in helping them when their old servant was taken seriously ill; chance, or what he preferred to call design, had enabled him to supply them with a new housekeeper, but there had been none of that neighbourliness Margaret had expected of them, and after the first two Sundays John had absented himself from church. This had disturbed Maurice, for he knew that he could preach. He was aware of his social disabilities but, aloft in the pulpit, in that place of authority where he was not subject to interruption and could not discern or imagine the changes of expression he so much dreaded in closer intercourse, he remembered only enough of himself for the fit management of his voice and the control of his gestures. He was happy while he preached, for he believed he had a message, and when he had prepared it carefully he delivered it earnestly, and he had seldom experienced the flagging of his congregation's attention. He had vexed himself over John's desertion, wondering how he had offended and seeking vainly for a cause, comforting himself, in spite of the widow's tribute to John's regularity, with the belief that Edward's laxity had infected his churchwarden, and Hilary now took this comfort from him. John had listened to four sermons and no more, yet, hitherto, he had not been known to miss a service! Gloomily, Maurice came to the conclusion that John Blunt, like old Sarah, had taken a dislike to him. His sermons were not good enough to counterbalance that aversion: his prayers, his little jokes, had done nothing to soothe the old woman, who only showed animation when she asked about the Vicar's return. It was Edward they both wanted. Nobody had ever wanted Maurice when they could get Edward, and he felt sick with anger and hot with determination.

'Much fonder of John than of James,' Hilary went on thoughtfully. 'I love John. And he ought to be very grateful to you,' she added.

He waved that suggestion aside with a movement of his plump hand. 'Tell me about your holiday,' he said in an unmistakable manner.

This time she took his hint, and when the meal was over he rewarded her by assuring her that he had no objection to the company of the dog, who was loudly bewailing his imprisonment.

'Yes, it's a dreadful noise, isn't it?' she said.

He was hurt. This was the kind of thing that was always happening to him. The noise, which had been distressing, might have acted on him subconsciously, but his intentions, as far as he knew them, had been kind. This was the way in which Edward had received his timid advances when they were boys, and he began to think that Hilary was more like her father than her mother. He could hear her talking nonsense to the dog, telling him he must be good and careful not to annoy his Cousin Maurice. She was putting him in the wrong even with the dog, paying him out, no doubt, for refusing to satisfy her curiosity; yet, when she came back, she wore no look of guilt or triumph: she simply looked too good, too happy, and at the same time, too sensible, to be true.

'Are you a Boy Scout?' she asked.

'No. No, I am not. I leave that to some of my young men. I'm not very strong, you know,' he said, and while she nodded sympathetically, he was sure she was picturing him, as, indeed, he was picturing himself, in the costume which, more than ill-health, had debarred him from that form of activity.

'Because,' she explained, 'you've done your good deed

for to-day, and we're grateful, the dog and I. Even if the Blunts aren't,' she added softly.

There she was again! he groaned inwardly, and once more she reminded him of her mother. Margaret had always given with one hand and taken away with the other: when he had hoped for sympathy, he received mockery; and then, expecting mockery, he was met by sudden kindness; and even now Hilary was looking at him almost tenderly.

'I'm so glad to be at home,' she said. 'I like this house. I like my own belongings, but I believe Mother is much happier in Uncle Alec's musty little parsonage. We've been staying with him, you know. It's a dreadful little house, all dark corners and narrow passages and untidiness. Nothing must be out of its place here, but there, she doesn't mind falling over Uncle Alec's fishing-boots, or finding his cap and flies among the dishes on the sideboard. She just laughs and says she likes it. And if you tell her she's inconsistent, she says she's sorry for anyone who isn't! I suppose it's really the place she loves, and everything else seems perfect because of that. Human beings are odd, aren't they? She hates parsons, but she adores Uncle Alec, and even listens to his sermons. At least, she goes to church, but the door is always left open, so perhaps she really listens to the sounds outside, sheep and water and plover; and I sometimes think Uncle Alec is listening to them, too, and thinking about the trout he hopes he'll catch to-morrow. Perhaps the reason she doesn't mind his being a parson is because he isn't like one.'

'But she's married to a parson!' Maurice exclaimed, feeling a new comradeship for Edward in the disgrace they shared, almost enjoying the disgrace because he shared it.

'Ah,' said Hilary, 'but she says she isn't. She says the parson part is just an unfortunate accident. And then,' she added contentedly, 'Father isn't much of a parson either.'

27

'Not much of a parson? That isn't very complimentary.'

She laughed. 'He's much more of a scholar, I think,' she said thoughtfully; 'he's more interested in the theory of religion than in the practice of it.'

Maurice's eyes, magnified by his spectacles, positively glared at a daughter who could speak such treason of her father, though it was exactly what Maurice thought himself.

'You mean,' he demanded in his full voice, which woke the dog from his sleep, 'you mean that he's not a practising Christian?'

'Oh,' Hilary said, 'he practises it naturally. He can't help it. He doesn't need to think about it at all. Not that he's a conventional Christian, though.'

'I should think not!' Maurice snapped, and Hilary lifted her delicate eyebrows a little and seemed to register this ejaculation for future thought and interpretation.

Maurice saw with regret that his hastiness had closed the fount which might have supplied him with more details about his cousins. He had always had a consuming curiosity about these two: all the memories he cherished, though most of them were unhappy, concerned them closely, and, as though he could not resist the subject, he said quietly, 'The first time I saw your mother was at a railway station. She was in a carriage and I was on the platform. I didn't know who she was then, but, as it happened, we were both on our way to your grandfather's house. She was standing at the carriage door when a woman with a baby and a lot of parcels came along. What struck me' – Maurice gave a little cough – 'was the way she almost invited the woman to come in. Most people would have tried to block the doorway. It – I must say it impressed me. I knew, to my shame, that I wouldn't have done it myself.'

'Practical Christianity!' Hilary said brightly. 'Shall

we go for a walk? I think the dog ought to have some exercise.'

It was plain that she was neither going to give nor receive any more confidences about her parents. He deserved the snub, but it was painful, and meekly he fetched his hat, changed his shoes and followed her to the door.

On the pavement Hilary hesitated for an instant.

'Shall we go and call on the Blunts?' she said.

'Certainly not,' he replied, with an authority to which, as he thought afterwards, she bowed with too considerate a readiness.

Chapter 4: *Caroline*

In the neighbourhood of the Vicarage the village street was very quiet. The few shops were beyond and all wheeled traffic was obliged to cross the river by the new bridge, to which there was a road behind the church, so that only foot-passengers went between the Vicarage and the Blunts' house, and of these, even in the holiday season, there were not many. It was the Blunts' father who had been chiefly responsible for the development of New Framling, and its broad sands and safe bathing had diverted visitors from the old fishing village, which had the disadvantages of a cramped, stony beach and deep water in the bay. And Old Framling had few natural attractions. The bay, formed by the high white cliff on the west and a curved breakwater on the east, and backed by the clustered cottages, had the charm of a place devoted to its fitting purpose and, from the sea, it had a certain beauty; but on a nearer view the cottages were squalid, the lanes were uninviting and, in the village itself, the Vicarage was the only ornament. It had a look of worldly serenity, of self-sufficiency, an effect heightened by the red-brick wall protecting the garden, which stretched behind it until it met the churchyard.

Maurice's bedroom faced the street and, after the milkman had clattered through his morning round there was not a sound except an occasional shout from the beach or the rolling of a boat across the shingle, and these faint reminders of other men's activities made Maurice's light slumbers very pleasant. When Alice came to draw his curtains, she brought reality with her, but in the precious interlude he was still sleepy enough to keep back unwelcome thoughts and to forget that another day of idleness was before him.

He was robbed of this delicious drowsiness on the morning after Hilary's return, for the sound of wrangling voices in the street roused him completely, and he was the more annoyed because, as so often happened, he had passed a restless night; but having, like a policeman, a professional interest in frays, he hastily left his bed, threw his dressing-gown over his shoulders – for he easily took cold – and, pushing his head through the curtains, leaned out of the window.

It was one of those autumn mornings with an exquisite hint of frost in the air, and the street, like a little gorge with the houses for its cliffs, was filled with a faint blue mist which was making a pretence to keep back the sun. Through this sparkling medium, Maurice saw Hilary standing on the cobbled road, her bright blue dress turning the mist's pale blue to grey. She was holding the dog with one hand and some kind of bundle in the other, and her strong young figure, giving easily to the pulling of the dog, was sharply contrasted with the loose one of James Blunt, who stood on the opposite pavement, and even Maurice could feel some complacency for his own appearance when he compared himself with James, who was probably a few years younger. James looked as though his Creator had tired of a work begun in an inauspicious moment and decided to waste no time in trying to improve it. His limbs were ill-fastened to his body, his fair, straggling moustache was like a false one, attached insecurely: he had a small, restless head on a thin neck and his voice had the uncertainty of his gestures; it rose to a squeak and fell to a mutter and there was no conviction in its emphasis. Wagging a finger weakly, he was threatening Hilary with every form of punishment if, through her dog, his cat should come to harm.

Maurice withdrew his head and shoulders, but not

his gaze, and peeping from behind the curtains, he saw and heard Hilary's laughter. Enviously, he enjoyed the sound of it and the sight of her fair, shining head. She was not really like her mother. Margaret's laughter was richer, suggesting amusement at more than the hearer could divine, and her head was dark and far from smooth. Only in Hilary's competent and tender management of that tiresomely buoyant animal was there any resemblance to the girl who had opened the door of the railway carriage to the woman with the baby, that air of understanding and knowing how to deal with natural things.

'My dog wouldn't think of touching your poor old cat,' she said, 'so don't let us quarrel any more.'

'Quarrelling? Who's quarrelling?' he demanded. 'And the cat's a fine cat! No, I'm not quarrelling, but don't you let that dog loose in the street, that's all!'

'Go and have your breakfast, Mr. James,' Hilary said. 'I'm going to bathe, and if I'm drowned you'll be sorry you were cross with me.'

'Now, now, you must be careful,' James said nervously. 'Drowning's a nasty death. Never do to have you drowned and your father and mother coming back to-day. It's to-day they're coming, isn't it?' he asked, and Maurice thought he heard an anxious note in the voice, to which his own heart responded.

'Yes, to-day,' Hilary said.

'Well, then, don't you get drowned. Don't you get out of your depth. You'll get cramp. It's cold before the sun gets up. Better wait and bathe comfortably off New Framling beach. Shallow water – bathing machines – much better.'

'I'm going in off the breakwater.'

James shook his head. 'Dear, dear, I wouldn't like to do that. John did, as a boy, but not me. I can't swim and I never cared for cold water.'

The dark doorway of the Blunts' house was enlivened by a white-aproned figure and Maurice saw the attentive turn of Hilary's head, her expectation of being made known to this stranger, but the Blunts' new housekeeper did not linger.

'Mr. James, your breakfast's waiting,' she said, and disappeared with her last word.

Maurice stepped back and sank on to the edge of his bed. He had not heard that girl's voice since the day of her coming to Old Framling, and that was the day after Sarah Scutt had been taken to the hospital. He remembered how he had found her sitting, strangely yet fittingly enough, in the very shadow of Edward's heretical books, a shabby bag at her feet, her hands composed on her knees, as though she were willing to wait there indefinitely, but more clearly still he remembered the expression of disappointment which had crossed her face at his entrance. He could not have been mistaken about it: his consciousness of his outward disadvantages had made him extraordinarily sensitive to facial changes and he did not need her first words, uttered in a tone which matched her look, to tell him she had expected a different kind of man.

'No, I am not the Vicar,' he said precisely, and with a sort of sigh, she murmured ingenuously, 'I thought you couldn't be.'

How much he had been influenced by that beginning of their interview, he did not know. There had been a tremulous pleasure in settling her with the Blunts, yet what choice had he? He could not send her to the workhouse or keep her under the Vicarage roof, and when John Blunt neglected his sermons and Sarah Scutt showed her indifference to his ministrations, because he was not Edward, it was good to think of her on the other side of the road, and Edward had seemed a long way off. But to-day he was returning, and all the phrases, accusatory, sorrowful or careless, which Maurice had, time and again, rehearsed, were now astonishingly inadequate to the situation. He had always been afraid of Edward, and, as he crawled miserably into bed lest Alice should find him out of it, he emphasized his belief that he had taken the only possible course. No one could blame him for that, and he had committed himself to no further action; but he was in two minds, and he knew it. When he wanted to punish Edward he reminded himself that God had cast a duty on him: when he shrank from doing it he admonished himself for spite, yet all the time he was honest in believing that, if he had been certain of God's will, he would have submitted to it at any cost.

'At any cost,' he said aloud, but he was glad that the uncertainty of God's purposes had left him a loophole for escape.

When he went down to breakfast he was beginning to be anxious about Hilary. It was nearly an hour since she had gone to bathe. It was half-past eight, and John and James Blunt, those punctual men, were setting out for work. As he stood at the dining-room window, Maurice saw James leave the house and stand on the pavement, his head cocked suspiciously towards the door, until he was joined by John, a burly figure with a firmly held head, and the two went down the street together. A moment later, the new housekeeper stepped from the doorway and looked after them.

In the shadow of the house, she stood very still, as though her thoughts held her in that admirable and unstudied pose. Thus Maurice had seen mothers in mean streets watching their children start for school. It was difficult to believe that she was only twenty-one. She had a mature dignity and development of body, and Maurice remembered that her manner had been quietly self-confident. Self-confidence, he thought, seemed to be the fashion of the age. Even Hilary had too much of it, and he regretted that his own birth had not been postponed for twenty years. Then, as though his very lack of the quality spurred him to action, he suddenly decided to step into the street.

When he opened the door, his habitual, professional

34

smile quivered a little, but he managed to steady it as he sent a loud 'Good morning' across the road.

The girl turned slowly and gave him a calm, comprehensive glance. He was at once aware of his felt slippers, his scanty hair and the shapelessness of his clothes and, losing his head, he became too friendly, as he realized before the words were out of his mouth.

'So you have been seeing your charges off to business,' he said jovially.

She did not reply. She looked at him steadily, without embarrassment and without insolence, and while he fidgeted with the cross hanging from his watch-chain, he was envious of her capacity for stillness. With her rather broad, short face, a definite but not obtrusive chin, the deep-set eyes under level brows, the dark hair falling in a dip on each side of her forehead, her perfect immobility, she was like a statue of a severely benevolent deity, and her height, and the firmness of her well-moulded body made Maurice feel smaller than he was and more than usually conscious of his physical softness.

'I really came out,' he explained hastily, and he wished he had omitted the qualification, 'to see if Miss Stack was in sight. She has gone bathing and she's rather late. She has the dog with her – a young dog – and it occurred to me that they might have got into trouble. You haven't seen her, I suppose?'

'I saw her before breakfast.'

'Yes? Well, we must hope for the best. I'm unduly nervous, perhaps. No doubt she swims well.'

'She wouldn't bathe in the bay if she didn't, would she?'

'No – no. I'm sure you're right. And my breakfast's waiting. Oh – ah – Miss Mather' – he swung round again, 'the Vicar is returning to-night.'

'Yes, so I've heard,' she said, and her lips tightened a little.

'So,' Maurice went on, and he gave her three little nods of encouragement, 'you will be able to plead your cause with the real Vicar at last.'

'I didn't know I did any pleading with you,' she said, and now she showed a little heat. 'I asked for work and I got it.'

Maurice made a sound of protest. 'You mustn't take me up like that,' he said. 'It was just a way of putting it, a *façon de parler*, as our neighbours say,' and he waved a hand in the direction of the sea. He smiled brightly, hoping she was not hurt by his use of a language she probably did not know.

'Well then,' she said, and the faintest smile broke her severity, 'I got work – thanks to you. And I'm very well suited where I am, Mr. Roper, so I shan't trouble Mr. Stack.'

'Oh, but really – !' Maurice exclaimed. 'Don't you think – if you'll forgive my suggesting it – that it may be your duty? Your mother – Well, of course you must do as you think right.'

'I'm going to,' she replied without offensiveness. 'Work was what I wanted, and now I've got it. And I mean to keep it,' she added in a lower voice.

'Yes – well –' Maurice began, but he was interrupted.

'I think this is Miss Stack coming up the street,' said Miss Mather, and she went into the house.

In spite of James Blunt's injunctions, Hilary had let the dog loose, and they came running side by side.

'I'm sorry I'm late!' she cried. 'We've had a lovely swim.'

He felt almost affectionate towards this girl who treated him so cordially. How pretty she was, and how young! It would be a shame, he thought, to cast a shadow over her. Caroline Mather did not mean to do it: his hope of leaving his responsibility to her had gone. It was he who would have to do it, and it was just a continuance of his ill-fortune that the burden should be laid on him now, when, by ignoring it, he might secure something valuable for himself.

He smiled at her. 'I was beginning to get anxious about you.'

'Were you? How sweet of you, but oh, Cousin Maurice, you ought to have come with us. You would have loved it!'

He looked at her sharply. Was she making fun of him? She could hardly mean what she said, and the weight of his burden eased itself a little.

Chapter 5: *The Hand of God*

HILARY was more fortunate than most of her generation in having parents whom she could heartily welcome back to their home, and she expressed her thankfulness by seeing that none of her father's books was upside down and by picking flowers for her mother's pleasure.

'But,' she explained to Maurice, who was watching her, 'I have to be careful. She doesn't like too many. She doesn't like a room to look like a flower show or a nursing home. On the other hand,' she went on, and Maurice noted with relief that she seemed to have forgotten her reserve of the night before, 'she isn't one of those people who put a snowdrop in an egg-cup and call it decoration.'

To Maurice this sounded like a quotation and, as sensitive to influences as himself, Hilary looked up.

'That's what she says herself.'

'Yes,' Maurice said with a faint asperity, 'I thought I recognized the style.'

'She's very amusing,' Hilary murmured.

'And easily amused.'

'Don't you think that's a good thing?' she asked.

'For your mother, yes,' he replied.

'But she's never unkind,' Hilary said quickly.

'I'm sure she doesn't mean to be,' Maurice conceded untruthfully, but he wanted to remove the slight trace of anxiety from Hilary's face, he was still more desirous of hearing everything she had to say.

'It's no good trying to judge people unless you understand them,' Hilary said.

'Tout comprendre c'est tout pardonner,' Maurice

38

said urbanely, and he peered sideways at Hilary to see if she were criticizing his accent. She looked as blank as Caroline had done at the sound of a foreign language, and he said kindly, 'You understand that, of course.'

'Yes, like God,' she said promptly.

'Oh, come,' Maurice protested, for he did not approve of this casual poaching on his preserve, 'I think that's a purely human dictum. God understands everything, of course, but his pardon depends on repentance.'

'I hate bargains,' Hilary said, 'and I don't believe it. I simply don't believe it.'

'Well,' Maurice said, 'if you put your opinion before that of the saints and the sages, there's nothing more to be said. Age may teach you wisdom.'

'I expect it will,' Hilary agreed cheerfully.

'And experience,' Maurice added threateningly.

'Yes,' she agreed again, and he felt a weak anger for her impregnable courtesy.

'But,' she went on, and she snapped the stalk of a pink and held the flower to her nose, 'I understand repentance to other human beings, being sorry for treating them badly and that kind of thing – and saying so. That's natural – and right. But repentance to God – there's something rather mean about that, on both sides.'

'Don't talk nonsense!' Maurice exclaimed. 'A girl of – how old are you? Nineteen – can't be expected to understand the problem of sin. You're taking a purely childish view.'

'Oh, I know,' Hilary said, 'but what else can I do – at my age? If you'll tell me what you think . . .'

'Certainly not!' Maurice said. 'I'm not your spiritual adviser.' With a great effort he took all sharpness from his tones as he added, 'You must go to your father for that. But we were talking about your mother.'

'Yes. You said she didn't mean to be unkind. I don't see why you should think she's unkind at all. Witty people, clever people, they're so quick, they make the

39

others feel they're being snubbed. For instance, she'll tell me how nicely I've arranged the flowers and then she'll alter them a little. You'll see. But not much, not enough to hurt my feelings, and it would be silly to be hurt. Besides, it would be conceited. We both know she does them much better herself. She always arranges the flowers for church.'

'Very beautifully, I'm sure,' Maurice said with a polite vagueness. Thinking of Margaret, the witty, the clever, and trying to fit Hilary's explanation to his own case, he began to walk, a few paces backwards and forwards, on the grass. He moved clumsily but lightly, and though there was no wind, his loose clothes seemed to flap about him. The sun was brilliant, and he had tipped his soft felt hat over his eyes, but Hilary was bare-headed and, as she bent over the flowers, he thought she was like a flower herself. Near her, the dog, his coat burnished by the sunshine, waited hopefully for this tiresome business to end, yawned now and then, suddenly rolled with terrific energy, lay on his back with his legs held stiffly upwards, and then resumed his mildly reproachful pose.

Maurice heard a gurgle of laughter, and thinking she was amused by the dog, he nodded in that direction with a paternal sympathy. Fortunately, she was not looking, for she said:

'Yes, she does the flowers beautifully, but funnily as well.'

'Funnily?'

She nodded.

'According to the lessons and the hymns. Father tells her what's coming, because she never knows, and then she tries to get the right flowers. Angry colours and sharp leaves for the fierce occasions, and soft ones for the gentle bits.'

'It seems,' Maurice ventured, 'rather a waste of time.'

'That's what Father says,' and at this Maurice was

quick to add, 'But no doubt she knows her own business best.'

'And that's what she says to Father.'

'I suppose she is a great help to him in the parish,' he suggested cunningly.

Hilary laughed again.

'I think you must have forgotten Mother,' she said. 'The only thing she does for him is to protect him.'

'Protect him?' Maurice repeated, and he halted in his walk, a plump finger at his lip.

'From all the silly little worries, so that he can get on with what he likes.'

'Ah, the theory of religion, I suppose.'

'Yes. He's writing a book.'

'And the parish has to take care of itself.'

'He's there if he's wanted,' Hilary said lightly.

'Yes,' Maurice said bitterly, 'they come when they want anything, but what do they want? Food and clothes and money. They don't want what we are ordained to give them.'

'Well, poor things,' Hilary began, but Maurice held up a hand, the palm towards her as though he were in the pulpit.

'Now, don't argue, I won't discuss it. I find you,' he said in a gently reasonable tone, 'extremely argumentative for a young girl.'

'It's a family failing. Father and Mother never agree about anything, and I've caught the habit. Family life is very difficult.'

'It ought not to be.'

'I'm not sure about that,' she said. 'Now, don't get angry with me, Cousin Maurice. I'm talking about something I really do understand because I've experienced it. Loving people is easy, but living with them isn't. Mother says we ought to love them and leave them.'

'I should have thought,' Maurice said slowly, and he found a great satisfaction in uttering the words, 'I should have thought it was your father who would have said that.'

'Oh, no. He's just the opposite. He's very – very retentive.'

'But perhaps his memory sometimes fails him,' Maurice said drily.

'It does!' Hilary exclaimed. 'That's one of our troubles. He has a very bad memory except for the things he wants to remember – the Kings of Israel and which prophet comes before which and what's in Luke and isn't in Mark.' She let out a light sigh. 'It seems as though he couldn't forget those if he tried, and I suppose you know all about them, too.'

'There are things to which I attach more importance,' he remarked, and he turned sharply away.

The lawn was bordered by a high privet hedge, pierced here and there for entrance to the shady grass path beyond, and up and down this path Maurice walked silently on his rubber soles. When he passed the gaps he could see the sunny lawn, the flower beds, Hilary and the dog, but these glimpses were no more than irrelevant flashes of light across his thoughts. He had often walked on that secluded path before, avoiding the gardener, hoping the servants would imagine he was out on parish business, ashamed that they should see him idle, though there was nothing for him to do. His anticipation of pleasant chats with picturesque old fishermen had been disappointed; the women, sitting in the doorways of their cottages, had looked at him with the hard eyes they kept for strangers, and a little girl, with a tangled head of hair, had made a face at him. He walked down those lanes in the constant apprehension of having a fish-tail or the claw of a crab thrown at him, and it was difficult to proceed with dignity. He discovered that these simple people did not necessarily see a clergyman, even when he was Edward's deputy, as a friend, and the only invalid in the place seemed to be Sarah Scutt, who did not want him.

Edward had been right in calling his visit a holiday, but it had been a lonely one. He would rather have been comforting the sick, ministering to the dying and wrestling with wrong-doers, than skulking in the garden and picturing the happy lives of his cousins. But now he was wondering if they were so happy after all, and though he was reluctant to part with any of his envy, he had a pleasant feeling that perhaps justice was being done.

Then Hilary called to him clearly.

'Cousin Maurice!'

'Yes?' He stood in one of the gaps.

'I've thought of a name for the dog.'

He was vexed by this childish interruption. She tried to argue with him on equal terms and, the next moment, she behaved like a baby, and he had no interest in the dog, no interest at all, he told himself, as he looked at her severely.

She came towards him, the bunch of flowers on her arm. She took a rose from the bunch.

'Smell it. That's for you,' she said. 'Were you thinking of a sermon? It suddenly struck me that he ought to be called Leander because he's such a good swimmer.'

'Yes?' Holding her rose, he had to forgive her. 'No, no, keep down, that's a good dog. Good dog! Good Leander! But Hero,' he said, and his mouth quivered with enjoyment of his own quickness, 'would be just as good.'

'So it would! How clever of you!'

'However, I think Leander is better,' he said generously.

'Do you really? Well then, that's settled. Don't you hate having things unsettled in your mind?' she asked.

'Yes, but it can't be helped,' he said, and he resumed his marching. He had not lived for more than forty years in a state of mental barricade without knowing the signs of attack, and when he came back he was not

43

surprised to see her looking at him wistfully over the bunch of flowers.

'I've picked too many,' she said.

'Well, well, you can put them somewhere.'

'It seems such a waste. I was wondering,' she said slowly, 'if I should take some to the Blunts. They have nothing but weeds in their garden, and the new housekeeper looks as if she might like flowers. I saw her this morning. She looks rather sad, and she spoke quite sternly to Mr. James. Perhaps she doesn't like being there. It's a dreary house. So dark, and I think the papers have been on the walls since their father and mother went to live there. Have you ever been inside?'

'No, I have not. Yes, once, just for a few minutes. And she needn't stay there if she doesn't want to, I suppose?'

'You know best about that,' Hilary said meekly.

This girl was like a wasp, he thought: she had a wasp's way of threatening or intending to sting and, as with a wasp, he did not know whether to ignore or punish her. In the meantime he grew hot. He took off his spectacles and wiped them, and as carelessly as he could, he wiped his forehead.

'I had a very bad night,' he mourned. 'I must sit down. No, not on the grass – it may be damp.'

'Aren't you well?' Hilary asked.

'I am never well,' he said sharply, for his fresh complexion, his look of heartiness, had deprived him of sympathy all his life.

'Oh, I didn't know,' she said. 'And you've been ill, haven't you? Come to the garden seat. I'm so sorry.'

He smiled bravely.

'It's all right, it's all right. Nothing to worry about.'

If he had looked at her he would have seen that she was not worrying; her mouth twitched a little as he sat, bowed forward, as if he had a pain, and anxious to offer a remedy which would be suitable without being too suggestive, she said:

'Would you like some hot water, Cousin Maurice?'

'Hot water! All I want is to get cool!'

'This isn't the place for that,' she said sensibly, for the afternoon sun was shining full on him: she could see the beads of perspiration on his face. 'And,' she pursued, 'it's a bad thing to leave the back of your neck uncovered.'

'Oh, please leave me alone!' Maurice begged, but he pushed back his hat, and under that black halo his face looked sulkily infantile. He was aware that Hilary was sitting sideways, delicately sparing him her regard, and it occurred to him that all she wanted was a little discipline: she had been allowed too much liberty with her elders, but she had the makings of a tender-hearted woman, and he had no sooner come to this conclusion than he heard her saying gently.

'What is that girl called?'

He sighed. She was very persistent.

'Her name,' he said with the precision of his irritation, 'is Caroline Mather.'

'I liked the look of her,' Hilary said; 'but you think I'd better not take her any flowers?'

'I didn't say so,' he retorted.

'No-o,' Hilary answered slowly, 'but perhaps you are right. Though it's rather mean of you, Cousin Maurice, because you let me give you one.'

It was hanging slackly from his hand and, as he looked at it, he pardoned the injustice of her words.

'I think it's the first flower I've ever had from a lady,' he said.

'And it's the first flower I've ever given to a gentleman,' she replied, and she laughed with a gay, sexless sound which hurt him, for it seemed to imply that he was a strange recipient of a lady's favour.

'Don't you want to go and arrange your flowers?' he inquired.

'I was waiting till you felt a little better. You know, I really wanted to take the flowers for an excuse to speak to her. I like talking to people. Isn't she a desirable acquaintance? Because, if she isn't you ought not to have sent her to the Blunts. They have always been so respectable.'

'I don't like to hear you talk in that way,' he said sternly, but he did not disturb Hilary's serenity.

'If she's as nice as she looks,' she went on, 'the Blunts were very lucky to get her.'

'Lucky!' he cried. 'In this world, there is no such thing as luck.'

'Isn't there? What is there, then?'

He took a moment before he replied weightily.

'There is the Hand of God.'

Hilary said nothing. He had silenced her at last. He sat back more comfortably on the seat. He looked complacently at the blue sky, the green trees, the tower of the squat little church beyond the garden, and then at this fair young girl, sitting in a submissive attitude and considering what he said. Her lips moved, and he prepared to clear her mind of difficulties.

'We'll have fruit salad for tea,' she said, 'that will be nice and cooling. I'll arrange the flowers first and then there'll just be time to take Leander for a run before the others come. We'll go up to the cliff. He'll enjoy rolling on the turf. Dogs always like rolling in strange places better than in their own gardens. Have you noticed that? And perhaps you'll come with us, Cousin Maurice, if you feel well enough.'

'Thank you, I think I shall stay in the garden. But Hilary,' he called after her, 'don't let that dog get boisterous and push you over the cliff.'

She laughed.

'It would be the Hand of God,' she cried gaily and, in his anger at this retort, held back so cunningly for the fitting moment, he had an instant's longing that the Hand of God would really smite her. And was she a child or a woman? Was that remark about fruit salad intended as a snub, or was she incapable of serious thought? His life was full of disappointments. She would not make a good companion after all.

Chapter 6: *Margaret*

THIS little episode was a poor preparation for his meeting with her parents. It was a foretaste of the kind of thing he must expect from Margaret, unless time had changed her much, and nothing Hilary had told him led him to believe that she had changed at all; but if time was powerless over her character, it must surely, he thought hopefully, have robbed her of her beauty. Then he grew hot again. 'I must get out of this glare,' he muttered, but he knew the sun was not to blame. He had committed the double weakness of acknowledging her beauty's influence over him in the past and his fear of it in the future. He had always told himself that he had fallen in love with the kind act of which he had spoken to Hilary and not with any physical charms she possessed, and on that belief he had based another – that the quality of his love was superior to that of Edward's. How could it be otherwise when Edward had earlier proved himself susceptible to another woman who had nothing but beauty to recommend her?

Maurice retreated into the shade of the green path and the refuge of noble thoughts. As he had loved her in that fine manner, why should he disturb her now with reminders of Edward's poorer one? Yet was it possible to leave her undisturbed? Was this impulse inspired by generosity or cowardice? And what was right and what was wrong? And was he never, never to be at peace? Perhaps God had not intended to give peace to men.

He raised his head and saw the church tower rising above the red wall laced with fruit trees: it seemed to beckon him to come there and find an answer to his question, and obediently, not without humility, he passed through the latched door which led into the churchyard.

No funereal trees, hardly a tree of any kind, grew there. The grey headstones and slabs were as little sheltered as the lives of the dead had been and, as these fishermen and their families had worked under the open sky, so stood or lay their plain memorials.

The aspect of the churchyard was almost as flat as a calm sea, but here and there a larger stone topped the others, like a wave, and, in a conspicuous place, a large white monument stood as prominent as a lighthouse, for those who needed one no longer. It had not, however, the beauty of a lighthouse, that beauty of a means sternly directed to one end; it was the figure of an angel pointing an attenuated finger at an open book, and on one page there was inscribed the name of Mary, the devoted wife of Andrew Blunt, whose own name, in stronger, later lettering, was engraved below.

Maurice blinked at this glaring structure, tried to avoid all thoughts of its connection with the living Blunts and fixed his short-sighted gaze on a chestnut tree in the field beyond. He had watched the leaves growing dry, their edges turning to gold, and now the tree was like a great flower of lovely symmetry, its petals coloured with green and red and bronze. Soon they would drop gently, crisply, to the ground, enriching the earth from which they came with their colour and then with their decay.

Very rapidly, he made the rough sketch of a sermon in his mind; the tender shoots of spring, the flower, the fruit, death and the resurrection of the body. He would be at home in time for the Harvest Festival services and the chestnut tree would serve as his text for the evening sermon. In the morning, while the decorations were still fresh, the note of his discourse should be one of gratitude for God's gifts, thanksgiving and praise; in the evening, when the dahlias were beginning to droop, he would speak solemnly of the renewal of life here-after.

He thought of his shabby church and his humble congregation with the affection of a man for his home. There he was accepted for his better parts, his eloquence and his will to serve, while here, even in God's house, he was a stranger.

Yet he stayed there for a long time. He tried to pray and found himself planning his meeting with Edward and Margaret, and set himself to pray again. But should he meet them in the hall and lay himself open to the charge of behaving as though the house were his, or should he hover in the drawing-room and be suspected of ungraciousness? He prayed for remembrance of his own trespasses and forgetfulness of those of others, and then he drifted into thoughts of Margaret. He saw her as she had stood at the door of the railway carriage, half smiling at the woman with the baby; he had fallen in love with her then and there, never guessing that Edward would meet her at the station and they would stand before him, hand-in-hand. He remembered the rough tweed suit she wore, of the same colour as her eyes, and the little hole in her wash-leather glove. He gave up his attempt to pray and gradually his body drooped, his knees slackened, his head was bowed on the book-rest; he felt sleep stealing over him and he made no resistance. It seemed to him that God wanted him to sleep, here, in his quiet house.

When he woke, he was cold, he had missed his tea, and Margaret and Edward must have arrived already, yet he took a turn round the churchyard for the revival of his circulation and to give himself that feeling of having done something brisk and hearty which would facilitate his entrance. He went into the house by the garden door and he hesitated only for a moment in the passage leading to the hall. He could hear voices and the excited barking of the dog and, practising his smile, he stepped forward.

Though the hall was dim, for the lamp had not been lighted, he saw at once that Edward was not there, and, with the relief of that absence, he tasted again the bitterness of his boyhood when, according to the circumstances of their last encounter, he hoped or feared to see his cousin, but Margaret's warm, soft voice was like balm, astringent, yet soothing to his spirit. To hear it, to watch her when he himself was not seen, had once brought him near to happiness, and now this gloom was kindly, for if he could not see her face, neither could she clearly distinguish his. He experienced again that sensation of being enriched, though it might be perilously, by her presence, and in this sudden happiness he forgot the clamminess of his hand as he took hold of hers.

'I'm glad to see you,' she said, and he felt the sincerity of her welcome, yet he protected himself from her possible mental reservation by saying, with a laugh:

'Perhaps that's because you can't see me properly.'

'No, no!' she protested. 'But why hasn't the lamp been brought? Light a candle, Hilary. Light two candles. I hate groping for people's faces in the dark.' She turned to him again. 'And are you better, Maurice?'

He could not answer at once. She had always given a special value to people's names: she slurred or shortened no syllables and, on her lips, his name sounded, when she chose, like an endearment, and few endearments had ever been addressed to him. He felt a little catch in his throat, and before he could clear it away Hilary, shielding the flame of a match, said in her cool young voice:

'He wasn't very well this afternoon.'

He disliked Hilary at that moment. He wanted to tell her she was a little tell-tale and, when he remembered the words with which she had parted from him in the garden, he was convinced of her desire to make him feel uncomfortable and physically inferior in the presence of Margaret, who, as he could now see, had kept her appearance of splendid but indolent vitality. She had seated herself on the chair with the curved legs and the dog had put his head on her knee. His tail went slowly to and fro like a feather fan as he gazed with mournful sentiment into her face; he was wearing, in fact, the very expression which Maurice had to suppress.

'It was nothing – nothing at all,' he said quickly.

'It was the heat,' Hilary explained kindly.

'But you're really better?' Margaret inquired.

'Perfectly well, perfectly well,' he replied, and he sent a hardly perceptible, warning frown in Hilary's direction.

With her hand on the dog's head, Margaret was looking at him, her own head thrown back. Her face had a certain effect of squareness, caused by the breadth of her forehead and the placing of her cheekbones, and in its tilted position it looked squarer than it was. A smile dented the corners of her full, sweet mouth.

'Yes, you are just the same,' she said.

'I'm afraid so,' he answered ruefully, and shifted from one foot to the other.

'Except for the spectacles,' she added.

He touched them, glanced again at Hilary,. and said, 'Yes. I find them more comfortable.'

'He looks much nicer in them,' Hilary said.

He had an almost uncontrollable desire to growl at the girl. He wanted to give the impression of having worn his spectacles regularly for years, but Hilary knew better and no doubt she would tell her mother.

'I'm afraid I've never given much thought to my appearance,' he said stiffly, and regretted the remark, but in the company of these people he seemed compelled to say what would urge them to secret laughter.

'I wish Edward did,' Margaret sighed. 'He has a positive preference for odd socks.'

Maurice felt a little easier, and when Margaret asked him whether he had forgotten Hilary's existence and had been startled by her arrival, he confessed that he had been momentarily surprised.

'And dismayed, Cousin Maurice.'

'Not at all,' he said sharply.

'You looked dismayed,' she persisted.

He forced himself into a playful manner. 'Well, how was I to know you would be such a charming companion?'

'And you were very kind about the dog,' she admitted. 'I'm going to call him Leander, Mother – he swims so well. We had a bathe together this morning.'

'Oh, Leander's a silly name for a dog,' Margaret said.

'Cousin Maurice and I agreed that it was rather good. Or what do you think of Hero? That was your idea, wasn't it?'

'A suggestion,' Maurice said. 'Merely a suggestion.'

'I don't like either of them,' said Margaret. 'Call him Bob. That's the right kind of name for a sheep-dog.'

'It's very ordinary.'

'So is the dog.'

'Oh, Mother, you know you love him!'

'I love you too, darling,' Margaret said.

Hilary laughed and Maurice marvelled at her insensibility.

'Well,' she said, 'you always have your own way, so we'll call him Bob.'

'Much better,' Maurice said traitorously.

'And what's in a name?' Hilary asked and, in the childish way which Maurice found so irritating, she knelt down and put her face against the dog's head. 'By any other name he'd smell as doggy.' She sniffed. 'I love the smell of him.'

'But don't let him lick you,' Margaret said quickly.

'I don't mind what he does,' Hilary crooned. 'I don't even mind if he kills James Blunt's old cat. We had quite a quarrel about it this morning.'

'Poor James! You mustn't tease him." She turned again to Maurice. 'Have you seen much of the Blunts?'

'No. Not very much,' he answered slowly.

'But I hope they gave you any help you needed. James' – she smiled – 'is rather odd, but we trusted to John to do what he could for you.'

'Really, there has been so little to do that I did not need to trouble them. A real holiday!' He rubbed his hands together. 'A giant refreshed!' He realized at once that he had said the wrong thing again. Was she hiding the laughter in her eyes?

She looked up. 'I'm glad you've had a peaceful time,' she said quietly. 'We generally come back to find some kind of trouble – somebody ill, or dead, or naughty.'

And now he saw that Hilary was looking at him with expectation. This, her look and attitude implied, was the moment when he would naturally speak of the Blunts' old housekeeper and of the new one he had supplied. It would be just as natural, he thought, for Hilary to speak of them herself, but though her lips were parted, she was silent. He wished she would speak, for he found it impossible to do so; and, he thought angrily, it was just like the child to reserve her remarks for when they were not wanted.

'And now I must go and get tidy,' Margaret said, and she stood up.

'And where is Edward?' Maurice inquired in the voice which gave him confidence. 'Perhaps I ought to go and render an account of my stewardship.'

'He's in the study, reading his letters." She paused at the stair-foot. 'Will you go in and see him?'

'I don't suppose he wants to be disturbed,' Maurice said, with the studied brightness of his reflection that, if Edward was in the study, he must have heard their voices and ought, in courtesy, to have come out to welcome him.

53

'Well, no, I don't suppose he does,' Margaret said, and she went smoothly up the stairs.

He was left in the hall with Hilary. 'It's rather chilly, isn't it?' he said, and again he rubbed his hands together.

'I hope you haven't caught cold,' she said gravely. 'And you hadn't any tea.'

'No. I was – I was occupied.'

'And Mother didn't mean that Father wouldn't want to see you. She just meant –'

'My dear little girl,' he said kindly, 'you need not interpret your mother to me. You must remember that I knew her long before you did.'

'And when Father's reading,' she went on, 'he never hears a thing. He might just as well be deaf.'

'Indeed?' he said. 'Remarkable concentration!'

'Yes, isn't it?' she said, and with a cheerful nod, in which he detected a touch of defiance, she followed her mother up the stairs.

After her he went soft-footed, pulling himself by the hand-rail, his brief exaltation gone. If Hilary, with her usual interference, had already felt obliged to explain her parents, how much unhappiness would the next few days hold for him, even if he left his doubtful duty undone? Yet Margaret had been kind, she had certainly been kind, and was it not possible that her last words had been directed against Edward, uttered in patient disapproval of his character? He was too ready, far too ready to be hurt, he reproached himself, and he determined to be braver in future, as he stepped on to the landing.

Across it, there was a shaft of light from Margaret's bedroom door. He heard a murmur, a little laugh, and then Hilary's cruelly clear voice:

'But he isn't nearly so funny as you said he was!'

He stood quite still until the door was shut and then went, very quietly, through the darkness to his room.

54

Chapter 7: *Edward*

No one but Maurice recognized a hero in the plump clerical gentleman who entered the drawing-room. He showed no sign of the miserable half-hour he had just spent. He was smiling, and if, still smiling, he looked round the room with little propitiating glances, it was easy to account for them: they had become a habit with a nervous man who had dealings with many kinds of people and wanted to assure them all that his intentions were good, and though the goodness of his intentions was buried to-night, and perhaps permanently, as regarded the Stacks, under a load of injury, the habit remained.

He was conscious, as he glanced, of that feeling of unreality which the sight of ordinary things gives to a person who has suffered from a shock, and the room, with its unnecessary wood fire, its shaded lamps, and Margaret standing at the open window, looked to him like the opening scene of a play. He was not used to people who stood in beautiful attitudes in beautiful rooms; it seemed as though she must have been waiting there for the curtain to go up; his own entrance became too significant, and he was pleased to discover a pair of homely grey flannel legs and shabby wool-work slippers stretched out in front of the hearth. That, for the moment, was all he could see of Edward, but when he had pulled his great length out of his chair, Maurice was touched and astonished by the kindness of his greeting, until he remembered that Margaret had been kind, too. But Edward had a frankness which was disarming: what Maurice called his youthful brutality had been frank: he never troubled to conceal his boredom, and when he pushed Maurice into a chair, took another himself and began to talk, Maurice had to admit that, with Edward, a mere sense of hospitality would have stopped at a hearty welcome. He felt the renewal of Edward's strong attraction. He had kept his boyish appearance. His fair hair, in which the grey was not apparent by lamplight, still had its absurd way of standing up, and this, with the nose of which Hilary's was a finer copy, gave him a look of eagerness and enthusiasm. His nose was the index to his character: it was ardent, optimistic, petulant, diverting attention from the rather visionary eyes and the humorous mouth. No one but Maurice would have called Edward a handsome man, but his enviable leanness, his possession of qualities which Maurice had always desired, his lack of the self-consciousness which was Maurice's bane, had always persuaded him that Edward was endowed with every kind of good fortune. For the moment his envy was in abeyance and, if it had not been for that girl across the road, he believed that the long-desired friendship might have been possible; for here was Edward, talking about his holiday, asking Maurice about his health, thanking him for his care of the parish, talking to him as he might have talked to a brother, easily and without formality. Had Maurice been misjudging him all these years? His reaction to this treatment had the force of his late misery, and though he thought of the girl and the heretical books in the library, these evidences of offence lost some of their horror through the proximity of Margaret, whose offence was of a more personal nature.

He stole a look at her now and then. He wondered why she did not sit down She moved indolently about the room, clad in a low-cut dress of some blue material threaded with gold, a garment quite out of keeping, he thought, with a country vicarage and, in his bitterness, he decided that she was trying to attract his notice.

She caught his eye and, advancing on tiptoe, she

whispered, 'It's all right, Maurice. It was a remnant and I made the dress myself.'

He blushed hotly. 'It's – very pretty,' he stammered.

'You see, Edward's so slovenly – look at his slippers – that I have to set a good example to Hilary.'

'I wish you'd sit down,' Edward said in a loud tone of exasperation. 'You've been fidgeting about the room ever since Maurice came in.'

'Ah,' she said sweetly, 'I wanted to remind you both that I was here,' and Maurice blushed again. 'I'll just pull the curtains –'

'Sit down!' Edward thundered.

She obeyed meekly, lifting her eyebrows pathetically at Maurice. He felt uncomfortable, for here were signs of those domestic differences of which Hilary had spoken; but he was flattered, for Margaret seemed to be inviting him to share her trials, and he balanced this against her unkindness and Edward's friendliness against his discourtesy to his wife. His sympathies swung painfully between the two, but they came to rest as Hilary entered the room. Hilary was a kind of neutral country, for, though she had consistently irritated him, she had found him – and a little shiver ran through him – less comic than she had been led to expect.

'I believe you've caught a cold,' she said at once, and lost some of her advantageous position.

'Hilary,' he said, 'is determined that I shall be ill.'

'I'm determined that you shan't,' she said. 'Mother thinks illness is a crime and Father and I are afraid even to sneeze.'

'It's only a crime when I have to nurse it,' Margaret said, and she got up again. 'You've arranged the flowers very nicely, Hilary,' she said, but she took a rose from one bowl and put it in another.

'There!' Hilary said softly to Maurice, in a kind of triumph.

He was incapable of understanding this pleasure in a

57

snub. He considered it another proof of Hilary's thick skin. Margaret, too, seemed to have recovered from Edward's reprimand with surprising speed. Maurice felt himself an alien among these people, yet how delightful it was to look at them and cozen himself into the belief that they were as charming as they appeared. He thought Margaret more beautiful than she had been as a girl: there was a ripeness about her, with no suggestion of decay: she had the same strong, lazy movements with a maturer grace, and both she and Hilary had an air of physical fastidiousness to which the women he met in the course of his work had not accustomed him. Maurice was short-sighted, but through his powerful glasses he saw much that Edward missed. Edward probably knew the colour of Margaret's eyes; he certainly did not know the colour of her slippers, while Maurice could have told him whether they were adorned with buckles or with bows, for his life, though he would have shrunk from the admission, had, like that of a wild creature, encouraged habits of observation in self-defence, and though, like such a creature's, his deductions might be wrong, he was constantly on the alert.

He would have felt still more out of place in the company of this decorative pair if Edward's careless clothes had not made his own formal black ones seem like festive garments, but even here there was cause for criticism: Edward wore a soft collar and a brown tie with his flannel suit, in pursuance, Maurice supposed, of the growing fashion among clergymen of advertising their common humanity. In Edward's case, he thought grimly, this was quite unnecessary, and no sooner had he hardened himself with this reflection, than he was softened by hearing Edward speak kindly of a clerical acquaintance of notoriously narrow views. It would have been impossible for Maurice to speak thus of anyone with notoriously broad ones, and he was first humiliated by this generosity and then angered by the impossibility of settling on a comfortably fixed state of mind in relation to his cousin.

When Margaret approached the hearth and knelt between the chairs of the two men to poke the fire, he saw her as the most potent cause of his bewilderment. Balancing the poker, she sat back on her heels and looked from one to the other with a half-smile which made Edward ask, 'Well, what's the matter now?'

'Nothing's the matter. I was just admiring you both. And look at Maurice's nice patent-leather slippers! You ought to be ashamed of yours, Edward!'

Expecting Hilary to inform the family that he had been wearing felt ones hitherto, Maurice was quick to confess that, if he had known such slippers were permitted, he would have sacrificed his appearance to his comfort.

'That's the only rule of conduct I never break,' Edward said.

'Except on Sundays,' said Hilary. 'You have to wear your uniform then.'

'You'll be staying over Sunday, of course,' Edward said, and, as Maurice hesitated, Margaret echoed, 'Of course!' on the kindest note of her voice. Hilary was silent, and quite properly silent, Maurice told himself; it was not for her to encourage or discourage her parents' guest, and he looked at her to see whether her attitude expressed this conviction. It expressed nothing: she was sitting in a low chair, her hands folded in her lap, her eyes cast down, and Maurice, feeling unreasonably dissatisfied, straightened his spectacles and said, 'You're very kind, but it's time I was getting back – time I was getting back.'

'And if you stay you'll have to preach.'

'He's going to stay,' said Margaret.

'But I won't preach. They won't want to hear me now you are back.'

'Nobody can listen to Edward's sermons,' Margaret said. 'He drones. He isn't interested in them himself.'

'Yes, I am!' he protested. 'But in the middle I begin to wonder if I'm talking sense, and that's fatal.'

'They don't want to listen to sense. They can get that at home. What they want is a nice cheerful entertainment.'

'I'm afraid I can't undertake to give them that,' Maurice said with a pained smile. He remembered that he ought to prepare the way for a possible retreat and he was depressed by all the implications in the thought. 'I'm not really sure that I ought to stay,' he murmured.

At last Hilary's voice was heard: 'And John Blunt says you're a very good preacher.'

'Oh, really!' Maurice turned and spoke sharply. 'I'm obliged to him!' Now, when had she had the opportunity of hearing that from John Blunt and, if he appreciated the sermons, why had he neglected his duties at church? Maurice's spirits sank lower still. He might have known it was some personal peculiarity which had upset the churchwarden, but what was it? There was surely something definitely unfortunate for him in this place.

'Well, then,' Edward was saying, 'John Blunt can have the pleasure of hearing you again. I'm lazy. I don't want to get back to work.'

'And that reminds me,' Margaret said, 'there's a note for you on the hall table.'

Edward rumpled his hair and moved his feet impatiently. 'I do wish I could have my letters given to me. As you saw it, why didn't you bring it in? It may be something really important.'

'That's what I thought,' Margaret said lightly, 'so you'd better go and fetch it.'

'But,' he persisted, 'why didn't you bring it?'

'Malice!' she said. 'Deliberate malice! I saw the letter, looked at it, turned it over, and wondered if it would annoy you more to have it and be obliged to answer it or to leave it there, and I decided that leaving it there would give you more trouble in the end, so, of course,' she ended in a matter-of-fact-way, 'I left it.'

Maurice blinked. He looked at Edward, who was still frowning, though less intensely than might have been expected; he looked at Hilary, who appeared not to have heard these astonishing remarks; at Margaret, who was still playing with the poker, and he was inspired to break the intolerable strain of the atmosphere by saying gaily, 'Ah, Margaret, you are just the same. You always would have your little joke.'

Hilary laughed, with a little gasp in which Maurice heard relief; but Margaret turned to him gravely, and said: 'Joke? I spend my whole life in trying to irritate Edward. It's my only occupation.'

'And the only thing you really work hard at,' Edward said. 'Hilary, fetch the letter for me, there's a dear.'

'No, Hilary! Sit still.' Margaret swung round to face her daughter. 'I won't allow you to pander to his laziness.'

'Then the best way out of the impasse,' Maurice said brightly, 'is for me to go and get it,' and, with his surprisingly light step, he went out of the room.

He did not know what to make of this little scene, except that it was one which Hilary should not have witnessed, and hastening to get the letter which he hoped would be a pleasant diversion, he returned to find the trio sitting in a solemn silence.

'Now, who can this be from?' Edward sighed. 'Thank you, Maurice. I'm ashamed of my family.' He read the letter and looked up. 'You didn't tell me Sarah Scutt was ill.'

Maurice spoke in a slightly strained voice. 'There hasn't been much opportunity. As a matter of fact, I wasn't going to trouble you with parish matters until you asked for them.'

'No,' Edward replied, apparently missing the rebuff.

'Well, she wants to see me. I must go to-morrow morning.'

'But if she's ill,' Margaret said, 'what have the poor Blunts been doing?'

The one person who was supposed to know the answer to this question answered it quickly. 'I believe they have been managing very comfortably.'

'But how?' Margaret insisted.

Hilary hesitated for an instant before she replied: 'They've got a new housekeeper. I've seen her, and John Blunt seems to like her.'

'But I wonder where they found her,' Margaret said as Alice entered to announce dinner.

Chapter 8: *A Delicate Question*

MARGARET thought she had never seen her daughter look prettier than she did that evening at dinner and, if Maurice had been a younger, or a different, man, she might have suspected that Hilary's exhilaration was due to him; but no girl, she decided with relief, was likely to derive from Maurice anything more dangerous than amusement. He had been the cause of much sly laughter in her own girlhood; though she had known men who were more obviously absurd, she could remember none who had so readily moved her to mischief, for he took his office, himself and everybody else with an immovable seriousness; there was not a spark of native humour in him. She knew she ought to pity him, and she might have managed to do so if his physical imperfections had not weighted the scales against him. Actual beauty in a man was of no importance, but she disliked Maurice's plump, sagging body, the soft rosiness of his face and the fat, tapering fingers which performed little exercises on the table, now and then, in a funny, old-maidish way. He looked determinedly genial, but he seemed preoccupied. It was Hilary who did most of the talking; she did altogether too much, and as this was unusual and consequently interesting, Margaret allowed it to go on.

Hilary seemed to have mislaid her customary tact and possibly that was the form of her reaction to Maurice. She had always had a highly developed social sensitiveness, and Margaret's secret regret that the child was not a boy had gradually changed to gratitude for this good companion. She had many of the boyish qualities and none of the tiresome tricks which Margaret

63

had expected and dreaded in her adolescence. She seemed to be unconscious of her sex and charm and, while she was often childish, her mother recognized something subtle in her simplicity. Margaret, who wished she had half a dozen children, had tried not to indulge herself with too lavish a display of love for the one she had. In this endeavour, Hilary had been sent to boarding-school at an early age, and now, her school-days over, she had returned, without apparent ambitions, willing to stay at home, to be the old-fashioned daughter in a new way. This, for the moment, was very well; but Margaret was not content that she should stay in Old Framling, slowly developing into her father's curate and having her bright spirit dulled. If she had no hankerings after a career, she ought to marry, and in Old Framling there was no one more eligible than the Blunts. Somewhere in the world there must be a man almost good enough to marry her, but how was he to be found?

Margaret's own meeting with Edward had been romantic, a chance one, in the hills, and she desired for Hilary a future as beautiful in its beginning and as continuously entertaining. She had been as free as Hilary seemed to be from hopes of possible lovers until she saw Edward sitting on a rock beside a mountain stream, with a knapsack by his side and a pipe in his mouth. Then she had felt a sudden doubt whether a life with her Uncle Alec in the country she loved was really all she wanted, and she had never regretted the unmaidenly way in which she had provoked Edward into conversation and an invitation to share his food. She had continued to provoke him, in one way or another, with undiminished pleasure, and she still shared all he offered; this was a good deal and Edward said it was all he had, but she was quite aware that what now kept her interest in him alive, a reserve, deep down, of which he himself was hardly conscious, was what had attracted her then. She divined more than she was told, while he expected her to tell him more than he divined, and she did not resent a state of things which Edward would have indignantly denied, for she knew the leavening value of a little mystery in the familiarity of married life.

With Edward's surface emotions she was intimately acquainted; she knew now that he was trying to be patient under Hilary's chatter; she wondered that Hilary herself did not avoid the coming rebuke with her ordinary quickness, and presently Edward sighed wearily.

'Hilary,' he said, 'we're all convinced that the dog is a wonderful animal, but can't we talk about something else?'

'Yes,' Hilary said amiably. 'What shall we talk about?'

'I am afraid this very unusual weather will end in a severe storm,' Maurice said adroitly, and tried to hide his pride in having saved the situation for the second time.

Edward leaned back despondently, and Margaret, quickly covering this movement, skilfully developed the theme; from the contrasting climates of Old Framling and Maurice's town, she led the conversation to his work and listened so attentively that Maurice thought Hilary must be mistaken as to her mother's dislike of clergymen. He was under no misapprehension about Hilary's silence; she was not listening; hurt at last, she was considering her wrongs, and for the first time he felt some sympathy for her. He knew exactly what she was suffering and, if Margaret had not kept him busy, he would have tried to show his sympathy with an understanding word.

Hilary, however, was not hurt at all. It was a pity her father should have to think her tiresome, but he had already forgotten all about it; his temper went as quickly as it came, and now both he and Hilary were thinking their own thoughts, while Maurice was telling

65

Margaret how he had raised money for the repair of the heating apparatus in his church. It was a long story, but her interest did not flag, and it occurred to Hilary that perhaps her mother was letting Maurice talk for the very reason that Hilary had talked too much herself; yet, wonderful person though she was, how could she have already discovered the cause of Hilary's uneasiness? Cause was too definite a word; Hilary simply felt uneasy. She did not find her Cousin Maurice so very funny; she found him a little sinister, though that word, too, was not the right one. Her perceptions, not yet overlaid by experiences which might be misleading, were vague, but quick, and she knew better than her father or her mother that Maurice's whole character was not reflected in his face. She knew there was a sort of ferment in his spirit. She was a little sorry for him, but she could not be more than a little sorry for a man who had revealed to her the signs of enmity for her father which he had hidden from Edward himself. That, to her ignorance, looked rather like deceit, and he had been strangely secretive about the Blunts' new housekeeper, though this had interested, without worrying her, until she had met John Blunt that afternoon.

At an hour when he was usually still in his office in New Framling, for the Blunts worked early and late, she was surprised to see his unmistakable figure outlined against the sky as he stood on the edge of the white cliff. She was pleased, too, for she was fond of him, and she called to him and waved her hand as he turned his head and, as soon as he recognized her, he strolled down the slope to meet her.

'Well, Hilary,' he said, in the kind voice he always used to her, 'I'm glad to see you.'

'I thought it couldn't be you,' she said, panting a little, 'and then I knew it couldn't be anybody else.'

'That's the fault of the man I get my clothes from. And I'm playing truant. It's a long time since I've been up here. That's a fine dog you've got. Mother and father back yet?'

'They'll be back in about an hour. I'm just exercising the dog. I'm glad you like him.'

'Yes, I like a fine-looking dog; but James has always had his cat, you see, and I'm a busy man, and a dog takes up a lot of time.'

'Yes, that's the best of them,' she said. 'They're really a great nuisance, but if they weren't you wouldn't like them so much. It's the same with babies, you know.'

'I dare say,' he said. 'Had a good holiday?'

'Lovely. And how have you been getting on without us? You don't look very well, Mr. John. You ought to have a holiday, too.'

'And what would I do with a holiday?'

'Enjoy yourself, of course,' she said.

'H'm,' said John.

She looked at him with the genuine anxiety she felt for those she cared for. He wore his familiar hard felt hat and a clumsy pepper-and-salt tweed suit. His close-cut moustache was of the same indeterminate colour; his mouth, grim, almost sullen, drooped a little; he looked worried, cross and stubborn; but she knew how far she could go with him, and she said gently:

'Perhaps your new housekeeper isn't looking after you properly.'

'What do you know about her?' he demanded.

'Nothing. I saw her this morning, for a minute, when I was talking to Mr. James. She has a nice face.'

John opened his mouth and shut it, then opened it again to say, 'Shall we go up to the top of the cliff?'

'Yes, but we must be careful,' Hilary said gravely. 'Cousin Maurice was afraid the dog might push me over. He seemed rather anxious.'

'He's an anxious kind of man.'

'Is he?'

'Yes. Look at his mouth. It's a good mouth for a preacher, but a poor one for a man. He's a good preacher – ' John said, and left Hilary to finish his sentence as she chose.

She controlled her smile and said, 'But he ought not to be anxious. He ought to feel very comfortable about everything. He doesn't believe in luck. He only believes in the Hand of God.'

'The Hand of God, eh?' John said absently.

They stood at the edge of the cliff and seemed to overlook an empty world. The sky, tired of its own deep blue, was growing pale; the sea was pale and no line marked the place where it met the sky. Away to the left, the pier of New Framling, with the pavilion at the end of it, like a long animal with a diminutive head, seemed to be wading feebly seawards, without progress and without hope. There was something desolate, exhausted, in the scene, but nearer, just below the cliff, the village of Old Framling huddled cosily in its shelter. The cottages lay under their own smoke, like banked fires, for from every variety of chimney, tall and squat, straight and distorted, a brave blue plume ascended without a tremor.

John looked out to sea, then down at the cottages. 'So he thought you might fall over the cliff,' he said. 'I was just thinking, before you came, how easy it would be to slip over. Easier than lots of other things,' he added in a mutter.

'But,' Hilary began, with her readiness to discuss any subject that cropped up, 'it would be the end of all the other things.'

'Just so,' said John.

'I see,' Hilary said thoughtfully, and John laughed.

'You mustn't see too much.'

'No,' she said with docility. 'That's one of the dangers. Of course, if you're like Cousin Maurice, you needn't try to understand. You just take things as they come; but I don't believe he's really like that himself.'

'Catchwords,' John said curtly. 'He believes them when he wants to. It's time I was getting back.'

For a minute Hilary did not move; then she said, 'Is it? Then I'll come too,' and they started down the slope.

Now the village was on their right hand and straight before them lay the open country. Here and there a dark clump of fir trees stood like an island in the sea of fields, a sea infinitely richer in colour than the one on which John and Hilary had turned their backs, for there was the green of the grassland, the red of bare earth and the gold of stubble, and the gentle rise and fall of the ground gave an effect of movement. Facing this, they walked in silence, slowly, while the dog made circles round them, rushed after a smell and stood with a paw uplifted, barked sharply to attract Hilary's attention and considerately desisted when he understood that she was occupied with business of her own.

'I wonder – ' she began, and raised her head. John Blunt was gazing straight before him and, realizing that he would not notice an apparent lack of sequence in her remarks, she said clearly, 'Cousin Maurice said you got that nice housekeeper from the Hand of God.'

He stopped. 'What's that?' he asked.

Hilary nodded. 'Yes, from the Hand of God.'

'So that's what he calls himself is it? He brought her across himself!'

'Yes,' said Hilary; 'but perhaps he means that God sent her first and he just – just passed her on.'

'Well, whatever he means, it was queer that she should come to see the Vicar and be wanting a situation the very day after Sarah was taken ill.'

'Very convenient, though.'

'Yes. Yes, it was very – very convenient. I don't know what we should have done, else.'

'And she's satisfactory.'

'Mr. Roper guaranteed that,' John said with reserve.

'He didn't tell me she was a friend of his.'

'Her mother was a friend of your father's, I believe. Mr. Roper knows all about her – not that I set much store by what Mr. Roper knows or doesn't know.'

'I'm afraid you don't like him,' Hilary said demurely.

'And I've been rude about your cousin. Well, I can't help it. He's an old woman,' was John's reply. They had left the grass and passed through the lane leading to the village street before he added: 'Of course, that's a way of looking at it – the Hand of God. I hadn't thought of that. Look here, Hilary,' he said, and again he stopped, 'would you mind very much if some one you – well, some one you liked had done something you didn't like at all?' Her eyes widened, she did not answer, and he said, 'Would it be much of a shock to you?'

'Yes,' she said, 'I suppose it would.'

'Some one you believed in, you know. Do you think you'd stop liking him altogether?'

She took a moment to consider this. 'It wouldn't make any difference if I'd liked him enough before,' was her decision.

He looked at her with an alarming wistfulness and she said, a little breathlessly:

'Why did you ask me that, Mr. John?'

'I just wanted to know how you'd feel about it.' He put his hand on her shoulder for an instant. 'There's nothing for you to worry about,' he said kindly, and he talked of indifferent matters until they parted at the Vicarage door, but he left her bewildered, vaguely distressed, afraid of having that vagueness clarified, yet roused into a general state of protectiveness against she knew not what. She only knew that she wanted to avoid any discussion of the Blunts' affairs.

Chapter 9: *Margaret and James*

EDWARD retreated to the study after dinner. His patience was easily exhausted and he had done his best for Maurice earlier in the evening. He did not want to be rude to the old fellow, but he knew he would be if he saw too much of him, and Margaret would entertain him more successfully and amuse herself at the same time.

Maurice, thus deserted, could not make up his mind whether he would rather be with all the Stacks together, with two of them, or with one only. He was excited and nervous, like a child who would have been broken-hearted if he had missed the party, but longed for the moment when his nurse would come to take him home. However, he was getting on much better than he had feared. Margaret had changed in the opposite way to the one he had expected: her beauty remained and her character had softened. He knew he must have detected the slightest sign of mockery or boredom, and she had shown none. It was possible, too, he thought as he took his coffee, that he had himself improved and that the peculiarities incident to his unfortunate youth had passed away. Had not Hilary said she did not find him very funny?

He made a wry face and Margaret handed him the sugar-basin.

'Thank you, thank you!' he said, 'how quick you are!' and he took the sugar he did not want. Forgetting his disbelief in chance, he told himself he was supremely unlucky, for now Margaret would be sure to over-sweeten his breakfast coffee and, in the Vicarage, the coffee was one of the few things of which he could not disapprove.

He did not approve of his own present state. He was being lulled into spiritual and physical indolence by Margaret's kindness, the softly lighted room and his restored confidence. He stretched out his feet and lay back in his chair, unconsciously imitating Edward, with that facility, which had been the cause of so much mysterious trouble in the past, of adopting and distorting the manners of the people he admired. He wanted to show Margaret and himself how much he felt at home and he deliberately ignored the problem which still faced him; he avoided any attempt to discover why his sense of duty had become less acute. This experience of sitting near Margaret, looking at her and listening to her voice, with a feeling of comparative safety, was unique, and he could not let it go, no, not even if his pleasure approached, very distantly, but recognizably, the sin of covetousness in its worst form, and he had a glorious moment of abandonment before that enchanting voice shattered his happiness.

'The Blunts will be coming in soon,' Margaret said, 'and then we shall hear all about everything. They always call on the night of our return,' she explained to Maurice.

He saw now that he had made a great mistake. Without comment, he ought to have told all he knew, for he had actually advertised his suspicions by his silence and he was suddenly very anxious not to be suspected in his turn. Only if he were considered free of any but the obvious motive of helping a girl in trouble could he hope to retain the precious gift, so lately won, of sympathetic kindness, and he had a dark vision of Margaret's changed face and Edward's anger. He was a coward: he was more afraid of man's near anger than of the distant one of God; but the thought of returning in shadow to his lonely life, with no bright compensating memories, was more than he could bear. He looked at Hilary, who was reading, and he fancied that her eyes did not move across the page: she was

72

listening for what he was going to say and he thought her face had an implacable expression, warning him that it was useless to hope she would not betray him. Then he roused himself. He had been brooding over this affair until he absurdly exaggerated his responsibility, and if he must suffer through Edward's fault, it would only be a continuance of his sad fortune.

'Ah, yes,' he began with his little cough, 'no doubt they will have plenty to say to you. Probably,' he went on waggishly, 'they will have some complaints to make about me!'

'The Blunts are very discreet,' Margaret said.

This was not the answer he had hoped for and he did not know what to do with it but, before he could decide whether there was any unpleasant suggestion in it, Mr. James Blunt was announced. He had come without his brother.

Whatever faults the Stacks might have, Maurice had to own that they knew how to greet a guest, and James, who stood near the door with the anxious air of a person who had come to ask for alms, was welcomed warmly and led to a comfortable chair.

'But where is Mr. John?' Margaret asked.

James lifted his eyelids for an instant.

'He's – well, I think he's rather busy, Mrs. Stack.' There was no conviction in his voice.

The churchwarden, then, was neglecting courtesy as well as duty, and Maurice's mouth dropped half open with the thought that Edward also was under John's displeasure. Margaret herself seemed puzzled by this absence.

'Isn't he back from the office yet?' she asked.

'Oh, yes, yes, he's back from the office.'

To Maurice's perspicacity, it was now plain that James felt the weakness of his excuse. John had refused to come and, searching for a reason, Maurice wondered if that girl, who made such a show of independence, knew more than he had believed, had told all she knew

73

to John, and delegated to him a delicate piece of business. That would account for her airy manner of this morning. He had never liked the girl, and he disliked her more now that he guessed her cunning, yet with his dismay there was a relief in which he almost forgot his bright professional smile.

But James was not looking at him.

'The fact is,' he said in a louder voice, 'John isn't quite himself. Well, of course, we've had a bit of an upset.'

'Yes, of course,' Margaret said soothingly.

He turned to Hilary.

'And where's that dog?' he asked.

'Having his dinner, Mr. James.'

'Ah,' said James. He drooped in his chair as though his body were hung together with threads, and Maurice looked robust by contrast: his moustache drooped, and his sad brown eyes were downcast.

'Yes, an upset,' he murmured. 'I'm glad you're back, Mrs. Stack. We've missed you sadly. There's no one like a lady in a difficulty. Mr. Roper did his best, of course, and I'm sure we're grateful, but there –' He paused, and Maurice, adroit again, looked inquiringly, rather eagerly, at Margaret and suggested that it would be a good thing if he and Hilary took the dog for a walk.

'Yes, do,' she said, and rewarded him with a smile, one of her best smiles, for she had not expected him to show such thoughtfulness for James. There was no one to give him much thought since his mother died: he was not attractive and Margaret found it difficult to like him. She had a natural shrinking from a person she considered not quite normal, while for John, with his sturdiness, his curtness, which always changed to a charming courtesy for her, she had a real affection, in spite of the things she knew to his discredit.

'Now, Mr. James,' she said when Maurice and Hilary had gone, 'you can tell me all about it.'

He raised his sad, dog's eyes.

74

'It's a comfort to have you back, I'm sure,' he said. 'You've heard about our trouble?'

'Yes. I'm very sorry. I hope she's better.'

'She'll never be any better,' James said, and he shook his head.

She was touched by this despondency. She had always believed James was devoid of feeling for anyone except himself and the cat.

'Is it as bad as that?' she asked. 'That's very sad. You and Mr. John will miss her very much.'

'Miss her?' James said, with his head on one side.

'I should think so; indeed, I should hope so, after all these years.'

'Are you talking about Sarah?' James demanded slowly.

'Of course.'

'Well,' he said, 'I wasn't. I was talking about that young woman we've got over there. It's not suitable, Mrs. Stack, it's not really. And the ideas she's got! She must have this and she must have that! She's not content with the pots and pans Sarah managed with – oh, no! They're not good enough for her! And now she's talking about one of those mechanical carpet-sweepers. Too lazy to get down on her knees, I suppose. And you know very well, Mrs. Stack, that those sweepers do nothing but wear out the carpets – made on purpose.'

Remembering the Blunts' carpets, Margaret said consolingly, 'I don't think it would hurt them, Mr. James.'

'But there's the expense!' James cried. 'We've got to think of that.'

'Oh, nonsense!' Margaret said sharply. 'Everybody knows you have plenty of money, Mr. James.'

He looked at her slyly.

'Is that what people say?'

'It's common sense,' Margaret replied. 'You can't own all that property in New Framling and have to count your halfpennies, and the best thing you could do would be to have the whole of your house cleaned and papered and painted.'

'Good gracious me!' James said softly.

'Yes, and new carpets and new everything else.'

'Well, I never!' James said. 'No, no.' Again he shook his head. 'We couldn't part with anything. Why,' he said indignantly, 'they belonged to our parents.'

This pious sentiment left Margaret unmoved. She had no illusions about the Blunts' regard for the memory of Andrew and Mary, who lay under the big tombstone in the churchyard.

'No,' she said firmly, 'you won't get any sympathy from me about expense. And I think the young woman ought to have her carpet-sweeper.'

'But don't you say that to John!' James begged with agitation. 'In fact, Mrs. Stack, all this is just between us two. I wouldn't like John to know of it. To tell you the truth, it's not so much the expense, though, mind you, we've got to be more careful than people think, but it's— well, it isn't proper. The girl's only twenty-one!'

'And how old are you, Mr. James?' Margaret asked gently.

'It's not myself I'm thinking about,' he replied. 'I'm safe enough; but d'you know that John's not much over forty?'

'Quite a boy,' she said.

James surprised her with his retort.

'If he was a boy it wouldn't matter. Just a bit of fun, perhaps. Not,' he added hastily, 'that I like that kind of thing, and John and I – we've always kept clear of it – but a man of forty – well, it's different. You can't tell what he'll be up to.'

'But if she's a nice girl –' Margaret began.

'Nice!' James exclaimed, and he gazed at her angrily. 'What's it matter if she's nice or not?' His voice rose a little. 'I tell you she's very good-looking.'

'Oh – good-looking,' Margaret said thoughtfully. She had noticed how, with an apparent indifference to the beauty or ugliness of his surroundings, John seldom liked a person without some physical charm, and she had sometimes wondered whether James would have had a happier life if the oddity of his mind had not been expressed in his appearance. John did not treat his brother with much consideration, and she had little doubt that James's sense of impropriety was really his dread of an influence which would leave him utterly disregarded. John was a hard man and part of her weakness for him lay in her ability to get a little way below the outer crust, for she, like the new housekeeper, was pleasant to look at, and suddenly she felt an absurd little spasm of jealousy of a rival.

'But, after all, Mr. James,' she said sensibly, 'if Mr. John likes the girl –'

'Likes her! Likes her!' James cried testily. 'I don't know anything about that! All I know is that he talks to her, goes into the kitchen to talk to her! What's he talk about? He never went and talked to Sarah.'

'No,' Margaret agreed, 'but there naturally wouldn't be much to say to Sarah. You can't find any amusement in talking to people who know as much about you as Sarah does.'

James looked her full in the face for a moment and she saw the suspicion she had expected in his own.

'I don't know what you mean,' he muttered, and he looked down again, and as she did not answer, he went on quickly, 'Sarah doesn't know – she doesn't know anything – anything we wouldn't like her to know.'

'I didn't say she did, Mr. James,' Margaret said sweetly. 'And what have you got to fear from that girl?'

'Fear? I didn't say I was afraid – certainly not! But I don't want her in the house. It isn't fit.' His tone became confidential. 'Two men, you know. It's hardly right. Well, now, do you think it is, yourself?'

'I should think it's better than one,' Margaret said, with what James evidently thought was a rather shocking cheerfulness. 'But doesn't she behave as she should?'

James spoke slowly.

'I don't want to be offensive, Mrs. Stack. I'm sure Mr.
Roper meant it kindly, and we were certainly in a fix –
Sarah gone to hospital, no food in the house, beds not
made, and all that. So we were glad enough to get her,
though I must say I was against it from the start. But,
of course, John had to have his way, and seeing that Mr.
Roper knew all about her and she'd got this message
from her mother for the Vicar, it seemed as though we
couldn't do any better. And to give the girl her due, I
must say she's a lovely cook. But there it is. She's only
twenty-one and she's good-looking. Tall,' James
straightened himself, bent his head sideways in what
was meant to be a feminine attitude and, lifting his
arms from his sides, managed, though grotesquely, to
give Margaret an impression of some one large and
gracious. 'Tall,' James repeated with a sigh; 'oh, yes,
she behaves herself all right. Very managing, though;
but there, I mustn't say anything against a girl who's
connected with the Vicar.' He became conciliatory.
'Poor thing, poor thing! She's had a hard time of it with
her father – if all she says is true – and it must be, it
must be,' he added. 'She'd hardly have come with a
string of lies to the Vicar; but you see, Mrs. Stack, we've
got to be careful, John and I – well known in the village
and the town, and anyone who'd leave her father, even
if he did drink, and come here without a word of warning, just because the Vicar knew her mother when she
was a girl – though, to be sure, she's got a letter for him,
written before the mother died, if you'll believe me, and
Mr. Roper will have told you all about it, anyway –
well, anyone like that – impulsive, you know. You can't
tell what she'd be up to, can you?'

'What's her name?' Margaret asked quietly.

'Caroline.'

'Caroline?'

Caroline Mather. Comes from somewhere in the

78

Midlands, so she says. But Mr. Roper can tell you more than I can.'

Margaret was ashamed to feel that the whole of her body had gone limp, but she managed to smile at James.

'Of course he can,' she said, and after a pause she asked pleasantly, 'And will Miss Mather be coming to see my husband?'

James looked cunning.

'Not she!' he said, 'not now! She knows when she's well off. Got John under her thumb. She thinks she's settled. But I want to get rid of her, Mrs. Stack. I want to get rid of her. What's he doing now, d'you think? Sitting in the study, working? Not he! He's talking to that girl. D'you think that's a proper way to be carrying on? It's not. It's not respectable.' He seemed near tears. 'But I thought to myself, I'll go and tell Mrs. Stack and she'll put things right. But you won't tell John?' he begged again.

'Don't worry, Mr. James.'

James nodded.

'That's right, that's right. I knew you'd help me. And now I must be getting back.'

'Won't you stay and see my husband?'

'No, no,' he said, 'I must get back to the house.'

'He's going to see Sarah to-morrow,' Margaret said clearly, and she was not surprised to see him stiffen as he rose.

'Ah,' he said slowly, 'it's not much use. John goes to see her, but I don't. Painful to see people when they're ill, and she talks a lot of nonsense, I believe. The Vicar won't get any sense out of her at all. You might tell him that, Mrs. Stack. Wandering in her head, you know,' and without bidding Margaret good night, he hurried out of the room.

Chapter 10: *Margaret Alone*

MARGARET sat quite still, with her eyes on the door through which James Blunt had gone, like a shabby little messenger of evil tidings. She was sorry for him: she was sorry for anyone who was afraid, and it was to emphasize her own refusal to harbour fear and to give herself time to be reasonable that she considered the Blunts' affairs before she attacked what seemed likely to be the problem of her own. Yet it was difficult to separate them. The people on both sides of the road were involved in each other's business. James was not only nervous of what old Sarah would say to Edward, but of what John might tell that girl, and she, apparently, was connected with Edward's past, as Edward was connected with the Blunts' future. James, with his fears, had justified Edward's suspicions about the brothers and betrayed Maurice's suspicions about the girl. It was more than difficult, it was impossible, to think of one group of people without the other.

Margaret was startled, but not greatly astonished by James's revelations. She knew of the woman whom Edward had once loved, who now, it seemed, had sent her daughter to him in the certainty of his willingness to help her, and while there were, doubtless, numerous mothers whom Edward had impressed during his clerical career, not many of them, surely, were also known to Maurice and had daughters of twenty-one called Caroline. It was Maurice's strange silence about the Blunts and their new housekeeper which, even while James was speaking, had assured her that this mother had a special claim, and she did a little simple calculation before, with an abrupt movement, she went to the open window.

The night was still, too still, she thought. The leaves hung from the trees in perfect immobility: they seemed to be waiting, listening, omniscient but indifferent. They had that callousness of nature which seems cruel to human beings who are bewildered or distressed, yet what was she and what was Edward but uncomfortable developments of the force which had made these trees, these flowers whose pale faces she could see in the darkness? He and she had been developed to the point where natural things became unnatural and interfered with the enjoyment of being alive. The trees carelessly dropped their seeds, saw little trees springing up about them, and looked down at them benignly: they were not concerned with the accidents of propagation, and she envied them. She felt a great impatience for civilization's readiness to criticize such processes: it caused more trouble than it prevented, and to her it seemed as radically stupid as any other form of frustration.

Aware that there were arguments on the other side, but indifferent to them, for with all her pleasure in outward seemliness she was naturally a rebel, she continued to look at the quiet trees, and now they acted as a screen on which she could project her visions. She saw Edward sitting by that mountain stream where she had first met him, a long, tanned young man, with something in his appearance so essentially innocent and clean, as he pulled contentedly at his pipe, that it was difficult to believe that he was suffering, as she learnt later, from a sense of sin. This was a malady with which she had little sympathy, and she did not want to hear the confession he felt bound to make when he asked her to marry him. She was rather irritated by the delicacy with which he spared her modesty, and she retaliated by concealing the fact that of modesty of that kind she had none, and was well used to her uncle's liberal comments on the village scandals. He would moreover, and quite naturally, have been hurt at having his very particular case likened to all those others which were of so much less importance, but to Margaret his apology was rather absurd and, at that stage of her affection for him, she did not accept his absurdity with equanimity. By the time she could do so, she had learnt that his reticence had been more for his own sake than for hers and that, excluding matters which at all painfully concerned himself, he could be franker and funnier than she would have cared for anybody else to be. This was a great relief: she would never have been able to adapt herself to the standards of which she had suspected him, and, for successful marriage, a certain amount of adaptation was as necessary as a reasonable difference in character and tastes. To act the part of the parson's wife, however, was too extreme an instance. She did not feel like a parson's wife; only when she was angry with him could she feel that Edward was a parson, and she sometimes wondered if he felt like one himself. Fortunately for him, his duties in Old Framling – and he did not neglect them – left him plenty of time to do the work he liked; but Margaret, in marrying him, had resigned her chances of the kind of life which would have suited her, one in which her charm and her ability would have been exercised and increased. She could, so Edward told her, employ them very well in Old Framling and, to some extent, she did. She had made fast friends of the Blunts and of several energetic women who were glad she did not wish to preside at sewing meetings and mothers' teas, and she could walk down the lanes among the fishermen's cottages without Maurice's sad experiences. The people liked her well enough, but they were no more anxious to receive than she to give the usual offerings of a woman in her position and, when she stopped to talk to them, they knew there was no sense of patronage or of duty in her neighbourliness. There was not even the desire, so easily detected, of assuring them that she considered them her equals, and she escaped, by a kind of miracle, the self-consciousness which might have resulted from her attitude.

She had had a quiet life, she thought, still seeing her visions against the trees, but she had made it amusing to Edward and herself, and now it seemed as though the excitement she had wanted had arrived in a singularly disagreeable form and her gifts must be turned to uses she had always disdained, though what these were she did not attempt to decide. She had a moment of suspension, without definite thought or feeling, in which her sense of the situation soaked into her mind, before she turned from the window and the indifferent trees. They were quite right to be indifferent, but they were too close to her, too stifling, and she thought longingly of the hills she had just left. Only a few slim rowan trees grew near her Uncle Alec's parsonage: a trout stream ran at the bottom of his rough lawn, and beyond that a vividly green strip of pasturage slipped into the moorland, the moorland into the hills. She saw the hills plainly, coloured with all the shades of bracken and heather, streaked with little streams like threads, and, farther off, their multitudes of colour gathered into one, a faint blue or a threatening blackness, they had the curves of waves which never broke the compactness of solid rock. This effect of movement in permanency was what the sea could never give her: its noise was repetition, the same words uttered in varying volume; its action was repetition in varying force: there was something futile in the ceaseless exhibition of its strength, but the hills told her that behind restlessness there was rest, and the peace which passed all understanding.

The hills were far away, but her love for them had given her the power to bring them near, and she forgot the lamp-lit room and seemed to be standing outside her uncle's door and listening to the stream she could not see. It sang through the night with the strange and lovely noise made by invisible water and, across the valley, the hills took solid shape against the sky's thinner darkness. She lost her sense of present time and place; she could smell the peaty earth and feel the softest of all winds on her face, until she was startled by a piece of wood shifting in the grate. Just for a second she thought the sound came from the house behind her. It was her uncle moving in the narrow passage, searching for something he wanted, and soon he would call to her to come and find it and she would respond with the good humour which never failed her there. The calm spaciousness of that country seemed to enlarge and quieten her own nature, but here she allowed small things to fret her far more than even Hilary had discerned, and no one, seeing her now as she smiled tolerantly at her weakness and went slowly towards the door with movements saved from voluptuousness by the impression of muscle under the flesh, would have divined her eagerness to escape from the room she had been at such pains to beautify. There were no hills in Old Framling, but there was the open sky: the darkness would hide the tormented sea with its insistence on the endlessness of struggle, and out of doors she would be able to deal more competently with the thoughts which were now assailing her.

Very quietly she went upstairs to get a shawl and, still more quietly, she slipped into the street. No one else was in sight; no lights shone from the Blunts' house. She thought of John, talking to that girl, and of James, consoling himself with the cat. She thought of Edward in his study, reading some theological review, absorbed, forgetful of everything except the immediate problem which, for him, was in the printed page, while hers, created and ignored by him, lay in the narrow space between the Blunts' house and her own. Her sigh was half a laugh. She had never felt the slightest jealousy for the other woman he had loved; she took no credit for her own single affection; she might have loved another man if she had met him first; she had no illusions about the inevitability of her marriage with Edward; it had been good, but another might have been as good in a different way, and she had a normal, though generally unconfessed, desire to be loved by any man who could do it with dignity and skill. The management of one man and one child was hardly enough to occupy an intelligent woman; she had a power of attraction which would have been dangerous in anyone less honest, and when she was dull she told Edward that her honesty was her cross. These were sentiments which Edward found very shocking, and he only half believed they were sincere. He saw himself as the pattern of steadfast devotion, which, indeed, he was; but he did not know, as she did, that her waywardness, though natural enough, was part of her plan for keeping him to that perfection. Marriage and motherhood were the only arts she had been able to practise, and what creative impulse she possessed she had spent on Hilary and Edward. They were her works, but other hands had meddled with Edward first, and while she felt responsibility for the results of a past in which she had no part, she had nothing but a tenderly impatient tolerance for their cause, and that, she told herself, was more than Edward, with all the love of which he so justly boasted, could have sufficiently eliminated himself to do for her. She saw his limitations and liked them. It amused her to think of him in the study, concentrated on theory, while she faced a fact of flesh and blood which was menacing his peace, but her amusement turned to sharp anger when she thought of Hilary, who was too young to be allowed to suffer for another's folly, too young to refuse to suffer for it. But perhaps no suffering was necessary for anyone; she was determined not to take a sentimental or a conventional view, the view which Edward himself would take, about the claims of Caroline Mather, whose name ought, in all probability, to be Caroline

85

Stack. Her present business was to discover how much was known or suspected by John Blunt, by Maurice and the girl herself. Maurice had been most indiscreetly discreet. John Blunt, that worthy churchwarden, lived in a glass house and was not likely to invite stones: Caroline Mather was a handsome girl and a good cook; and this was the extent of Margaret's knowledge as she went down the street, with the points of her slippers darting in front of her, like gilt fish swimming on the pavement; but when she reached the old bridge she saw that the man who might tell her more was standing there.

She never saw John Blunt without a conscious increase of her femininity: he had that effect on her and, with a little hitch of her shoulder, she let her shawl fall more gracefully.

Just as Hilary had recognized him that afternoon against the skyline, knowing that the square figure could belong to no one else, Margaret was sure of him in the darkness. Wherever he stood, he looked as though he had grown there; his hard felt hat seemed to have grown on his head; he looked fixed, immovable, and Margaret wondered if James's grievances were imaginary. If not, why was John standing on the bridge, when he might have been in that girl's company? And again she felt her absurd little spasm of jealousy, not of Edward's past, or Hilary's future, but of the influence of any other woman over John, and the moment for the feeling was so ill-timed, so irrelevant to her present urgency, and so foolish in itself, that she laughed aloud and saw John turn slowly at the sound.

Chapter 11: *Margaret and John*

HER voice, greeting him, both completed and prolonged the laughter. 'Did you think it was a ghost jeering at you?' she asked, as he took her hand.

He gave the question a moment's consideration. 'No,' he said, 'not exactly. I was a bit startled. It seemed – rather strange. I'd been thinking.'

'So had I,' Margaret said, 'and my thoughts made me laugh. They often do. It's a great resource to have thoughts like that.'

'It needs practice, I suppose.'

'It would for you. You're a serious-minded man. They come naturally to me.' She was growing used to the darkness and she saw him smile.

'You are a very merry lady,' he said, making the statement, without knowing it, into a caress.

Perhaps it was his simplicity which made him attractive, Margaret thought; a masculine simplicity, without the womanly qualities which crop up in the nicest men and annoy their women with a reminder of themselves. If he talked like that to the girl, she was bound to love him and Margaret envied anyone who was freshly in love. New love was like dew on sunny grass – it made the world sparkle, and old love, which was better, though less exhilarating, was like hay, spread out and drying, in a fair field; warm, scented, with the beauty of the past in it and the comfort of the future. She wished she could tell John that, but what she could see of his face betrayed nothing of the lover. And why should he be standing there alone, watching the water?

'You didn't come in to see me, Mr. John,' she said.

'Mr. James did. He said you were busy, and I find you here!'

'Yes, I was having a look at the river.'

'Is it doing anything special?'

'It turned a little while ago, I think. Going out. I don't know why, but I'd rather see it coming in.'

'Ah, yes, it seems more hopeful,' Margaret said. 'In my country, there isn't any of this foolish going out and in. There's just more water or less. And it's clean. You can drink it. I don't know why you should waste your time over water like this.'

'Well, I haven't been here so very long,' John said. 'I felt as if I must get outside the house.'

'So did I.'

'To think,' he said.

'That was what I meant to do, and now we're interfering with each other. What a pity!'

'Not for me. I'm very glad to see you, Mrs. Stack. I never like it when the Vicarage is empty.'

'But it wasn't empty.'

'Well – no,' John conceded slowly.

She smiled with a gradual widening and tilting of her mouth which she was afraid John could not see. 'I hope you were kind to Mr. Roper,' she said gravely.

'I don't know about that,' John said, and he looked over the parapet. 'Yes, it's going out. It would be nearer the truth to say he was kind to us. He'll have told you all about that. Did James give the Vicar Sarah's message?'

'Edward had heard already, from the hospital.'

'But did James give the message?'

'No,' Margaret said. 'Now, don't be cross with him, Mr. John.'

'Oh, I shan't say anything to him,' John replied curtly.

'Poor Mr. James!' Margaret said softly, as she sat down on the low parapet of the bridge. 'I don't think you ever say much to him, do you?'

John stood over her, his hands in his pockets, and looked at her fixedly. 'No,' he said, and he walked to the other side of the bridge and back again. 'What can you say to a man like James?' he asked.

'He's lonely,' Margaret said.

'And who isn't?' John asked with a roughness she had not heard from him before.

'I'm not,' she said. 'And you wouldn't be, if you'd come and sit here by me.'

'You oughtn't to be sitting there. That parapet's not safe.'

'It's as safe as anything else.' She patted the stone beside her.

'I shouldn't like you to fall into the river,' he said, and he sat down.

'Then it would be Edward who would be lonely. He'd have the consolation of saying, "I told you so," but I shouldn't be there to hear it, so he wouldn't get much fun out of that!'

'He'd still have Hilary,' John growled.

'Mr. John,' she said and, bending forward, she turned towards him with a prettily persuasive movement, 'what's the matter? It's a bad sign when a man compares his lot with someone else's, even by implication. I'm going to talk to you like a mother.'

'No,' he said, 'like a friend.'

'Very well. Like a friend; but I shall sound like a prig. Don't you know that when strong people are lonely, it's their own fault? They put up barriers. They're so proud of being able to build them well, all by themselves, and the walls go up and up, higher and higher, thicker and thicker, and behold, the poor things have shut themselves inside! That's real loneliness. Not Mr. James's kind. He's prowling about outside, trying to get in.'

'So you think I've bricked myself up?'

'I didn't say so.'

'By implication,' he retorted.

She laughed. 'I must take to writing Edward's sermons for him. If you'd called on me in the proper way, you would have escaped this lecture.'

'I like this better,' he said, 'even with the lecture.'

They could hear the water running under the bridge, in a hurry to reach the invisible sea. The village on their right was an indefinite mass of walls and roofs, studded with lights. New Framling, on their left, was a constellation, and nothing could be seen of the gaunt pier but the lamps marking its continual, unprogressive stride.

'This place is almost bearable, in the dark,' Margaret said.

'You're sure you're not cold sitting here?' John asked. Her shawl had slipped back a little, showing her bare neck. 'I can't understand how ladies manage to keep warm.' He glanced down at her feet. 'And those thin slippers! But they're pretty,' he said.

'Yes, I think they're pretty,' she said, following his glance.

'They look very small,' he said seriously.

'They're smaller than Hilary's, though I'm bigger than she is. Girls' feet are larger than they used to be.'

'Yes, I've noticed – something of that kind,' he said in a slight confusion. 'But I like a large hand,' he remarked, a moment later.

'Do you? Why?'

'It seems right, somehow,' he muttered.

So the mysterious Caroline had large hands and feet! Margaret smiled to herself, but not happily. Perhaps she had inherited them from her father, she thought grimly, and her anger flared up again. What a terrible nuisance Edward was! If he had been a different kind of man she would have told him everything, for she hated secrecy, but with his readiness to feel sinful and to make atonement, he would rush across the road and take that girl into his arms, and then into the Vicarage, proclaiming her his daughter, and what would Hilary think of that? Hilary had as much right to consideration as Caroline, and if Caroline's mother had been light in her affections, there must have been other lovers as well as Edward. It was possible that she had sent the girl to him because the same simplicity which had made him her victim would constrain him to acknowledge the child, and convenient as it might be to suspect someone else, Edward's pride would forbid that. Just as he scoffed at Margaret's suggestion that another man might attract her, he would refuse to believe he had shared another woman. In his own way he, too, was thoroughly masculine.

'I'm getting spiteful – about the woman and about Edward,' she said to herself. 'The woman was probably as good as I am, but less discreet, less fortunate. All the same, it's true about Edward. No real sense of humour.' She laughed again. 'More funny thoughts,' she said to John.

'Were you laughing at me?'

'You? No!' she cried indignantly.

'You might very well,' he said quietly. 'I'd laugh at myself if I knew how, but I've never learnt. A pity, that. There was never any laughter in our house when I was a boy. Smiles, you know – my mother used to smile – but no noise. Everything very quiet.'

'Yes, I remember your parents,' Margaret said.

'Of course! Of course! But you don't remember James and me as boys. Mrs. Stack, I never opened my mouth in my father's presence without a struggle, and then I wished I hadn't.' He was silent for a moment. 'That's when I began to build the walls, I suppose.'

'You can begin to pull them down.'

'I'm doing it now,' John said, 'talking to you. But what's the good of pulling down one lot and finding another one outside? A steel fence. That's worse. People can see through that and still you can't get out. I'd rather not be seen at all.'

'It depends who's looking at you.'

'That's just it,' he said. 'That's just it. But I've talked enough. I hope you've had a pleasant holiday, Mrs. Stack.'

'A steel fence,' Margaret said thoughtfully. 'Yes, very, thank you, Mr. John. Well, you know, you can always blow it up. One explosion and you'd be a free man.'

'Yes, and a lot of other people would be wounded, as well as me.'

'You've got to risk something,' she said lightly. 'Here we are, sitting on this crumbling old stone, and and we're not in the river yet! Life's all risks, and the prizes fall to the brave. Why, your new housekeeper – Miss Mather, isn't it? – took a risk in coming here, and she found a home on the Vicarage doorstep. And you and Mr. James risked taking her into your house, and I hear she's a lovely cook!'

'James tell you that?'

'Her cooking seems to have made a great impression,' Margaret replied.

John stood up again. 'She's only twenty-one,' he said.

'Yes,' Margaret said, patiently. Twenty-one years ago Edward had asked her to marry him. She was not likely to forget the girl's age.

'She seems older.'

'Perhaps she is.'

'No, she says she's twenty-one,' John said simply. 'And it's only when ladies are getting on, isn't it, that they begin taking off a few years. It's very young, Mrs. Stack, to be alone in the world. If it were Hilary now – her mother's dead. She seems to have had a great liking for her mother. A fine woman. But you must know all that. I've been thinking it would be a good thing for her to have a friend, a lady. If this father of hers comes after her – Oh, well, you never know what might happen. And she might want –

she might want a change. I'd like to think you would be willing to help her.'

Margaret looked at the points of her slippers and then into John's face. She thought, as Hilary had thought earlier, that there was a look of strain about it. 'I'll do what I can,' she said, 'but won't she be expecting Edward to go and see her? Or will she come and see him? I'm told she has a letter for him.'

'She doesn't want to see the Vicar,' John said abruptly.

'She doesn't want to see him?' Margaret repeated slowly. 'Then why did she come here?'

'She came to get work and now she's got it. She's very independent. If you'll excuse my saying so, Mrs. Stack, she doesn't seem to think much of clergymen.'

'No? Neither do I. But she came to get help from one.'

'I think she was pretty desperate. A bad lot, her father. She wouldn't have left him if he hadn't been past bearing.'

'And she's desperate no longer?'

'No-o,' John said, 'not at present, certainly.'

'And when she is, she'll appeal to Edward again?'

'I don't know what she'll do,' John said more loudly. There was a sharp edge on his voice.

'It sounds very mysterious,' Margaret murmured. She wanted to make John say more, she wanted to find out how much he knew. She wondered if he were struggling between loyalty to the girl and to Edward, and, suddenly, her doubts and fears turned into fury against Maurice. If, as his silence implied, he suspected Caroline Mather's origin, how could he have blundered into the arrant folly of installing her with the Blunts? It seemed that her estimate of his intelligence, low as it was, ought to have been still lower. It was not surprising that he had been nervous at dinner, playing a tattoo on the table and glancing from face to face. She was sorry she had listened to his dreary story about his defective furnace. How could he expect it to be anything else? Silly old woman! she thought, and she tapped her toes on the road.

'You're getting cold, Mrs. Stack,' John said.

'No, but it's time I went home. And I haven't asked after Sarah. Is she going to get better?'

'I shouldn't think so,' John said indifferently.

'You don't seem to care much,' she said sharply, for she felt it was her turn to hurt somebody.

'No, I don't care,' he said.

'Mr. John! You sound quite heartless. Sarah has served you faithfully all your life. Is that your gratitude?'

'Yes, that's my gratitude,' he said stubbornly.

'Poor old woman. I hope she doesn't know.'

'Ah, she's got other things to think about,' John said.

Margaret stood up and gathered her shawl more closely round her. Now she really did feel cold. The chill of John's callousness had invaded her body. He seemed remorseless, cruel, capable of any disloyalty, and she said bitterly, 'Yes, you've built your walls thick and high.'

'And you think I'd have made them lower, if I'd told a lie?'

'What's a lie?' Margaret demanded. 'It's sometimes truer than the truth.'

'Oh, I've told plenty in my time,' he said, 'but not to you, not in words, at least. I shouldn't find that easy.'

'And I suppose I must feel honoured,' Margaret said dryly.

'Not by me,' John said at once, 'but by yourself.'

She was softened and she was shamed by this tribute, and quickly, half in apology and half in explanation, she said: 'It was for you I felt sorry, Mr. John, more than for Sarah, yet I have no right to feel sorry for you. That is presumption. You must forgive me. You have been very patient.'

'Have I? I didn't know it. You said you were going to talk to me – like a friend.'

'But did I?' she said, and she asked the question more of herself than of him. Her kindness to John had not been quite disinterested. She liked him, she felt he was suffering from some strange, new pain and she wished to help him, but she could not pretend she had not been probing him for her own purposes. 'But did I?' she repeated, in a desire for reassurance.

'Yes, you did,' he said briskly. His voice became gentle. 'I'm not entirely devoid of gratitude. And you've promised to help Caroline – she likes us to call her Caroline – if there's any need. Now you must let me see you home.'

Chapter 12: *Margaret and Hilary*

As she shut the front door on the figure of John Blunt, standing on the pavement, hat in hand, Margaret wished she had someone to share and appreciate the irony of the situation. She could hear Edward and Maurice talking in the study, but to neither of them could she explain the humour of her promise to John. She was to help the girl who should have been her enemy, the girl who had no desire to see her mother's old friend to whom that mother had sent her. Margaret, stepping towards the stairs, stood still, caught by a thought. Something had changed Caroline since her arrival in Old Framling. Was it possible that Maurice had been even more foolish than she feared and told her what she had not known before she came? He was a born blunderer; it was just the kind of thing he would do, and now he was afraid of being found out. She nodded her head wisely, then shook it angrily in the direction of the study, before she went upstairs and knocked at Hilary's door.

The room was in darkness but for two lighted candles on the table by the bed in which Hilary lay, with pillows behind her back and a book against her raised knees, and to Margaret, coming from that dim interview with John and the confusion, and what seemed now the murkiness, of her own thoughts, the sight of Hilary in her clean fairness was a reproach for anything less clean and fair. To Hilary, her mother's entrance brought life and beauty into the room, and they were both aware that each was half a mystery to the other.

'You've come early to bed,' Margaret said.

'Yes, I was tired,' said Hilary.

'You don't look tired.'

'Not in my body,' Hilary said. 'I find Cousin Maurice very exhausting. You have to be so careful with him.'

'Do you? I'm not.'

'But you were wonderful at dinner about the heating apparatus. You seemed really interested.'

'Well, I was, in a way,' Margaret said, and she sat down on the end of the bed, throwing her gay shawl behind her. 'I'm lucky. I find it hard to get really bored. One can always speculate on how much duller a person can be, and when I was listening to Maurice to-night I was forestalling his next sentence in my mind, saying the most obvious thing I could, and I was beaten every time. There was a kind of brilliance in his banality.'

'But nobody could be very amusing about warming a church,' said Hilary, doing her best for him.

'Couldn't they? I could! And if they can't make things amusing, they shouldn't talk about them at all.'

'Then most people would be dumb.'

'I suppose that's what they really are, and the noises they make are attempts at human speech.'

'You sound hard-hearted, but you're not,' Hilary announced solemnly. 'I'm not surprised that poor Cousin Maurice is afraid of you. He's afraid of you and he doesn't like me. I irritate him. I try not to – most of the time – but I do.'

'I shouldn't try too hard,' Margaret murmured.

The candles were burning steadily, for the air was still and no wavering of theirs could be blamed for the shadow which passed over Hilary's face. Her feeling of discomfort had not been lessened by her walk with Maurice. Under the kind cover of the night, he had tried to give himself confidence by talking, not of the things actually pressing on his mind, for of those he did not wish to think, but on the past which had occasioned his present difficulties, and in his reminiscences of her father and her mother, Hilary had detected an acid flavour under his heavy gaiety. She could not guess that the very kindness he had received had roused all his old resentments as soon as he left the presence of her parents. So it had always been with him. The kindness which soothed him while he enjoyed it turned to condescension when he was alone, and to-night, the sight of Edward in a home shared with Margaret had waked his weak desire to ruffle all its smoothness and dim its brilliance, while his dread of doing it, his dislike of responsibility, his fear that James Blunt was doing what he should have done himself, and his longing for appreciation, aggravated his distress. With a subtlety of which he was hardly aware he had found relief in disturbing Hilary, or rather, for he doubted her sensibility, in giving her the chance to be disturbed. She had taken her chance, but she did not understand it. For the first time in her life she had a sense of danger, and Maurice and the Blunts' new housekeeper, her father and John Blunt's question were concerned in it. John Blunt had asked her if it would be a shock to learn something dishonouring to one she cared for, as though on her answer some action of his depended, and when she had answered he had told her not to worry, but how could she help being worried after such a question, when it followed Maurice's suggestive silences and was followed by his suggestive talk? She would not try to express her fears, for they were vague, and to speak of them would be like turning fancy into fact, but here, sitting on her bed, was someone cleverer than herself, someone alert though lazy, carelessly beautiful, wise and witty, and she would know what to do with a hint, so Hilary, wriggling her toes under the bedclothes, said slowly, 'I don't think he's very happy.'

'Nobody who is irritated by you deserves to be happy,' Margaret said at once, but with a sly change of expression she acknowledged her prejudiced point of view.

Hilary laughed with a clear little peal of sound. 'I annoyed Father at dinner!'

'Yes. What did you do that for?'

'Well – to hide Cousin Maurice. I felt as if he ought to be covered up.'

'Yes, that's what he likes,' Margaret said, 'and, all the time, he's so obvious, poor dear.'

'I think he's a poor dear, but I don't think he's so very obvious. Only on the top,' and slowly she repeated, 'I'm sure he isn't happy. And I don't see why everybody shouldn't be. I wish you'd be very kind to him.'

Margaret widened her eyes and lifted her hands. 'Haven't I been? What about his cold church? And the draught in the pulpit? It whistled down his neck and blew round his feet, and at the end of his sermon he hardly knew how to walk down the steps. But I knew how he did it, just as usual – like a duck! Have you noticed how he turns his feet out? The first time I saw him, at a railway station, he was walking along the platform like that – flap, flap! I didn't know who he was, except that he belonged to the duck family –'

'And he didn't know who you were. He told me about that,' Hilary said, and there was a slight constriction of her throat. She felt the sadness of the contrast between Maurice's memory of that occasion and her mother's, and to say more about it would have been to strike Maurice in the back. 'And you ought to be extra kind to him, because of his feet,' she said.

'Ah, that's just where I fail,' Margaret said. 'I don't like physical imperfections. Even a saint ought to have a beautiful body. I'll try to be nice, but I can't help laughing at him.'

'But don't, don't!' Hilary cried with her first display of emotion.

'You're much too tender-hearted, my precious,' Margaret said. 'Don't worry about him. I'll do my best. Go to sleep. Shall I put out the lights?'

'Yes, please. And tuck me up.' She kissed the hand smoothing the sheet. 'It isn't tender-heartedness,' she confessed in a low voice.

'What is it, then?'

'Oh – I don't know. But I wish he'd go away.'

'The nicer I am to him the longer he'll stay,' Margaret said, smiling as she looked down. 'Now, what am I to do?'

Hilary shut her eyes. 'You know best,' she said, and Margaret kissed her daughter's eyelids before she blew out the lights.

She went to her own room and sat there in darkness, by the window. It looked on to the garden, but the trees, which had oppressed her before, were more distant now and seemed to have a kindlier wisdom, and she could imagine that the flowers, pale patches on the black lawn, were looking up at her in appeal, as Hilary had looked up from her bed. Margaret sat very still, and the sense of her love for Hilary flooded her like a sea. She had refused to be sentimental about her child and their relationship; she had a genuine scorn for women who considered themselves sanctified by the common experience of having borne a baby; it was right that the child should be sacred, but the child should not know it, and Margaret had seldom indulged herself in a consciousness of maternal passion. Only now and then it took her unawares, at a note in Hilary's voice or some slight play of her features, and she was caught up in a sort of ecstasy of possession. To-night, she told herself that while she did not want to keep Hilary unspotted from the world, she would do all she could to shield her from the kind of spot which threatened her from the other side of the road. It was Hilary, not Edward, whom she wished to protect: her love for Edward was like her love for herself; it could stand buffeting, it could suffer temporary eclipse and shine out again. Marriage was warfare, and the periods of peace were chiefly valuable for the opportunity of sharpening weapons and practising their use. It was impossible for her, at least, to love a man as she loved Hilary, with a willingness to give and get nothing in return, with obligations on her side and none on the other, and a deep respect for the child's reserves, a respect which forbade her to dwell on them more than was necessary for their protection. But with Edward's thoughts she flagrantly played the spy. She had the right, for though she constantly mocked his assertion of their unity, it was true enough: she made fewer claims than he did and, secretly, she acknowledged the justice of his, for they were friends as well as lovers, but at times the independence of her spirit rebelled against the bonds of her own making, and then quailed at her primitive consciousness of their existence. A really civilized woman, she thought, would have accepted the physical relationship more calmly, but with her it meant a complete, if passing, surrender, and her reaction had the same strength. These characteristics had their advantages both for her and for Edward. Their love had never lost the element of surprise, and her clear-sightedness and his forbearance had welded them into a companionship which could not break. Even now, when her love for Hilary was at white heat, and she could see Edward's past folly menacing the child's peace, she could think of him tolerantly, and find an irritated pleasure in picturing him, down there in the study, talking to Maurice, stretching his long legs and pulling at his pipe, in a state of ignorance which was, after all, rather endearing. It was strange that, in some ways, he was more her child than Hilary had ever been. No excuses were necessary for Hilary but, if they had been, Margaret would not have troubled to find them, while for Edward, who was part of herself, allowances had sometimes to be made.

She was not grudging with them over this affair of Caroline Mather, but she was determined that he should have no hand in it until she could see it all more clearly.

Downstairs she heard the opening of a door and Edward's voice continuing some argument from which, she was sure, Maurice was trying to escape. She heard the creaking of a stair under Maurice's flat feet, and Edward's voice still following him in his retreat.

'I am not convinced,' Maurice said loudly from the landing, and Edward laughed. Then he shot home the bolts of the front door, and Margaret hastily lit her candles.

Chapter 13: *Margaret and Edward*

HE appeared in the doorway, holding his candlestick aslant, and Margaret took it from him with an air of patience.

'Grease all over the stairs, I suppose,' she said, but he, ignoring or not hearing the reproach, wanted to know where she had been hiding herself all the evening.

'When did you begin to ask yourself that? I'll tell you. As soon as Maurice went into the study.'

'I always want to know where you are.'

'It's fortunate that your anxiety doesn't take an active form. I've been sitting on the bridge with John Blunt.'

'I do wish you wouldn't be so foolish.'

'We weren't nearly so foolish as I should have liked.'

'But you know that parapet isn't safe. I've told you not to sit on it before.'

'It's safer than John is.'

'Don't be absurd,' he said sharply.

'You're rather cross, aren't you?' she asked sympathetically.

'Of course I am. If you'd nothing better to do than endanger your life on that bridge, you might have relieved me of Maurice.'

'Oh,' she said easily, 'we have to shuffle him about. It's only fair to take turns. And he's your cousin, not mine.'

'Well, I endured your Aunt Agatha yesterday.'

'But Maurice is your brother in the Lord, and that makes a lot of difference.'

Edward snorted. 'There's a lot of difference in our ideas of the Lord.'

'I heard you arguing,' Margaret said sweetly, 'all the way up the stairs.'

'And I haven't finished yet,' Edward assured her.

Margaret went to the window and raised her hand to draw the curtain. 'It's a lovely night, Edward. Look at it. And there's your church – modest little emblem of peace and goodwill! You mustn't quarrel with Maurice.'

'Arguing isn't quarrelling, and the church doesn't want lies even for the sake of peace.'

'H'm,' said Margaret, 'I don't believe it knows what it wants. Don't look self-righteous, Edward. I can't bear your nose when you get into this mood – it looks so pious. And you know perfectly well that you can't help arguing, so don't pretend you're the Church Militant, with truth for your banner. Hilary says we've to be kind to Maurice.'

'Hilary always echoes you,' he said as he went into the dressing-room.

Margaret took off her dress and hung it up. She let down the thick, wavy hair which reached no further than her shoulders, and walked slowly to the communicating door. In her short silk petticoat she looked very young, and he moved towards her appreciatively, but she stopped him by saying quietly. 'That's one of the stupidest things I've ever heard you say, and it reveals a gross ignorance of your daughter. I can assure you, my dear man, that Hilary's thoughts go their own way, and you and I shall never know what that is. She's docile, but deep.'

'When I said she echoed you, I was saying the nicest thing I could about her,' Edward explained.

'No. You think so now, because you like me in my petticoat, but I wasn't in my petticoat then.'

'You're both adorable,' he said, 'and if Hilary were hideous and disagreeable, I should still adore her because she's yours.'

'Only because of that?'

'I'm afraid so – in those circumstances.'

'Couldn't you like a child if you didn't like her mother?'

'Luckily I needn't consider the problem.'

Margaret checked the quick words on her tongue, and murmured as she turned away. 'But you'd do your duty by her, all the more conscientiously.'

'And would that be wrong?' Edward demanded.

'No, quite right, quite right,' Margaret said soothingly, from the shadow of the hair she was brushing.

She felt rather mean, but determinedly remorseless as she brushed. He was sitting down and watching her, with that perennial interest and admiration which made him pathetic to her, while she was planning the introduction of a subject he would not like.

'Did Maurice render an account of his stewardship?' she asked with faint mimicry of his tones.

'No. No.' Edward rumpled his hair. 'I suppose I ought to have asked for it, but he came in and found me reading a review, and then we began talking about it.'

'You mean you began telling him about it.'

'I didn't! He asked intelligent questions.'

'How unwary! I've learnt not to do that. I don't put my feet in the water unless I'm prepared to swim for a long time.'

'Well, he didn't swim – he floundered. I'm fond of the old fool, but his attitude towards Biblical criticism is tragic.' He took his head in his hands. 'Tragic! However,' he looked up cheerfully, 'I've persuaded him to preach on Sunday. He preaches very well.'

'Then I shall have to listen, and when you preach, I needn't.'

'Oh, I know you think nothing of my sermons,' he grumbled.

'You are so much better than they are, my angel,' she said softly.

He looked at her with a sort of wonder. 'What a genius you have for saying nasty things.'

'We shall certainly have to get rid of Maurice,' she said thoughtfully.

He sighed. 'I wish I could be angry with you for more than a minute at a time.'

'But you can't,' she said, 'and I take advantage of you.' She dropped on to his knee and put her cheek against his. 'But I wouldn't if I didn't love you.'

'Are you sure of that?'

'Nearly,' she said.

'Then don't take advantage of poor old Maurice. He's very fond of you.'

'Everybody's fond of me.'

'Not in love with you, though.'

She sat up with a jerk. 'Edward! Really? What makes you think so?'

'I've always known it.'

'I don't believe it.'

'So much the better for Maurice. But I know he's been in love with you ever since he saw you. I'm not so dull as you think.'

'Oh, why didn't I know?' she cried. 'You might have told me!'

'I thought women always knew these things. And, anyhow, I had some consideration for him.'

'And I might have had such fun, and by now he must have got over it.' She was silent for a moment. 'I see no signs of love, Edward.'

'I don't suggest that he's suffering acutely.'

'I could make him, though! For if I'm middle-aged, he's more so. Yes, I could make him, Edward.'

'That's why I didn't tell you.'

'Then why tell me now?' she asked, but she knew the answer better than he did. Her beauty still moved him to confidences and demonstrations, and though he would have scorned the suggestion that candle light was kind to her, she was without illusions and, leaning away from him, she said reproachfully, 'Yet you always pretend to keep nothing from me. Have you any more secrets? I rather like them. But I shall never be able to trust you again,' she said sadly. 'Never, never! And what a pity that it's only Maurice. I can't expect you to be jealous about him.'

'I believe I could be jealous about anyone,' he confessed.

'Except John Blunt.'

'Oh, John Blunt's in love with his money bags. I'm not afraid of him. No, my trouble is that you're so sure of me.'

'Though I have less reason,' she said, very quietly. She was tempted to use a note of sorrow, but even Edward, innocent of such frauds as he was, might have suspected sorrow, and the quiet gravity of her voice made him loose his hold of her at once.

'What do you mean?' he asked.

She stood up and smiled down at him. 'Well, Edward, my – what shall I call them? – my amatory experiences have been limited.'

His face clouded heavily. 'I'm sorry to hear you say so. I thought I had no limitations as a lover.'

'Darling, you're wonderful,' she said effusively, for she could never take him as seriously as he took himself, 'and if I'm less resourceful than you are, you must remember that you've had more practice.'

'I don't know what you're talking about.'

She picked up her dressing-gown and flung it round her, for she felt suddenly cold, but the unintentional effect was to put a little distance between them. Her tone was light enough. 'I was thinking of that girl you were in love with. What was she called? Caroline? Yes – so old-fashioned. I often wonder if she was like her name.'

'I don't wish to talk about it,' he said stiffly, and he passed her abruptly on his way to the dressing-room.

'No, Edward, don't run away!' she cried. 'You are rather a poor exponent of your own theories. Perfect confidence on my part, selected confidence on yours?'

This was a challenge she knew he would not refuse, and he said wearily, 'I told you all I ought to have told you ages ago.'

'Yes,' she agreed, 'but you were rather cryptic, and I want to know some more. Were you engaged to marry her?'

'I suppose you might call it that,' he said with a kind of humour.

'And why didn't you?'

He made a gesture of distaste. 'Because it was all wrong. I found out, too late, that I'd made a great mistake.'

'Too late?'

'Too late to retreat honourably, but not too late,' he said warmly, 'for her generosity.'

'Ah, she let you go,' Margaret murmured.

'Yes. I hadn't the decency to pretend properly.'

Margaret refrained from telling him that it was ability he lacked, and she said gently, 'Did she think she had made a mistake, too?'

'That is what she said, but how do I know? Can't you see I don't want to talk about it? She went away and I never heard of her again. Can't you see that I don't want to think about the wrong I did her, and the second one she forced on me? It's gratifying neither to one's pride nor one's self-respect.'

'You were very young, Edward.'

'I can't see what difference that makes, from her point of view. She was young, too. She was a little older than I was, and she chose to blame herself. Now, is that all you want to know?' he asked with a curbed impatience.

'Not quite. How well did Maurice know her?'

'So it's Maurice who has been talking, is it?'

'My dear, he wouldn't mention any episode so shocking. But he was living with you, more or less, wasn't he, at the time?'

'Oh yes, I suppose he was somewhere about, but he

hardly knew her. She would have frightened him with her bigness and her gaiety and noise. She wasn't what he would have called a lady.'

'She behaved like one,' Margaret said.

'Yes,' he said, and his stubborn look passed away. 'Yes, she did,' he said eagerly. 'I was right about her all the time, about her character. She was more like you than anyone I've ever met, but – well, there were things I couldn't stand. I loathed myself for noticing them, for not having noticed them at first, but there they were and she saw quickly enough. I don't know how much she cared. And all I could do was to make her promise that she'd send for me if she – if she needed me. Do you think,' he asked in a child-like manner, 'she would have kept her promise?'

'I don't know,' Margaret said slowly. 'A woman doesn't keep that kind of promise to the man she loves if she knows the man doesn't love her.'

'Oh, don't take away the only bit of comfort I've got,' he begged.

'It's a long time ago,' she said.

'Yes, but I don't like it, I don't like it,' he said, between petulance and sadness. 'And I feel as if I've robbed you of something.'

She felt she could bear the loss with equanimity. Sentimentally, the episode only affected her because it troubled him: practically, its consequences were taking shape in her mind as the colossal figure of a woman casting a deep shadow. 'It's a long time ago,' she repeated, thinking that the shadow stretched unfairly far.

'And then,' he said, smiling whimsically, 'think how I've robbed myself! I could have told you I loved you after the first minute, but the other thing was too near. I felt I still belonged to her, if she wanted me. I had to wait a little longer, in case she called me back.'

'A little longer! I'd almost resigned myself to spinsterhood! Was she nice to look at?'

'Well, of course,' he said with simplicity. 'She was big – tall –,' and he made a movement which reminded her of James Blunt's attempt to describe her daughter. 'Dark, I think. Yes, dark.'

'And do you think you were her first lover?' Margaret asked, finding him more amenable than she had hoped.

He looked surprised, a little hurt. 'I don't know. I should think she had had lots of fun, innocent, hoydenish sort of fun, before. But don't let us talk about it any more,' he said, like a child who has been scolded enough, and she kissed him with a tenderness which, for him, was the sign of her forgiveness.

'Bless you!' she said. 'I'm afraid Hilary has inherited your conscience. But, tell me. You say she wasn't a lady. Would you call John Blunt a gentleman?'

'What on earth has that got to do with it?'

'It just occurred to me,' she said.

'If John Blunt had three times his breeding, I shouldn't call him a gentleman if what I suspect of him is true.'

She put up a hand. 'Ah, but it's only a suspicion.'

'And I've another that I shall hear more about it to-morrow.'

'From Sarah?'

'Yes.'

'Tiresome old woman! I hope not. And whatever you hear, I shall always love John Blunt; but I wonder if I should love him if I saw him getting undressed.'

'I take some pride in having survived that test,' Edward said dryly.

She laughed. He had survived more than that and she had a feeling of exultation, not entirely born of kindness, in keeping this new test from his knowledge.

Chapter 14: *The Blunts*

MARGARET'S thoughts did not keep her awake that night but, in the misty period before sleep settled down on her, she had the dark visions which come to imaginative people then, and she saw John Blunt and Edward, in fixed attitudes, threatening each other with exposure, their fingers pointing, their mouths open, like figures cut out in black paper. They had an intenser reality than things seen in a nightmare, and when she opened her eyes to get rid of them, they gave place to men in shirt-sleeves and green baize aprons who were moving the furniture from the Vicarage, while on the other side of the road a large young woman watched them.

She sat up in bed and lit a candle. 'Edward,' she said clearly, and a sleepy voice answered from the dressing-room:

'What's the matter?'

'How much money have I got of my own?'

'Something like a hundred pounds a year, I suppose.'

'Well, we could live on that – in a caravan. I was thinking I'd rather like to live in a caravan and wander about the country, and you could preach, from the steps, on village greens, and Hilary and I could take round the hat. If you're giving people the Bread of Life, there's no shame in taking a few coppers for it. Do you think we could do that?'

'Do you think you could let me go to sleep? I thought you'd heard burglars, at least. Keep your nonsense for the morning.'

'I never talk nonsense that hasn't sense in it. I've

often envied gipsies. We'd bake hedgehogs in clay and wear handkerchiefs round our heads – except for the meetings on the village greens. Then hats. But after the meetings we'd harness the old horse and pull out to some open place beside a stream, with hills not far off. And one fine morning the young squire would come riding by, and he'd marry Hilary out of hand, and you and I could jog along to the end of our days – and give up the prayer-meetings because we shouldn't need the extra coppers. I should like it, Edward. The only thing I should mind would be parting from my furniture.'

'Go to sleep,' Edward said. 'I believe you care more for your furniture than for Hilary or me.'

'It was so much harder to come by,' she said with a chuckle, and she lay down again; and now the visions, prolonging themselves into dreams, were of green places and clear water, and the threatening figures did not return until the morning, when she woke to that heavy sense of trouble which waits doggedly for the sleeper who has known it overnight.

But the day had come and it was going to be a fine one, and she slipped out of bed in the assurance of her capacity for dealing with events and men. She had the optimism of her superb health, and, though she would not have admitted this lest she should be punished for her flippancy, there was a certain amount of pleasant excitement under her anxiety.

She went to the window and looked down at the garden with the mist lying over it, and through this, as though it had been blue water, she could see the dimmed green of the grass and the subdued colours of her roses, like subaqueous plants, living a secret life of their own. Above the mist, the privet hedge made a green frame for the lawn; above and beyond that there was the red boundary wall with its fruit trees. In the field she could see the chestnut tree, like a torch lighted to dispel the mist or to guide those who were wandering in it, and the little grey church had the look of a large, sleepy beast just about to struggle to its knees after a night's rest, while all around it the tombstones, smaller beasts of the same colour, were lying flat, cramped into inactivity by the heavy dew. She could not hear a sound and it seemed to her that this was like the stillness before a storm.

Barefooted, she went into the dressing-room and looked at Edward. His head had slipped from the pillows and he lay like a child, with nothing but his fine fair hair showing above the sheet, and it was almost a shock to see that the hand which was hanging down was the hand of a man, long and thin, but a little blunt at the finger-tips. 'Extreme sensibility,' Margaret said to herself as she looked at it, 'combined with unexpected obtuseness.' She touched him and he woke with a groan.

'You'll get cold out there,' he said. 'Come inside.'

'I daren't. Alice will be bringing the tea in a few minutes. She's very proper.'

'Do her good to know we're not,' he said, and he shut his eyes. 'I've just remembered Sarah Scutt. Why didn't you let me sleep? I don't want to go and see her a bit.'

'Perhaps she only wants you to say a prayer over her.'

'No such luck. She's going to tell me what I don't want to hear.'

'Then tell her you know all about it and there's no need for her to tire herself. Yes, Edward, that's the thing to do. Gently, but firmly, with a kind, understanding smile, and I hope she'll have the sense to leave well alone.'

'You're a callous brute,' Edward said. 'I shall let the poor old woman talk as much as she likes. It's unpleasant, but it's my duty. I'd certainly rather not hear that my churchwarden is a thief, but if she wants to tell me so, I must listen.'

'But such a nice thief,' Margaret said tenderly. 'And

I dare say he had very good reasons for what he did.'

'I don't understand you,' Edward said in despair. 'I – don't – understand you. I suppose a woman has no abstract sense of justice.'

'Abstract fiddlestick! You have no tolerance for the sins you're not tempted to yourself. If John Blunt were guilty of seduction, you'd find excuses for him; and what's that but another form of stealing?'

'I really don't think I have deserved this,' Edward said, and, sitting up, he thumped his pillows into place behind his back. 'But I do think there's more excuse for a hot-blooded sin than for a cold one.'

'John's temperature probably rises at the chance of getting money, and one's point of view depends entirely on one's own tendencies. Now I' – she smiled mockingly – 'being free from all temptations, can judge them fairly. And I don't want you to quarrel with John.'

'I shan't quarrel unless he makes me, but if Sarah brings any accusation against him, he shall hear about it.'

'You'll tell him?'

'Of course. I should have to give him a chance of refuting it.'

Margaret was silent. It seemed to her important that, at this juncture, John and Edward should remain friends, for if John knew nothing against Edward, the knowledge was very close to him: Maurice had it, and his discretion was not to be trusted: Caroline's unwillingness to see Edward was an indication of suspicion at least. No, they must not quarrel, but Edward was quick-tempered and John was a hard man, capable of using any weapon in self-defence.

She went into her own room, knowing that Edward misunderstood her silence. He thought it came of her loyalty to John, and really it was Hilary of whom she thought. If it had not been for Hilary, she would have disdained this caution. She had an intense personal pride which detested subterfuges and considered fear the worst infirmity, but of the weakness of supporting her own pride at any cost she was not guilty and, for Hilary's sake, she could cast her prejudices aside. And what advantage would there be to anyone in acknowledging Caroline as Edward's daughter? She had very little doubt that she was, for Edward had parted from her mother nearly twenty-two years ago: the girl was twenty-one years old, and the mother had sent her to Edward – with a letter. Margaret had promised John to help her, but did that mean she must claim her as a step-daughter? And was the girl ignorant, or merely biding her time? The position was awkward enough without the John Blunt complication, and she suspected that he would be as bitter against a sexual sin as Edward against a financial one; and again she saw the two as she had seen them in the darkness, shouting and gesticulating at each other angrily. Well, there was always the caravan, but that did not solve the difficulty about Hilary. She had a great admiration for her father and she could not be expected to understand a youthful folly; the discovery of it might warp her character in some odd, incalculable way, and it seemed to Margaret that, if she had a duty towards anyone, and she disliked the word, it was towards Hilary, though no doubt Hilary herself would be enthusiastically, if sadly, on the side of truth.

She went to the window again, and she thought of Andrew Blunt who lay under the gleaming angel in the churchyard. She found a little comfort in putting on him some of the blame for this confusion. She had thought it strange, and now she thought it abominable, that he, who was chary of words and gifts, but had never been known to break a promise, should have left unfulfilled the sacred one he had made to his wife. In the bitterness of his grief at her death, he had talked to Edward about her. He had done so little for her, he said, and all she had wanted was for other people. She knew he was accumulating wealth and she thought it a sin to keep it. It had been sent by the Lord to Andrew that he might use it in His service. She had asked him to build almshouses for the old people of the village – what happiness to think of them in a safe haven after their stormy lives at the mercy of the sea – and she was anxious that the future of Sarah Scutt should be assured. She had what Andrew considered an unnatural fertility of ideas for spending money, but it was Sarah's pension, the almshouses and a new organ for the church on which she laid most stress. The squeaks and groans of the old organ pained her ears, and was it fit that the Lord should suffer under it, too? The Lord should be offered lovely sounds of praise, she said, for with her severe simplicity of dress and the frugal habits so much appreciated by her husband, there went a strong belief that it was a duty to be lavish in the worship and the service of the Lord. This was a duty which Andrew did not readily recognize. He had made his money hardly and he could not easily let it go, and his wife, finding her persuasions useless, trusted to the Lord to touch Andrew's heart in His own good time. This time came when she was dying and, in a passion of sorrow, he swore that she should have all she wanted – for other people. He had loved her in his dour, grasping way; how much he did not know till she had gone.

Margaret remembered her better than she had known her, a small, neat woman in Quakerish clothes, to whom she found it very difficult to talk. Mrs. Blunt seemed to be living in another world and listening to a language with which she was not quite familiar. Margaret had liked Andrew better, in spite of his close-fistedness, and, apparently, he had liked Edward, for, as though in that house, where, as John said, there had been no laughter, there could be no confidences, it was to Edward that Andrew came with his loneliness, his little stories of his wife's goodness, his fear that he had not shown his love for her and his plans for the redemption of his promise, but when Edward, like a conscientious clergyman, suggested asking the advice of an architect and an expert in organs, Andrew hesitated. It might not be easy to raise the money at present, he said; he would have to see; but, lest he should be prevented from achieving his purpose immediately, he would make provisions in his will. Edward, never doubting that the promise would be kept, realized at once that this meant postponement until Andrew's death; yet when he died, after a short illness, no will could be found. It was disappointing to be mistaken in his estimate of the man; he was vexed, too, about the money, for he wanted the organ badly, and he told the brothers what their father had meant to do and assumed that they would see that it was done. James sent twenty-five pounds to the Vicarage, for parish charities, in memory of his parents, and John sent nothing. Margaret remembered Edward's outburst of temper on that occasion. He had marched across the road and told John what he thought of him, and John had coolly replied that he had no wish to carry out his father's plans and no intention of doing it, but he seemed to bear no grudge for Edward's outspokenness. He might be mean, but he was a man, Margaret told Edward, and increased his anger. He was himself generous to a fault and he was almost as much puzzled as enraged. Living as the Blunts did, they could not spend a quarter of the income derived from their property in New Framling, and what could they want with Andrew's hoards?

'They're just natural-born misers,' Margaret said. 'They like to think about money.'

'And that poor old woman, left without a penny!'

'Serves her right – she's a slattern,' Margaret said, but she was kinder than her words and she went to condole with Sarah at the loss of her master. This was just an example, she said afterwards, of the folly of doing good deeds, for Sarah, sobbing convulsively, had explained, as one cause of her distress, that the boys, as she called them, had never loved their father.

'It isn't my money I'm minding about, it's burying their father without a tear. And Mr. John hates him, I do believe,' she said, 'or he'd never have done what he did – and before my eyes.' Then, as though her words made an echo to which she listened in fear, she stared at Margaret, her lips trembling. 'I don't know what I've been saying,' she said. 'I'm all upset.'

'Yes, you're upset,' Margaret said soothingly. 'And perhaps you have misunderstood them.'

'Perhaps I have,' Sarah said a little grimly, but there was appeal in her look and Margaret managed to reassure her. Women always trusted her and she wondered if she had been false to Sarah in telling Edward what had happened; but in telling him there was relief and little danger, for he could say nothing to the Blunts without betraying Sarah, and, after all, there was not much to go on – only the broken words of an old servant who was in trouble. And now she was calling Edward to what was probably her death-bed, and he would march across the road for the second time and in a still more violent temper.

'Tiresome old woman!' Margaret said again, as she began to dress.

Chapter 15: *A Skirmish at the Breakfast Table*

WHEN she went down to breakfast, she was meditating on the strange power of human wishes. Sooner or later, they bore fruit which ripened without sweetness. Wishes, it seemed, should be vaguely virtuous, with no keen personal desires behind them. There could be no harm, surely, in wanting happiness for her family, but her hankering after change and excitement for herself was rewarded with this unpleasant growth on the other side of the road. For nearly fifteen years she had lived in Old Framling and day had followed day with no enlivenment but what she had created, and now there was a subtle sense of stirring in her own house and the one opposite. She felt as if an invisible wire stretched between the two and there was no knowing what communications passed across it.

Yet, when she went into the sunny dining-room, with Edward and Maurice and Hilary already seated at the table, the spirit kettle purring gently and the sound of Maurice discreetly crunching toast, there was no evidence of this disturbance. The scene was placid; it was pretty, too; for if she allowed her glance to skim past Maurice, who, hastily wiping his mouth, had risen to greet her, there was not an ugly thing in sight, and for most of the beauty she was responsible. She could take no credit for Edward or the dog, but in Hilary, the furniture, the primrose curtains at the window, the gay breakfast china on the table and the brightness of the silver, her personality had prevailed, and she stood there with a little air of triumph, conscious of her beauty in her frock of yellow linen, more warmly conscious that Edward and Hilary were happier for her presence.

'What? All silent and all damned?' she inquired pleasantly, and looked at Maurice with a penitent expression. 'It's a quotation,' she said kindly.

Maurice blinked, his mouth quavered a little. 'Yes,' he said, and in a slightly strained voice he added, 'But that doesn't make it any the less true.'

She was surprised. Maurice was not so obvious, after all, and she murmured: 'Yes, we're all miserable offenders,' before she looked at Hilary, caught her lip to show that she was sorry for teasing Maurice and lifted her eyebrows in a question. She and Hilary found this mute language useful when remarks not fit for Edward's ears, or comments on his behaviour, had to be made, and Hilary gave an almost imperceptible shake of her head, implying her inability to account for Maurice's manner.

Beyond the knowledge of either was his restless night, through which the thought of Margaret had buzzed like a persistent insect. He tried to get rid of it with prayer, indignation and defiance, but it came back, and he saw her in her dress of blue and gold, sumptuous, lazy and quick-witted. She was all that the woman he loved ought not to be, he was the object of her mirth, yet she came swaying towards him through the darkness, her tender mouth smiling at his lack of pride. He groaned aloud and muffled the sound under the bedclothes. He was a clergyman, he was middle-aged, he was ashamed, and his shame was increased by his secret certainty that what he called his love was half compounded of old jealousies. If she had been the wife of another man, she would have seemed less desirable; but that she should have married Edward who had cruelly deserted another woman, at once tempted and excused him, and there was a barren comfort in thinking of Margaret kneeling before the fire and saying she spent her life in irritating

Edward. Maurice was never sure whether she told the truth or not, but he hoped she told it then. Edward was unworthy of her; he doubted her worthiness of himself; and, since they were both unworthy, why did he hesitate to do his duty by that girl who was doing menial services for the Blunts? He knew the answer, but he stopped it with a prayer, and at last he fell into a fitful sleep, to rise in a state of physical feebleness and mental misery. The sight of Edward and Hilary, with their clear skins and bright eyes, was an offence to him; the dining-room was no fit place for a dog; the smell of bacon sickened him and Margaret's entrance was a renewed reproach. He felt that he was indeed of the company of the damned and his words had a personal application which Margaret did not suspect, or she would have felt merciful instead of mischievous.

She sat down beside him, facing the window, and there, on the other side of the road, like a reassurance of normality, were John and James Blunt setting out to work as usual, John striding boldly with his head held up, like a man who could face the world, and James shuffling a pace behind him, with his head down.

'The glorious company of the Apostles,' she said, with a faintly clerical inflection, and at the familiar words Edward looked up from his letters.

'Only the Blunts, dear,' she said suavely, and with a grunt he looked down again. She turned to Maurice. 'When they say that in church, I always bow slightly in the direction of the Blunts' pew. I don't bend my knees, as they do in the Creed,' she was careful to explain. 'I don't like that. It always makes me think of a lot of inefficient bathers bobbing at a wave. I just bow my head a little – like that.'

'Now, Margaret, be careful,' Edward begged. 'You might remember that you're talking to a clergyman.'

'A clergyman!' Maurice exclaimed loudly, accenting the first word. 'Then what do you call yourself?'

'You see,' Margaret said hastily, 'I never talk to Edward at breakfast. He's so bad-tempered!' He had a definite gift, she thought, for hearing when he should be deaf and speaking when he should be dumb. He lived, at certain times, in an atmosphere of his own, impenetrable by the sparks given off by other people. A look, a frown, a stealthy pressure of the foot, only evoked a spoken desire to know what was the matter, and it was long since she had tried to establish a secret code with him. The very carelessness of his last words, with their suggestion that Maurice had a narrower mind than his own, was affronting and, like most people who were adept at teasing, she thought other people did it very clumsily, but, unfortunately, Edward had been innocent of the attempt. He had quietly and naturally pushed Maurice on to another plane of comprehension, and been, according to Maurice's view, disloyal to his profession.

'Then what do you call yourself?' Maurice persisted, staring at Edward through his spectacles.

'I don't know. A wolf in sheep's clothing,' Edward said good-humouredly.

'I don't observe the clothing,' Maurice said, and he drummed on the table and smiled wanly at his little jest.

'Margaret's fault. She doesn't like it.'

'A disguise has its advantages, I dare say,' Maurice said blandly, then frowned, for Hilary was calling her mother's attention to the fact that Cousin Maurice was eating nothing but dry toast.

'And it isn't Friday!' Margaret said. 'What's the matter, Maurice?'

'I was sure he didn't feel well, yesterday,' Hilary said, and Margaret received the impression that her anxiety had a touch of malice in it.

'I – I slept badly,' Maurice confessed.

'Ah, a guilty conscience,' Margaret said; and when he saw that she was smiling he did his best to laugh.

'Ha, ha!' he began, and stopped suddenly with his eyes on the window. 'Ha, ha!' he said again, more feebly, like a mechanical toy that was running down, looked furtively at Edward and said the day was going to be very hot.

Leaning her elbows on the table and wearing, she hoped, a natural expression of interest, for Hilary's as well as Maurice's benefit, Margaret took a careful survey of the womanly figure which had startled Maurice with its appearance on the pavement outside the Blunts' house. The girl was standing in the shadow and her features were indistinct, but there was something splendid in her pose, something a little formidable in her stillness, and Margaret could understand her attraction for John Blunt, though the promise he had wanted seemed unnecessary. Caroline Mather looked as if she could take care of herself and the visit Margaret had planned to make became an adventure in which there might be danger.

Hilary had her back to the window and it was past her fair head that Margaret looked at the other girl. She disliked the link her own glance made between them, but Caroline vanished in a moment and Hilary remained, looking at her mother, with her wonderful willingness to understand, to do or say the right thing, or none at all.

'I think we ought to have a bathing-party,' Margaret said. 'There's nothing else to do.'

'H'm, you're lucky,' Edward said. 'I wish you could go to the hospital instead of me. And Maurice won't bathe. He hates cold water. Do you remember how we used to take you to the river and throw you in?'

Maurice remembered well enough. He could still shiver reminiscently with dread of his cousins' jeers and the river's chill contact with his puny body, and his sense of that past cruelty returned so strongly that he had hard work to answer amiably.

'Ah, I'm fatter now,' he said ruefully, 'and you couldn't expect a miserable little fellow like me to take to cold water kindly. No, I won't bathe to-day, thank you.' He smiled arduously. 'I won't revive painful memories.'

'Not on dry toast,' Margaret said. 'Of course not. Then I won't, either. Hilary, you can go alone.'

'But I've bathed already,' Hilary said.

'Then bathe again, darling,' said Margaret sweetly. 'Maurice and I will sit in the garden.'

'But you mustn't let me keep you from anything you have to do,' he protested, putting temptation from him.

'I've told you I've nothing to do. I never have – except to pick flowers for the church, and I can't do that until you've told me what you're going to preach about. They have to be suitable, and there aren't many flowers left. Do you think you could fit your sermon to dahlias?'

'I'm afraid not,' Maurice said with reserve. On the subject of his sermons he felt himself safe enough and he was glad that Margaret was to hear him preach. Even Edward, who had thrown him into that icy water and laughed at his struggles, might be impressed by a Maurice in the pulpit. 'I'm going to talk about sacrifice,' he said weightily, and now he played his five-finger exercises more firmly and set his lips.

'Red roses,' Margaret said at once. 'Blood-red roses, if there are any. Hilary, I hope you didn't pick them all yesterday.'

Hilary did not answer. She was looking at her father and she recognised the signs which were gathering on his face. He was going to be aggressive and there was no hope of staying him.

'Sacrifice?' he said. 'You're going to preach about that? Well, what's your view about sacrifice?'

Maurice's fingers went faster. 'Is there more than one view? I thought the meaning of the word was pretty generally' – he paused and looked steadily at Edward – 'pretty generally, though not universally, understood.'

'Ha!' Edward snorted like a war-horse. 'I thought so! I thought so!' He leaned back in a state of triumphant despair. 'My dear man, you don't know the original meaning of the word. Hilary, where's that article of mine? You might find it for Maurice and let him read it. I must go to the hospital now, but we can discuss it when I come back. You mustn't preach that sermon till you've read the article.' He sighed. 'We ground half our ideas of morality on misconceptions. It's terrible! Good-bye. We'll talk about it when I come back. You won't be out, Margaret?'

'No,' she said. 'But if you're going to talk about sacrifice, it will be a long time before you want me,' she added as he shut the door.

'I'm not so sure about that,' Maurice said, and he looked at her humorously twisted mouth and Hilary's grave eyes. 'I shall not read the article,' he said stubbornly, 'and I shall not preach about sacrifice. I shall preach about Jonah.'

'But there are no flowers suitable for Jonah – except seaweed. We can't have seaweed, so we can't have Jonah. Don't be inconsiderate, Maurice. Come and pick the roses.'

He cast down his eyes before the twinkle in hers. 'You make a joke of it. It is not a joke to me. I can't preach that sermon now, and I don't want to discuss the question with Edward. I'm not at all sure that he would like to hear what I have to say.'

'Oh, yes, he would,' Margaret replied. 'Discussion is meat and drink to him, isn't it, Hilary?'

'No,' Hilary said, unexpectedly. 'What he really wants is to find out the truth – about everything.'

'Really?' Maurice said politely, and his eyes looked large and watery behind his magnifying glasses. 'Really about everything?'

'Yes,' Hilary said, with an emphatic nod, and Margaret felt that somehow she had assumed control of the situation and had her reasons for taking it seriously.

'You seem to know a lot about it,' Maurice said acidly, for it was time this child was taught her place. 'Then perhaps you can tell me on what particular misconceptions your father bases his own morality?'

Hilary's face flushed, and before she could answer Margaret laughed. 'I don't think he would claim such a possession. He's a very modest person.'

'And what does it matter,' Hilary asked in her clear, child-like tones, her colour deepening, 'so long as he is really good?' And, calling to the dog, she went out of the room.

Maurice looked up to find Margaret considering him with an odd expression. She was smiling, but it was not one of the smiles he knew. She had the look of a fencer who enjoyed a fight, but would press home her strokes remorselessly.

'I think you ought to go to bed,' she said. 'You're not well.'

'Nonsense!' he muttered. 'I'm well enough.'

'Then you're cross,' she said.

'I've had a bad night.'

'I expect that was your own fault,' she said, and saw that she had touched him. She changed her tone. 'Come into the garden. The air will do you good and the sun isn't too hot yet. You shall sit in the shade while I pick the flowers and I won't worry you – at least, I don't think I shall – with questions about your sermon. I'll pick whatever flowers there are, and you and I' – she looked down and he saw her soft, dark eyelashes – 'you and I will know that they represent brotherly, or shall we say cousinly? love. Will you come?'

'I will come,' he said solemnly, ignoring her little gibe, 'as soon as I have changed my shoes.'

Chapter 16: *Margaret and Maurice*

AND this was the man who was supposed to be in love with her! Strangely enough, for she liked admiration, yet not so strangely, considering the more important matters on her mind, she had forgotten Edward's statement until this moment. She did not feel flattered and she was not convinced. It might explain his manner towards Edward, but a bad night more easily accounted for that, and the idea of his caring for a woman he had not seen for twenty years was as absurd as the idea of him as the lover of anyone at all. He might have been a kindly husband to some woman who asked for nothing more, if he could have managed the preliminary stages and, amusing herself by picturing his probable mode of making a declaration, she was merciless in her imaginings because he had not been nice to Hilary.

She went to the hall cupboard to fetch her garden gloves and scissors, and she listened attentively for sounds of her daughter. Perhaps she had gone away to cry. Margaret did not know whether Hilary ever cried, but her own youthful rages had found relief in tears and there was no doubt that Hilary had been angry, angrier, Margaret thought, than she need have been, particularly as she was so anxious to make Maurice happy. This was a proof of her loyalty to her father and a spur to Margaret's determination to protect Edward for her sake, but in her heart she knew that the abstract sense of justice, denied to her by Edward, might lead her to deal fairly by the other girl, if recognition constituted fairness. But why should it? she asked, as she opened the garden door and took in the freshness of the morning. Her shaded glimpse of Caroline Mather had been of an independent person who would prefer to stand alone and would not enjoy the doubtful privileges of an illegitimate daughter. It was true that her face had not been clear and it might deny the magnificence of her body, but that remained to be discovered before the day was out and, in the meantime, here was the garden, and it was nearly two months since she had set foot in it.

If it had not been for the view of the church tower at one end and of the Blunts' chimney-pots at the other, though these were screened, to some extent, by the Vicarage itself, she might have been in a world which knew nothing of Old Framling, and when she stepped on to the dewy grass she felt like a lady whose whole life had been sheltered in this green enclosure. She wondered if she were peculiar in adapting her surface moods to her surroundings and her company. Alone, in the garden, she was a lady, with no cares beyond those of her house and flowers; when Maurice appeared, she would imagine herself changed into a mysterious feminine creature of brilliant intuitions; with Edward she was everything by turn and nothing long; with Hilary she took pains to be as much a sister as a mother, and she felt at ease in all these parts. Was this variability the sign of a frivolous nature, or of an idle life, or perhaps of both? Edward was always himself and his faults were more evident than other people's, because he never thought of hiding them: he was incapable of pretence, though, to treat herself fairly, pretence was not the right word for the cause of her fluctuations: she simply did not know whether she was the simple human being she felt herself to be when she was among the hills, or the more complex person she had taught Edward to believe her. It did not really matter, but she came to the conclusion that no one who was vividly interested in other people could preserve that unity of character so evident in Edward, who was much more concerned with the words of the Hebrew prophets than with the thoughts and emotions of his neighbours. Why this absorption in Jeremiah when John and James Blunt lived across the road? Jeremiah was a great man and they were small ones, but they were alive, sinning, suffering, falling in love, experiencing fear, their destiny unknown, the impulses of their past a mystery, and she had a curiosity about them, and everybody else, which forced her to give them something of herself so that she might get something from them, and in that process it was impossible to be stable.

She had settled this point to her satisfaction when she saw Maurice coming towards her, flat-footed, across the lawn. She had to admit that with him she had not taken the trouble of which she had been boasting and she waved a gauntleted hand in welcome; but there was something in Maurice which impelled her to tease him, and she knew she put too much solicitude into her voice as she asked him where he would like to sit.

She stood, smiling, before him while, with his hat tipped over his eyes, in spite of Hilary's advice, his spectacles flashing in the sunshine, he answered, brightly reproachful:

'You needn't treat me as an invalid, you know.'

'Then how?' she asked, and his chubby face, the cheerful cast in which his features had been set, prevented her from divining his desire, which was a pain, for love, for friendship, for some relationship with some one, without the need for calculation or carefulness. 'If I treated you as I treat Edward, you wouldn't have a minute's peace.'

'He seems to thrive on it.'

'You think he looks well?'

'I've never seen him look anything else,' he replied.

'He has been very fortunate,' Margaret said, and

at that complacent statement from her lips a stealthy anger rose in him, creeping up his body like a living thing, and before he realised where the words might lead him, he said slowly:

'Yes, very fortunate, yet I remember his looking – well – harassed – a good many years ago.'

'Really?' Margaret said, with what seemed a perfunctory interest, and she went towards a bed of roses and held up the scissors. 'You've settled on Jonah?' she asked, and began to cut the flowers.

Making no reply, he dropped on to the garden seat with a bump and, like a child frustrated, he said loudly :

'You don't seem very curious about him.'

She cut another rose and smelt it and, as she looked at him over the dark red flower, he saw that it had the softness and colour of her mouth.

'About Edward?' she laughed. 'You can't tell me anything I don't know.'

Seeing her thus, standing in the assured grace which seemed to him to belong to no one else, the sunshine on her head, her face, to his partial eyes, as smooth as a girl's, unmarked by age or trouble, the one romantic figure in his life, he wanted to make her suffer as he did, he wanted to have power over her, for once. It would not be the kind of power he would have chosen, but it would change her view of him; she would learn that it was not safe to laugh at him and, remembering his hope that she did not care for Edward, he recognized, as she had already done, the vanity of human wishes, for, if she did not care for him, it would be impossible to hurt her in the one way which would be satisfactory.

'You have his complete confidence,' he half stated and half asked, and she thought he looked like an owl with a good complexion. Under her brightness she was wary; she wanted him to tell her everything without the help of questions and she was not sure how she could best make him do it.

'What a question to ask!' she exclaimed. 'You ought to know better with all your experience.'

'Well,' he said, and at this compliment his smile was natural and irrepressible, 'I hardly expected an answer.'

'No one would like to admit failure,' she said, and he watched her turning up the head of a rose with hands the gauntlets could not make clumsy, discarding this flower and picking that. It was a lovely morning. The mist had gone, but its coolness still lay on the world. Behind the perpetual green of the privet hedge, the trees were changing colour: among them birds chirped with the sharp little notes of autumn as though the early frosts had put an edge on their voices, and the autumn had touched the roses, too, giving these last blooms a subtler beauty. Out of sight, the gardener was trundling his barrow, carrying refuse for the bonfire which sent up a slim spire of smoke, and the smell of roses, damp earth and burning leaves hung on the still air.

'Do you burn incense in your church?' she asked suddenly.

'Good gracious, no!' he cried. 'What an extraordinary question!'

'Tit for tat,' she said. 'You asked me one. It was all these good smells out here made me think of a stuffy one in a church. Such is the ingratitude of human nature! Or do you think,' she asked seriously, 'that it's a salutary provision, this trick of thinking of nasty things, when one might be happy, just to keep us in a proper state of subjection – or apprehension?'

'I shouldn't have thought it was necessary,' he said, speaking from his heart, and he got up and began to walk up and down. 'Do you think it is, yourself?' he demanded, stopping beside her as she stooped over the roses.

'I was asking you – as an expert. In my case it works the other way. When I think of incense, I like the earth all the better, and I'm not afraid of what life may bring me. No, Maurice,' she said, 'here's a rosebud for you – I'm not afraid. Don't you want the rose?'

'Why do you give it to me?' he asked painfully, and still he did not take it, for, with her gift, she seemed to be shaming his intention of robbing her.

'Because it's beautiful,' she replied.

He said mournfully:

'Hilary gave me a rose yesterday.'

'You're being spoilt,' she said briskly.

'Spoilt!' He could not withhold the word, and having uttered it, he indulged himself again. 'Spoilt! I was spoilt – in the other sense, long ago.'

She looked at him with a new interest, but he allowed her no more than a glance before he turned away, giving her a view of a stout back, thick neck, and the back of a head sparsely covered with hair which was a little damp, and, for the first time, she detected a tragic element in the man she had considered merely comic. She laid her roses in a shady place and waited for him to return, and then, gently, without raillery, she said:

'You sound unhappy.'

'No,' he said firmly, and he adjusted his spectacles.

'Come and sit down,' she said coaxingly, and she led him to a corner of the lawn where a tree sheltered the garden chairs. 'It must be something more than a bad night,' she said thoughtfully. 'What is it, Maurice? Why did you speak like that?'

He clasped his hands across his waistcoat and she regretted his lack of the dramatic sense. He should have clasped them, if they must be clasped, about his knees, or dropped them despairingly at his sides, but he folded them across his waistcoat, and her sympathy lessened while her interest remained.

'What is it?' she insisted.

'It doesn't matter,' he said patiently.

'But it does – to me. You're Edward's cousin and so, of course' – she smiled narrowly – 'you're mine.'

'So you adopt all his relatives?' he asked with the sudden sharpness she had noticed once or twice before, and she did not miss the possible implication.

'It is my duty,' she said demurely.

'You mean that you do Edward's duty for him,' he said, and quickly, answering his own thoughts, he went on: 'I owe nothing to Edward – nothing – except much – much of my misery.'

'Misery?' she repeated, softly lengthening the word.

'Yes – misery. As a child. As a boy. All my life. You won't believe it. You don't know. You've never been unhappy. Imagine Hilary, an orphan, delicate, timid, thrust into a family of rough boys and girls, snubbed, teased – thrown into the river! You heard that for yourself! Thrown into the river, her spirit broken, and no one – no one to understand. Where has my self-confidence gone?' he asked loudly, and there was no response from the sunny garden at which he gazed or from the woman at his side; but, as he fell into a silence which he seemed unlikely to break, she said:

'But you were children! All children are cruel. I'm sure he didn't mean to hurt you.'

He turned with a swiftness of movement so foreign to him that it gave her some measure of his emotion.

'No,' he said, 'but he was a man when he deserted that woman' – he pointed a shaking finger in the direction of the street – 'whose daughter is over there. That wasn't the callousness of a child. It was the cruelty of a man. I don't wonder you wouldn't answer my question! He hasn't confided in you – he daren't!'

She straightened herself and sank back again with the letting out of a long, silent breath.

'What woman? What daughter?' she said.

He hesitated.

'It's not a subject I care to talk about.'

'I'm afraid you must subdue your feelings. You've said too much.'

'It's very awkward,' he mumbled. He regretted his outburst. His feelings were relieved and the energy of his resentment had almost gone. 'I – I would rather say no more about it.'

'Possibly, but I must hear everything. You needn't be delicate about it. Who is this woman, and who is this daughter? Are you referring to the Blunts' housekeeper?'

'I am.'

'Jehovah Great I Am,' she murmured. 'I beg your pardon, Maurice. It's that ridiculous hymn. It always makes me laugh.'

'You can laugh now!' he exclaimed.

'Well, why not? We've only got as far as the Blunts' housekeeper.'

'The Blunts' housekeeper,' he said quietly, 'and Edward's daughter – they are the same. Yes, that's the man you married, Margaret, the man who dared to marry you.' He waited a moment that he might steady his voice. 'And now the woman he deserted – oh, I was there, I saw the whole thing – she sends her daughter – their daughter – to him, thinking, I suppose, that he will care for her. She must have forgotten her own experience.'

'But perhaps he will,' Margaret said encouragingly; 'we mustn't despair. He may be reformed. We shall have to introduce them to each other.'

'Ah, you don't believe it!' he cried. He had looked for astonishment, bewilderment, indignation, anything except this flippancy, and in his disappointment he lashed out angrily. 'Oh, of course you can't believe such a thing about Edward – the good Edward!'

'I should like to know what proof you think you have,' she said coolly.

'Proof enough! The girl's age, her mother's action,

Edward's anxiety all those years ago, and,' he paused and said slowly, 'a distinct likeness to Edward himself.'

He could not keep a little triumph out of his voice, and at the sound of it she said :

'How pleased you must have been to see her and settle her with the Blunts.'

'That's not fair! That's not fair!' he cried. 'I did my duty. What could I do with a girl like that? Could I send her back to a drunken father? Could I turn her into the streets? I could not ask her to wait here, in the Vicarage with me, until Edward's return.'

'Why not?' she asked sweetly, and her smile stung him.

'You think there's no danger of scandal about a man like me?' he said quietly. 'Perhaps not. I have neither Edward's attraction nor his morals.'

At that she stood up, trembling a little.

'Be quiet, Maurice! I don't believe a word of it, and even if it's true, who are you to judge Edward? You can look after your own sins' – again she smiled annoyingly – 'if you have any, and leave Edward's to God.'

'Not to God, but to John Blunt,' he said, and he walked, flat-footed, yet a little jauntily, across the lawn.

Chapter 17: *In the Garden*

SHE took an immediate revenge in considering his retreating form. She longed to tell him that with his appearance, dramatic effects should be avoided, for she knew no other words would hurt him more, and then, suddenly, she felt sorry for him, and only pride kept her from calling him back. She was sorry for the past sufferings of the child and their continuance in the man but, with the flippancy of mind she could never subdue, she more deeply regretted his inability to see that pathos suited him no more than drama. She felt that if nature had not fitted the outward appearance to the man, the man should have the sense to adapt himself to nature, and Maurice, in taking the hint of his rosy chubbiness, would have found and given cheerfulness. As a fat, chuckling, tolerant priest he would have been a success; as a fat, miserable one he was ludicrous, and for a few minutes her mocking humour dulled her apprehension of what action a stubbornly resentful man might take. By the time he had disappeared, she realized the tactlessness of her dealing with him. A little sympathy would have gone a long way, an appeal to his generosity would have gone farther, yet she had sent him off with a gibe and received in return a threat. A threat was a new experience; it enraged her, and her determination to protect Hilary's sensibilities was stiffened with her anger and her loyalty to Edward. Maurice had declared war and she would fight him with every weapon at her command – with smiles, tears, lies, forfeiting her personal integrity to the necessity of beating him, not because her cause was

136

just, though she believed it was, but because he was Maurice and she was Margaret Stack. It would be intolerable to see him triumph, and while she had an acute suspicion that nothing, in the end, would make him more wretched than the spectacle of his success, she could not afford to indulge herself with failure.

She thought of Edward with exasperation and with tenderness; she was a little annoyed that Maurice's detractions had power to rouse her appreciation of the man she had married, but she allowed herself to enjoy the contrast between his physical hardness and Maurice's flabbiness and traced a corresponding difference in their minds. Edward was going with Sarah's story to John Blunt; Maurice had come to her with his!

She made a gesture of distaste and, moving away from the retreat she shared with him, she stooped to pick up her roses. It seemed to her that all her past life had been spent in the pretty pastime of picking flowers and now her hands were thrust full of sterner matter; but she was ready to deal with it, she told herself, and when she saw Edward coming towards her, wearing the aggrieved look which told her that he had had some difficulty in finding her, she smiled at him with a radiance which immediately removed his frown.

'You look so nice,' she said.

'I don't feel nice.'

'That doesn't matter – not a bit. I've been counting my blessings, Edward, and one of them is that I've never known an instant's physical repugnance for you. For your mind – yes, but for your body – no. The next time you irritate me, I shall remember that and behave myself.'

'But why should I irritate you at all?' he cried. 'You never irritate me!'

'Because I'm so charming,' she explained. 'You're not charming, but you're thin, and you look clean,' and thinking of Maurice's damp head, she added, 'and dry.'

'But I'm not dry. I'm wet through. It's abominably hot.'

'And we're standing here in the sun, and I expect the servants can hear you shouting at me. Come and sit down. No, not in that corner – in this one. I've been sitting with Maurice in the other.'

'With Maurice! And I've been looking for you all over the house!'

'Did you see him? I wonder where he is,' she said. But reflecting that John Blunt was beyond the reach of a man who would hesitate to walk to New Framling in the heat, she could give her attention to Edward when he said, 'And how dare you tell me that my mind is repugnant to you?'

'Because I'm a brave woman, darling! And only parts of your mind and only sometimes, just enough to leaven the lump of my admiration for you. Now tell me about Sarah.'

'I was wondering when you would remember that,' he said grimly.

She had a chance to feel hurt, but she did not take it. It amused her to hear the cause of her anxieties accusing her of lack of interest in his affairs, and she said meekly, 'Forgive me. Half an hour with Maurice benumbs one's faculties. It's bad news, I suppose.'

With his legs outstretched, his hands in his pockets and his hat tilted over his eyes, Edward answered, 'Yes. John found the will and tore it up.'

'Before her very eyes?'

'Yes, before her very eyes.'

'And the master not even in his grave! Did she say that?'

Slowly he turned his head to look at her. 'Something of that kind.'

'Ah – temper,' Margaret said.

'Greed,' said Edward.

'Greed is careful, temper's hasty. He put himself in that old woman's power; he's been in her power for years, and he's held his head up all the time. I like him more than ever! Greed would have been more calculating, Edward.'

'But he knew she was afraid of him and it was greed that made him angry.'

'I'm not so sure about that,' she said. She saw John tearing the paper with his strong, square hands in a gesture of defiance, of freedom, proclaiming that now he was the master of the man who had mastered his sad youth and for the first and the last time he was able to thwart his father. She liked this interpretation of his action, and when Edward said that, whatever the cause, the result was the same, she disagreed with him.

'Well,' Edward said, 'it's no good splitting hairs or arguing with you about John Blunt, but I haven't got my money and Sarah hasn't got her pension and, anyhow, John's motives don't affect what I have to do.'

'Can't you forget you're the vicar of this parish?' she asked a little wearily. 'Really, it's rather presumptuous to think it's your job to save souls.'

'But I'm not going as the vicar, I'm going as a man.'

'How hard you all try to be men,' she murmured. 'Poor dears! It's rather pathetic. There's something wrong with a profession that has to insist on its sex. Have you ever heard a greengrocer declaring he's a man, or a butcher, or anyone else? No. And I don't go about explaining that I'm a woman.'

'You don't need to, thank God!' Edward said warmly, 'and if you weren't so good to look at I wouldn't put up with half your insults. You know perfectly well that I'm not angling for John Blunt's soul. I shouldn't know what to do with it. He must fish for that himself, out of his hoards of ill-gotten gold. I'm going to treat him as I should like him to treat me.'

'So that's how you would like him to treat you, is it? My dear, you'd be simply furious.'

'John will be furious, too. I'm quite expecting him to knock me down.'

'Then, Edward, get your back against something while you talk to him and then he can't. But he won't attack you. I'll tell you what he'll do. He'll listen and not say a word, except, perhaps, to thank you.'

'Yes, he's capable of that!' Edward said.

'And you mustn't lose your temper. But really and truly, need you do it? There's Sarah to think of.'

'She wants me to do it. She's looked at death and found it much more terrifying than John Blunt. It's she who's thinking of his soul, not me.'

'Ah, she wants a family reunion in Heaven – Andrew and Mary and James and John and herself, in Heaven as they were on earth, and that's just what John would do anything to avoid. Perhaps he tore up the will to make sure he wouldn't meet his family again. And that's why he won't disgorge the money either. But seriously, Edward, if there was a will, there must be some solicitor who knows about it.'

'No, everything was arranged very nicely for John. Andrew made his will himself and saved a lawyer's fee. Just like him!'

'Then John destroyed it because he saw it wasn't legal.'

'Legal enough if there were witnesses. Sarah knows nothing about them. They were people, I should think, who hardly knew how to sign their names and might not know what they were doing. That would be in Andrew's character, too. He was very close about his affairs. But that's neither here nor there. I don't want to prove John guilty; I'd do a lot to prove him innocent – I've simply got to tell him what I've been told.'

She put a hand on his knee. 'Don't let your righteous indignation master you. Promise me you won't.'

'I've told you I'm not going as his judge. But why this anxiety? Can I flatter myself that it's for my safety?'

'Yes,' she said, 'you can,' and she laughed softly and bent to kiss the hand she had been holding.

'Thank you very much,' he said. 'I don't often get that kind of thing unless I ask for it. And now' – he laughed lest she should do it for him – 'I can go to John wearing my lady's favour!'

'But not to-day,' she said. She dared not let him offend John before she had done something to stop Maurice from presenting John with a retort, and assuming an air of earnest simplicity, she said, 'Don't you know that nothing of importance should be undertaken on a Saturday? It's a well-known fact. And to-morrow's Sunday and Maurice is going to preach, and perhaps John will discover a sense of sin. That would be convenient for everybody. A voluntary confession, Edward, must be much more salutary than an enforced one. We must give him every chance.'

Edward, growing sleepy in the sunshine, chuckled lazily. 'I can never understand why you bother to talk such a lot of nonsense. Why don't you put your brains to a better use?'

'And bury my one talent and a rare one at that? No. Any fool can be serious, but it takes some wit to be a fool if you're not one. We'll have Sunday in peace, Edward, and to ensure that, you'll have to be nice about Maurice's sermon.'

'Not if it's on sacrifice,' he said firmly.

'But it isn't. He's hurt. He's going to preach about Jonah.'

'And a nice hash he'll make of him!'

'No, he'll turn him out, as the whale did, compact and comfortable. And if John Blunt is susceptible to suggestion, he'll hiccough up his sins. And what a triumph for Maurice! But in any case, we must be complimentary about the sermon.'

'I shall say what I think, or nothing at all.'

'But he's our guest, Edward.'

'I'm not going to tell lies, even to a guest.'

She could not see his features very well, for his hat shaded them, but she knew his nose had subtly responded to this virtuous statement, becoming smoother in outline, more complacent, losing the impetuosity which made his face so boyish. She did not know how this could happen to a naturally immobile organ, but she knew it always did, and she said sharply, 'What rectitude! Then I shall tell a double quantity. You make me angry, Edward. If you can stretch points about the Virgin Birth and all the rest of it, why shouldn't you stretch one to please Maurice? I've no patience with mental reservations and mystical interpretations if they can't be used outside the creeds.'

'You've no patience with them inside, either.'

'No, I haven't. A kind little lie slipped out to make the wheels go round is very well, but making public affirmations that need really expert mental juggling to save your conscience – no, no, no! If I didn't love you very much, Edward, I should hate you when I hear you uttering what, to me, are no more than a witch's incantations. Yes, it needs a stalwart affection to stand up against that! Let's buy that caravan, and then perhaps I should love you all the time.'

'You wouldn't! Don't deceive yourself. No woman who is as much interested in herself as you are would be able to give anyone else enough attention for that.'

She was silent and, fearful that he had unexpectedly hurt her, he sat up and pushed back his hat to look at her. She was smiling at the roses on her knee with an air of secret wisdom, and whether it expressed her consciousness of her folly or her satisfaction with herself he did not know; and, realizing that she did not mean him to know, and that he could not find out without her help, he uttered a sound, a kind of groan, of admiration, irritation and bewilderment. Her beauty and the mystery which must reside in beauty if it is to endure, were as potent as they had ever been, and with that groan he acknowledged his bondage and exalted in it.

'I should like to squeeze the life out of you,' he said viciously.

'Not in view of the windows,' she said demurely, with the slightest increase of her smile and her eyelashes still dark against her cheek. 'Though I might allow it' – she looked up – 'I might allow it if Maurice's bedroom looked on to the garden.'

'Oh, you're incorrigible,' he said, and he sank back in his chair; but at once he jerked himself upright, to cry, 'And if you will talk like that, I'll take the first opportunity of embracing you, violently, in front of him.'

'No, you mustn't!' she said through her laughter, and again she put her hand on his knee, 'You mustn't!'

'Why not!'

'Well –' she reserved the imperative reason and said sweetly, 'It would be profanation, wouldn't it? And, Edward, don't you think your love lacks the spe-eritual quality so commendable in a parson?'

He jumped to his feet. 'Oh, damn my being a parson! I'm tired of hearing about it!' he said, and he went with long heavy strides across the lawn.

She looked after him, her eyes still merry, but her mouth severe. 'Yes, damn it!' she said fervently.

Chapter 18: *Maurice Takes Stock*

MAURICE was shaking horribly when he entered the hall by the door which, last night, had opened into a hall where Margaret sat, enriching its sober beauty, yet, with her vivid presence, diminishing its personality. It was empty now and it had resumed, for Maurice, its somewhat daunting dignity, like that of an aged being who, surviving passion, preserves the power of observing it coldly and criticizing it in others. The clock, in its tall, polished case, ticked with a steadiness which reproached the hurried beating of Maurice's heart: on the table there was a bowl of dahlias, stiff-petalled and precise, their self-assurance matching that of the clock, the furniture, the house itself and those who lived in it. He had felt himself an alien when he first crossed the threshold; he was doubly an alien now, by his own act, and that ghostly Margaret who had haunted him then, with her remembered gaiety, had changed into a spectre with hard eyes. Never again would she look kindly at him or pronounce his name as she had done last night and, as though he were in the dark, he gazed about him blindly and hoped for human sounds to allay his loneliness. But it seemed that he had killed all life when he destroyed his faint chance of occasional happiness, for there were no sounds and, pulling himself by the handrail and chilled by the cooling of his nervous sweat, he went upstairs to seek the shelter of the bedroom which had become a kind of home to him.

He dropped into the arm-chair and covered his face with his hands. He could offer himself no consolatory reminders of duty done: if Edward had not jeered at his projected sermon, if Margaret had been less serenely poised in her beauty and her surroundings, he would have held his peace, but, fulfilling the desire of years, he had struck at Edward and seen scorn and anger on her face. Worst of all, though for this he had to try to feel an adequate sorrow, his last words had been blasphemous. Not to God, he had said, but to John Blunt, must Edward's sins be consigned, and he dropped his hands and stared in front of him, his spectacles pushed on to his forehead, and all the objects in the room became blurred before his un-aided sight. His thoughts were in the same confusion, one running into another before he had done with the first, and not until he had replaced his spectacles and taken a few turns up and down the room could he control his reflections.

Instructed in the unbounded patience of God, he deferred the consideration of his blasphemous utterance until he had contemplated his immediate prospects. Before long, it would be time for luncheon and he would have to face the family. He did not know how to share a meal with a hopelessly estranged Margaret and a possibly enraged Edward, and the fears of his childhood returned to him, his misery increased by his consciousness that a man should know how to deal with them, and once more the perspiration broke out on him. 'I'm going to be ill,' he said to himself. That would solve his problem. No one could be angry with a man who was really ill; he could not be ex-pected, he would not be allowed, to take any action; his threat might be attributed, the whole story might be attributed, to the agitation of approaching sickness and, if any storms broke over the household, the invalid would be sheltered from them in common humanity.

He felt disappointingly better as he pursued this thought and he gave up the chase, not wholly in the hope of feeling ill again, but because he forgot his own words about the Hand of God and was sure no such happy provision would be made for one who was consistently unlucky. No, he had to face what he had done, he had to confess that he wished he had not done it. It was better, cried his lonely heart, to keep a friend than to avenge old insults, and all his carefully nurtured convictions that Edward's sin must be paid for had ended in his paying for it himself; and at that, for he never learnt by experience, his anger came back and he welcomed it, while secretly he knew that he would never have the courage to go to John Blunt; he would have all he could manage in existing at all until he could make his escape.

He must suggest departure before it was suggested to him, and Edward, who was so critical of sermons, could preach his own. But this, he realized in despair, was Saturday morning: his bags were not packed, he knew nothing about the trains, and it always took him a long time to decide what he ought to give the servants. No, it was impossible to rush off like that, unless he was actually shown the door. He would have to live through the rest of this day and the whole of to-morrow, suffering any martyrdom Margaret chose for him in addition to the one he had self-inflicted. And this one was of a new kind. Hitherto, he had always seen himself blameless; now, though he could find excuses, he knew he was a coward and, from the safety of his determination to do nothing more in the matter of Caroline Mather, he told himself that he should have attacked Edward directly and not through Margaret.

It was terrible to be forced to blame himself, to feel that he was shut up in this room like a naughty child and, like such a child, he did not know how to leave it with a good countenance, whether to assume an air of carelessness or contrition. He raged against this extra load of self-consciousness; he walked up and down the room with short, emphatic steps, stamping his anger into the carpet, ashamed of his futility, his shame gradually changing into hatred of Edward and of Margaret. He remembered her as she stooped over the rose with a mature grace which seemed to promise womanly sympathy and gentleness and gave no warning of the mockery which sprang so suddenly into her face, transforming her into some one dangerous, seductive and a little cruel. He remembered the flippancy with which she had received his story, and then the incredulity of her loyalty and, with a sharper pang, he imagined those hardened eyes watching his retreat across the lawn. At the moment he had been sustained by his own anger; now he measured the distance he had traversed and the endurance of a gaze which would miss no awkwardness or oddity in his appearance.

He took a glance in the mirror and turned away hastily. He was not a man to whom much would be forgiven: he was not like Edward, whom even Sarah Scutt preferred. What could Edward give her that he could not? he asked, and, like an answer, he had a vision of his cousin, long-legged and clear-eyed, striding up the hospital ward as naturally as he moved at home, and he saw himself going on tiptoe in deference to the sufferers, glancing from bed to bed with nervous readiness to be friendly with anyone who would let him, conscious that his calling set him apart from other men and losing, in the consciousness, what might have been the power of his position. He recognized the difference between himself and Edward; he saw that Edward's mental attitude was more comfortable and actually more effective, but he could not, he did not want to change his own; he wished only that he could hide it from other people, and if he had been quite candid he would have owned that, for him, one of the attractions of his profession had always been the inherent authority he could find, ready-made, in no other calling. He might be nothing in himself, but he was an official representative of a great and sacred organization and he was twice wounded when this peculiarity was ignored. In his own parish, if things were not all he wished, they were tolerable, at least; but here, in this house, among people who could remember him before he had received the Church's guarantee, it had been difficult to produce even a pretence of self-assurance. Stupidly hopeful that he was, he ought not to have risked meeting Margaret again. Fool that he was, and still hopeful, he was now counting his chances of forgiveness! She was worldly, she took serious things lightly; he doubted whether she would call herself a Christian; worst of all, she had told Hilary he was funny; but he could not bear to be for ever denied the sight of her. Against the darkness of her displeasure, she stood out very brightly: he saw the moulding of her face, the texture of her skin and her slow but supple movements, more conscious, perhaps, but no less easy than those of a healthy animal, and while he was shocked at his insistence on these physical attributes, his mental disorder was such that he did not care. A man does not consider the conventions in the midst of an earthquake and Maurice neglected his conscience in his present state of upheaval.

He would have been astonished to learn that this strange confusion of love and hatred from which he suffered was the same, in different quantities, as the one produced at that moment in the bosom of Margaret's lawful husband, who, a very short time afterwards, banged the door of his study with a violence which made Maurice jump. Only Edward, he decided would shut a door like that, and he wondered if the noise expressed indignation against himself. He almost expected to hear the door opened again and Edward's heavy footsteps on the stairs, and he rose from the edge of the bed on which he had sunk and took up a careless attitude by the window, in preparation for attack.

There were no passers-by in the street; the only living thing in sight was the Blunts' cat, sitting outside the dining-room window, and the house which had alternately been the symbol of his duty and of his triumph had lost its significance. He felt drained, but not purged, by the loss, for fear and not generosity had resigned him to it. The girl in that grim old house would not speak: she had told him so, and she was not likely to change her mind before he had left Old Framling, and he had only to possess his soul in patience until that desired, yet miserable, hour. Then, in the dull lonely house which, after all, was his own place, he could settle his account with God as it was impossible to do here, where duty and inclination were indistinguishable, and once more he could teach himself not to think of Margaret; he might even be able to convince himself that she was not worthy of his thought. He drew in a deep breath, but it was some time before he let it out.

A figure clad in a yellow dress and crowned with a large hat was crossing the street, standing at the Blunts' door and raising a hand to the old-fashioned bell. His breath issued in a low hiss of anxiety which was not entirely for himself, for there was Margaret, walking nonchalantly to the lioness's den, parleying with the lioness and disappearing into the dark recesses of the lair. What possessed her to do that? Was it wifely jealousy, torturing suspense, or a belief that she could disprove his statements? Or had Edward confessed his sin and Margaret set out to acknowledge the girl?

Speculation was idle, but inevitable and extraordinarily agitating, and he stood at his post, motionless except for the beating of his fingers on the windowsill, until she reappeared, and then he realized that his muscles ached with stiffness and apprehension.

She stood on the doorstep for a few last words with an invisible Caroline before she sauntered across the street, glancing up it and down with a ·repetition of her manner – how long was it ago?

Maurice let out another sigh. She had not been eaten by the lioness, there was nothing to indicate that she had even been mauled, though, from his position, it was impossible to see the face shaded by the large hat.

She disappeared and the luncheon-bell summoned Maurice to what might be his last meal in the Vicarage. He cast a look at the bed in which he longed to be lying, insensible and cherished, and just for a flash of time he wondered if he could feign the illness he desired; but no, that was too gross a deception and he was aghast at the ease with which dishonesty attacks the troubled. Moreover, he was acquainted with the callous accuracy of the thermometer.

Chapter 19: *Margaret and Caroline*

IN this somewhat sordid business of calling on Caroline Mather for her own purposes, Margaret, who was unused to justifying her actions, found some compensating pleasure in her suspicion that Maurice would see, and be puzzled by, her passage of the street: there was no pleasure in the knowledge that John Blunt would be grateful for a visit which was not exactly the friendly act it appeared, and though she was exhilarated by a feeling of adventure, she had a great dislike for her task.

She wore a hat as a sign of respect for her foe and she prepared herself with an apology for calling at an hour which was really recommended by the absence of the Blunts, but as soon as the door was opened she decided not to offer it, for when she looked at Caroline she divined that a call which needed an apology would not be appreciated, so she merely smiled, told Caroline her name and asked if she might come in.

Without returning the smile, Caroline said 'Yes,' and led the way through the dark passage and up the stairs to the drawing-room. Only once or twice had Margaret been in this pale apartment, which reminded her of a bouquet of wilted flowers with its suggestion of past romance and a past conception of beauty. Time had taken the colour from carpet, walls and upholstery; the chairs, with hard seats and curly legs, had a conscious propriety of demeanour, like genteel ladies ; a little, slender writing-desk was set crosswise in the darkest corner; a walnut, silk-fronted piano stood against one wall and a gilt clock, of tortuous design, was mute on the mantelpiece. Mrs.

Blunt might once have produced tender tinklings from the piano, but the clock looked as if it had always been too proud to tick.

In this room the two tall, ample women faced each other, and the neat little chairs, the faded water-colours on the walls, seemed to grow smaller and paler, shrinking from the intrusion of so much vitality, and only the clock maintained its usual expression of unshakable arrogance.

'I wanted to come and see you,' Margaret said, and again Caroline said 'Yes,' and Margaret, looking at the comely young woman and understanding John Blunt's visits to the kitchen, wondered if her share of the conversation was always monosyllabic. She was not helpful, she was not encouraging, she simply stood there, without awkwardness, courteous but silent, and there was something alarming in her self-possession. She seemed to imply that it was not for her to speak or act and Margaret felt herself producing as little effect as on a statue. But this statue had intelligence; it might have grievances; it certainly had power, though it might have no inclination, to hurt, and she did not know what to do with it. It made her feel small and insincere, a sensation to which she was not accustomed, and suddenly careless of consequences, she said frankly: 'This isn't an official call. I never make them. I've come because I hear my husband knew your mother.'

'Yes,' Caroline said, 'but I suppose he knows dozens of people's mothers.'

'Yes, I suppose he does' – Margaret was pleasantly obtuse – 'but they're not all strangers to Old Framling.'

'But did you know my mother yourself?' Caroline asked, as though she were a little puzzled. Taller than Margaret, she bent forward and looked down on her as she said the words, with a trace of anxiety, or of wistfulness, on her smooth forehead, and Margaret shook her head regretfully. 'And I expect Mr. Stack has plenty to do,' Caroline went on in a determined tone. 'There's no need for him to bother about me. I'm settled here very comfortably with Mr. John. And with Mr. James,' she added, remembering him, as everybody did, with an effort.

'Nobody is thinking of interfering with you,' Margaret said quietly. She was not sure how she was meant to interpret these decided statements, and whether they were inspired by resentment or independence. 'But you might like to know that if you want anything –'

'I want to stay here,' Caroline said, and she shut the big bow of her mouth firmly.

And now Margaret thought she could find another inspiration, more powerful than either of the others, in Caroline's manner, and she hoped the control of the situation would pass into her own hands when she said lightly: 'I happened to see Mr. John last night and he talked to me about you.'

To this Caroline replied at once: 'Yes, he told me,' and then flushed a little at this easy confession of his confidence.

Margaret was careful not to watch the flush until it faded. She looked at the mantelpiece and murmured, 'That's a terrible clock! If it belonged to me I should break it. I used to live with an uncle who had a short way with ugly things. He always took them outside and smashed them against the stable wall and said there was one sin less in the world.'

'But he might have given them to somebody who would have liked them.'

'That would have been encouraging sin,' Margaret said gravely.

'Well,' Caroline said, and she glanced over her shoulder at the offensive clock, 'I don't like ugly things myself, but that clock belonged to Mr. John's mother.'

'And so it's very precious?' Margaret half queried.

'It would be to me. I wouldn't destroy anything that belonged to my mother,' Caroline said; then, and plainly it was as much to her own astonishment as to Margaret's, she flushed again, more vividly.

This embarrassment at the renewed mention of her mother startled Margaret into remembrance of what, with her absorbed interest in a character, she had been in danger of forgetting – that this girl was probably Edward's daughter, and her blush and her unwillingness to see him suggested that she knew and was ashamed of the fact; and that though she was confused by her own confusion, she was determined to brave it out, for she looked at Margaret and said, with a strained note in her voice, 'My mother was everything in the world to me.'

'Was she?' Margaret said gently. 'I wonder if my daughter could say that about me?'

'No,' Caroline said with authority, 'she couldn't. Because she's got more than I ever had. She's got a father – a real father, I mean.'

They were at grips now, Margaret thought, and she felt that all the blood in her body was running into her feet. They were leaden, and the rest of her was so light that she feared it was going to topple over like a jelly and fall round those leaden feet on the floor. Hating her weakness, she hoped her distress was not apparent, but, surely enough, Caroline said kindly, 'Sit down here, Mrs. Stack. You don't look well, and I'm sure it's no wonder.'

Margaret obeyed meekly, and it seemed a long time before this strangely magnanimous enemy qualified her sinister words by remarking, as she sat down herself, that the heat was enough to make anybody faint.

'Oh, I'm not going to faint,' Margaret said. 'I don't know how to. But I've been sitting in the sun – with Mr. Roper.'

'Oh – him!' Caroline muttered.

This seemed to be a satisfactory explanation of any indisposition and Margaret laughed. Whatever quarrel there might be between her and Caroline, there was at least one bond; but it seemed as though Caroline, who, though she had not joined in the laughter, looked calmly amiable, was taking this extraordinary situation as Margaret had meant, and failed, to take it. Mentally, her view of it had not changed; she had simply overrated the strength of her nerves. She could not dislike this girl; she was vexed, but not horrified, at Edward's part in her; she was still anxious to save Hilary from grief and Maurice from triumph; Edward's trouble would be hers and his remorse extremely irritating; she dreaded a collision of accusations between him and John Blunt; but Caroline was a daughter of whom anyone might be proud, and Margaret looked at her, seeking that likeness to Edward of which Maurice had spoken, without finding it. The shape of Caroline's face was rather like that of her own, and only last night – and how long ago it seemed – Edward had said that Caroline's mother was more like Margaret than anyone else he knew. He had been faithful to the type, then, if not to the woman.

Caroline's hair was smooth and dark; it fell in a flat wave on each side of her forehead and under it her face, in repose, was inscrutably maternal, but when she turned her head, her hair, drawn upwards, looked like a dark wing, lifting her face into youthfulness. Yes, here was a woman who might well attract John Blunt, and it occurred to Margaret that there was a similarity between his calm embezzlement of his father's money and, except for those blushes, her matter-of-fact acceptance of peculiar conditions. About them she seemed unlikely to say more, and while Margaret was content to leave the offensive to her, she determined to make a feint in another quarter.

'Mr. John didn't ask me to come and see you,' she said, 'but I think he will be glad to know I've been. Will you tell him? When I saw him last night, he seemed a little worried about you. He said he wanted you to have a friend in Old Framling.'

Caroline separated the hands which had been folded on her knee and, as though this were the one subject which could loosen her tongue, she began to talk. 'I don't know what's come over Mr. John this last week or two,' she said. 'You'd think he wasn't satisfied with me, but I've asked him and he says, yes, he is. He says the house is a different place and even Mr. James says I can cook. Well, I can, you know. My mother was a good cook and she taught me. And I've cleaned the house from top to bottom. You never saw such dirt! I think perhaps Mr. John isn't feeling very well, or why does he begin to say he thinks the work's too much for me and I'd be happier somewhere else?'

'I don't know,' Margaret said. 'If I were you I should find out.'

'He's not the man to tell you anything if he doesn't want to.'

Margaret knew that, from her own point of view, her advice was unwise, for confidences beget confidences, but she was recommending what, in Caroline's place, she would have liked to do. She had most of the feminine attributes and she could imagine few more delightful occupations than making John Blunt confess he loved her. She was envious of this girl who had the opportunity, though, as her next words proved, she might not have the skill, for almost piteously, losing, amazingly, her mature look of experience, she cried, 'But I don't know how to do it!'

Margaret felt the impatience of an actress who sees a fine part wasted on a novice. 'Perhaps he's afraid of you,' she said.

'Oh, I wouldn't like to think that!' said Caroline, innocently revealing her young ideal of the man who is afraid of nothing. She looked searchingly at Margaret and seemed to decide to trust her. 'He hasn't been himself for the last week or two. I believe he's got something on his mind,' she said, and Margaret, ignoring the possibility that John was oppressed, like James, by dread of what Sarah might divulge, became convinced that it was indeed Caroline, and only Caroline, he feared. He was afraid to tell her of his past, he was too scrupulous to offer her a future which the past would shadow, and little knowing that she was echoing John's own words to Hilary, she said slowly, 'If you knew that Mr. John had done something you didn't like, would you want to leave him?'

'No, I'd want to stay,' said Caroline, 'but Mr. John wouldn't do anything he oughtn't, if that's what you mean.'

This simplicity almost moved Margaret to tears and changed the stalwart young woman, who had seemed so formidable, into a child. 'I didn't say he would. In fact,' she said with a smile, 'I'm sure he won't, but if you let him know that's how you feel about things he might tell you what's disturbing him. He hasn't many friends. He would be glad to have one – some-one he can trust. Everybody wants someone they can trust. Poor Mr. James doesn't count.'

'I don't believe Mr. James is quite right in his head,' Caroline said with native frankness and a slight broadening of her speech. 'You should see the way he looks at me!'

'Ah, you'll get used to him,' Margaret said easily, but under her light manner she had a queer feeling that this vision of herself and Caroline in friendly conclave, these words they uttered, existed, like dreams, in her subconscious mind. She could not reconcile Caroline's present guilelessness with her earlier manner, her acknowledged difficulty in dealing with John and the ease, the worldly tolerance of her references to Edward. Was it possible that the knowledge of her origin seemed to her as impassable a barrier between her and John as John's dishonesty seemed to him, to be broken down, in her case only by ignoring it? And, if that was her intention, would it stand the strain of learning, as, if she took Margaret's advice, she well might learn, of Edward's mission or Maurice's disclosure?

Margaret smiled without concealment at her own folly, but, even when she remembered Hilary she could not regret it for she wanted John to have his chance of happiness: she had had her own and surely a generous impulse would not rob Hilary of hers.

'I must go back,' she said quickly. 'And remember that I'm just across the road if you want me.'

'Yes,' Caroline said thoughtfully, 'I might want you,' and once again Margaret heard something a little disturbing in the coolness of her tone and, spurred to meet it with a challenge, she stood up and said, 'I understood from some one – was it Mr. James or Mr. John? – that you had a letter for my husband from your mother. Would you like me to take it to him?'

'No,' Caroline said. 'I burnt it.' This time she turned white instead of red, and there was defiance as well as appeal in her face. 'I had to. There was something in it I didn't want anybody to see. I told you I wouldn't destroy anything of my mother's, but she wouldn't mind. If she knew everything she'd say I'd done right. She always said there were people who set too much store on the truth.'

'And there I agree with her,' Margaret said slowly.

'And I daresay,' Caroline went on, checking a sob, 'she knows a lot more than we do.' She nodded her head vigorously. 'She understands all right. I like to think that.'

'Yes,' Margaret agreed, but she wondered whether the dead woman, if she heard and saw, was smiling ironically from her place among the blessed at all these living creatures who were playing their own hands – at Maurice, who was willing to advertise her slip from virtue to gratify his spite, at Caroline who destroyed her letter because John Blunt, who was a thief, had become of more importance than the mother who had been everything to her, and at Margaret herself, who was trying to save the happiness of her own child. And perhaps, in her omniscience, the Edward she had loved years ago shone again, not as a lover, but as the man she was not ashamed of having loved.

Chapter 20: *A Skirmish at the Luncheon Table*

THAT thought, born of her own belief in Edward's goodness, did not prevent her from making a little face at him when she met him in the Vicarage hall and followed him into the study. She had not seen him since their parting in the garden and her grimace defied his displeasure. Her spirits were high for she felt she was absolved from any awkward duty towards Caroline and she was sure she could manage Maurice.

'Are you better?' she asked sweetly.

'Much,' Edward replied, 'I've written about three hundred words. However, that won't interest you.'

'But I love your harmless hobbies!' she cried, looking reproachful. 'You don't know what a resource they are – to me!'

She thought, as he laughed, that she had very little chance of becoming a nobler character. Edward had his faults, but he had the great virtue of finding her irresistible and the only discipline she received was self-imposed: this was in bearing with his weaknesses while she neglected her own, which he accepted, when he saw them, as imperfections not seriously marring the perfection of the whole.

'And where have you been – in a hat?' he asked.

'On my lawful occasions, my lawful occasions! Keeping an eye on the parish while you play with the prophets. It's nearly time for lunch. I hope dear Maurice will be able to eat some.'

'What's the matter with him?'

'I don't know. Feverish, perhaps. He had nothing but toast for breakfast – and sacrifice. Don't let us have any more of that. Of course, it's a fascinating subject to me, but it doesn't agree with him. Let's talk about – well, really, I don't know what we can safely talk about. Was he always as difficult as this?'

'Is he difficult? I should call him dull but harmless. Don't bother about him. Just be natural.'

'Oh, just natural? I see,' she said gratefully. 'Is that how you treated him when he was a child? What was he like, Edward? I imagine him as rather a wretched little being.'

'I don't think he was. He seemed happy enough. He was just one of the family, like the rest of us.'

'But he said you threw him into the river. I shouldn't think he enjoyed that.'

'Oh, he didn't mind it,' Edward said casually, 'and anyhow, he had to learn to swim. We were all thrown into the river – girls and boys. It would never have occurred to us to make a special case of him.'

'But I expect you laughed when he was struggling.'

'Laughed! Of course we did. We always laughed at him. He must have known that. You did it yourself! And last night you were trying to make the old idiot think we were unhappily married.'

'That was tact, so that he shouldn't be envious.'

'And was it tact to say you'd let me kiss you in the garden if there was a chance of his seeing us?'

'That incident is closed,' she said, 'I regret the remark. I'm going to turn over a new leaf. I'm going to be kind to him.'

'Then you'd better not be too nice,' Edward said, with his simple faith in her charm.

'It's a wonder I'm not a vainer woman,' she replied.

As a matter of fact, she was humbler, if gayer, than she had been an hour ago. She had mismanaged Maurice in the garden and the weakness she had displayed in Mrs. Blunt's drawing room was a further shock to her self-confidence, shaking her faith in her ability to pursue a settled policy, for, determined to appease Maurice at the cost of her own pride, she no sooner saw him than

she found she had not reckoned with his power to provoke her laughter. And what a waste, she thought, to
have a perfect object for her particular kind of banter
and to be forced to take him seriously.

Under this necessity she managed to meet him with a
look in which, she flattered herself, there was gravity
without resentment. Yet how, she asked herself in
comic despair, was she going to keep him so steadily
occupied that he would have no time to seek John Blunt?

It was Hilary who at once made a happy suggestion,
though her manner in making it showed that she had
not forgotten her annoyance with Maurice and knew
how to make him pay for it, and it seemed to Margaret
that this miserable affair was bringing out all the worst
sides of their characters, for there was no mistaking
Hilary's gentle spite when she said:

'You don't look any better, Cousin Maurice. Don't
you think you ought to go to bed?'

He did, in fact, look ill; his face was yellow where it
ought to have been white and Margaret felt genuinely
sorry for him.

'Would you like to go?' she asked kindly.

He blinked and straightened his spectacles. Here was
the chance he wanted but he could not take it from
Hilary and, faced with this encouragement from Margaret, who would have no scruples about visiting him,
he did not know how he could endure the embarrassment of letting her see him in bed. And that child – he
looked severely at Hilary's sunny head and the tilted
nose challenging the serious eyes – that child should be
taught not to take liberties with her elders.

'You really don't look well,' Margaret went on, 'it's
the weather, I suppose.'

'Weather? Nonsense!' Edward exclaimed with the
intolerance of the man who always feels well.

'But I think it must be the weather,' Hilary said,
'because you remember, Cousin Maurice, you began
feeling queer yesterday afternoon in the garden and I

told you it wasn't safe to leave the back of your neck uncovered.'

'Don't be silly, Hilary. You talk as if we live in a tropical country. It's hot, yes, but I had a long walk this morning and I never even thought about the back of my neck. I never have and I hope I never shall think about it.'

'But,' Hilary persisted, 'some people's backs of their necks are more sensitive than others!'

'Oh, don't argue,' Edward begged, 'it's too hot for that, anyhow.'

And Maurice, who had been listening to these remarks with the calmness of helpless anger, almost loved his cousin at that moment. It was painful to be discussed, agonizing to have the back of his head criticized, and feebly smiling, he said.

'It might prevent further argument' – he looked at Hilary without his smile – 'if you would allow me to speak. I am not suffering from the heat. I rather like it than otherwise, but I slept badly last night, and I'm afraid I don't easily throw off the effects of a bad night.'

'Then what you want is a sharp walk,' Edward said. 'Walk into New Framling and back as I've done, and you'll feel a new man.'

'A nice dusty walk without a spot of shade anywhere,' Margaret murmured. And at the end of it there was John Blunt for whom there was no such thing as a half holiday!

'Sea breezes,' Edward said.

'Tasting of salt,' said Margaret.

'Unrivalled views of New Framling on the way.'

'Hateful place.'

'And of Old Framling on the way back,' Edward continued suavely.

'Only bearable by contrast. Don't be tempted, Maurice. Stay at home.'

Edward put down his knife and fork.

'It's a strange thing,' he said, 'that neither you nor Hilary can ever agree with me. I have only to open my mouth and one of you contradicts me.'

'Because we love to hear you talk and we know that's the way to make you. Stay in the garden, Maurice.'

'But it's exercise he needs!' Edward cried. 'He's putting on flesh. You're putting on flesh, my boy, and a walk will be better for you than a Turkish bath.'

'In the garden,' Margaret said, 'there's nothing to remind one of Old or New Framling. That's why I like it.'

'But I think,' Maurice said politely, but with the break of lost control in his voice, 'I think it's possible to see the Blunts' chimneys, isn't it?'

'Oh, you can't get away from the Blunts in Old Framling,' Edward said, and his face clouded at the recollection of what he had to do. 'Not even at lunch,' he added in a mutter. 'And that reminds me, Margaret. Sarah sent some sort of a message about the new housekeeper. Is she looking after the boys properly, she says. I didn't know they'd got a new housekeeper.'

'Yes, dear,' she said patiently, and longed to shake him.

'Then you'd better find out what she's like and I can report to Sarah.'

For a moment, Margaret hesitated before she spoke and it was not so much her conviction of the wisdom of answering frankly as the sight of Hilary very studiously looking at her plate, which made her say briskly.

'You can give a favourable report. I went to see her this morning.'

Edward opened his candid eyes a little wider.

'So that's where you'd been – with your hat on! Why didn't you tell me?'

Here Maurice interrupted his hurried five-finger exercises to shield a cough and Hilary, looking up, cried reproachfully:

'There! Now you're coughing, Cousin Maurice, and

you won't be able to preach. You'd better have some of Father's lozenges.'

Margaret was grateful for this diversion, but a little suspicious of it. No one except Edward could have mistaken the sound for what it was and he, though not easily alarmed by symptoms of illness, quickly produced a little box.

'Of course he's going to preach,' he said, handing it to Maurice. 'Excellent things! You can keep one in your mouth while you talk and it's too small to bulge.'

'They're very nasty but they're good for you,' Hilary said persuasively.

'But really,' Maurice began, and he looked helplessly at each of the three faces in turn. He was getting the attention he had always wanted but he was getting it in the wrong way. He felt he was being baited; he did not know where the next dart would prick him and once more he longed to make them suffer in return and his pitiful anger grew with the knowledge that it was his own weakness which lay between that suffering and them.

'Really,' he began again, as he fingered the little box, 'you are all very anxious to make me ill – and then to cure me. I don't need any lozenges, thank you,' and slowly he pushed back the box, enjoying his own restraint in not throwing it in the face of the man who had had the callousness, the cruelty, of telling him, in front of Margaret, that he was fat.

But Edward had apparently fallen into one of his fits of abstraction. He did not notice the box; he made no protest when Margaret said, in the low delightful voice which immediately soothed Maurice:

'Of course you don't need them. I'm afraid we're all worrying you. It's a mistake to try to be kind and one's belongings are always so interfering. I'm fortunate in having so few. My Uncle Alec is an angel, but my Aunt Agatha – she's a horror. Isn't she, Hilary?'

Hilary let out a little burst of laughter. One of the

charming things about her mother was that she demanded from Hilary no more respect for her elders than they deserved.

'Yes, rather a horror,' Hilary agreed, 'but I should miss her. At least I should miss the things you say about her.'

'Yes, after all, I suppose relations have their uses,' Margaret said thoughtfully.

Edward looked up.

'Uses? What are they?' he demanded aggressively.

No one replied. Margaret was blaming her folly in making a remark which Maurice could apply to himself, still more for introducing a subject on which Edward was sure to be indiscreet. Once more she noticed his curious trick of entering a conversation at the most inconvenient point and, apt as she generally was at changing the current of his thoughts, her mind was numb and she could think of nothing to say.

Edward glared at his silent victims and assured them that the time would come when no such thing as blood relationship would be acknowledged.

'And why should it?' he asked, hoping for a protest which no one offered. 'There will be no relations, no aunts — '

'I shan't mind that,' Margaret said.

'No uncles — '

'I shall insist on keeping my uncle.'

'And no cousins,' Maurice suggested, 'and, having eliminated them,' he said with an irony which was lost on Edward, 'I suppose you would be content?'

'Not in the least,' Edward replied promptly, and he pushed his fingers through his hair, one of the signs of battle.

Margaret and Hilary looked at each other and raised pained, sympathetic eyebrows. There was no stopping him, at present, they signalled, and he must be given his head for a little while before the curb was applied.

He was already off at a gallop.

'Why should brothers and sisters have to live together when they could find more congenial companions elsewhere? Mothers and sons, fathers and daughters . . .'

But Maurice, finding this more than he could bear, interrupted in a loud voice.

'And what about the Home?' he boomed. 'The Home is the foundation of all that is good in the national life. Take away the Home and the – the whole edifice collapses. We can't,' he looked round at his audience, 'we can't do without the Home.'

'What do you know about it, my dear fellow?' Edward asked patiently. 'You don't know what a nuisance a home can be. You've never had one.'

'No,' he said quietly, and Margaret, touched by his tone, seemed to unite herself with him when she said:

'Maurice and I each had a good uncle. We'll keep the uncles, Edward.'

'You won't be allowed to keep anything. Plato was right. Parents won't know their own children and children will be common to the State.'

'And that,' Maurice said, still more quietly, 'will be highly convenient – to the wrong people. I'm not surprised at your views. They are just what I should expect. Highly convenient,' he repeated ominously.

'But the important thing,' Margaret said earnestly, 'will be to get rid of the husbands,' and at that Maurice frowned stealthily in the direction of Hilary.

Margaret laughed.

'Hilary is used to this kind of thing,' she assured him. 'In fact, she's heard it all before.' She sighed. 'We both have. Several times.'

'And you'll hear it again,' Edward promised her. 'Sooner or later, there must be an end to this tyranny of parents over children and children with absurd claims on their parents.'

'You think a child has no claims on its parents? You think a parent has no responsibilities?' Maurice inquired pressingly.

'He should have no hampering ones,' Edward replied and Maurice uttered a portentous:

'So that's what you think about it. I see!'

Satisfied that he had given his cousin something to consider, Edward fell silent and, as it was plain to Margaret that Hilary, also, was supplied with occupation for her mind, she quite agreed with Edward that the family, as an institution, was doomed.

Chapter 21: *Margaret Takes Stock*

THERE was more sense than he knew in what he said. If there had been no such thing as family loyalty and parental jealousy, and the respectabilities they involved, Margaret would not have been wandering about her own house on a kind of mental tiptoe, afraid to make a noise lest she should startle an idea into some one's head or rouse some one else to action.

She had seen Hilary follow her father into the study to help him with his work, she had given Maurice every chance to make an apology; she had even been ready to apologize to him for the unpleasantness at luncheon, but he had gone upstairs and she had heard him shut his bedroom door, and now she was hovering on the landing, like a spy, to see if he came out. And how long did the wretched man intend to stay in Edward's house? No doubt he would stay until he had carried out his threat and it was her business to prevent that as long as possible, yet the longer he stayed, the more his irritation would grow under the natural treatment which Edward had recommended and meted out to him. It was no use suggesting that something a little less natural would be kinder. She knew her Edward. He would stare at her and say that if a man was fat there was no harm in saying so and, if he did not know it already, he ought to be told to do something about it. If she advised the avoidance of controversial subjects he would tell her they were the only ones worth talking about and the man who was upset by the honest opinions of another man was a fool, and then he would become more argumentative than ever. And this was family life! She was seldom discontented, for she had practised the art of being happy, but, at this moment, when she hated, yet half enjoyed, what she was doing, doubted the wisdom of her diplomacy and despised it and saw the possibility of still more harm in frankness, she looked back at her life and saw it marked by innumerable small doings which ought to have been insufficient to satisfy a normal human being; yet there were thousands, tens of thousands, of men and women who were doing no more, and she saw them all like ants, busy, intent, and infinitely tiny. But, if she had the choice, what else would she do? Her only gift was for this family life at which she was railing now and of which Edward would deprive her. She ought to have had half a dozen sons and daughters, to tease, quarrel and play with, manage and mismanage, as the whim took her, and Edward was wrong in believing she thought too much about herself to be consistently devoted. She loved Hilary, she could have loved that half-dozen, consistently, but marriage without fluctuations in affection would have been no better than a prison, enclosed, stifling, with no variety in the daily fare and the bonds always pressing on the prisoners. Edward's affection, as he always boasted, was not subject to changes in degree, and she thought it was rather lucky that, in his more serious moments, he definitely bored her, and so those variations necessary for a spirited life came without artifice, though she encouraged them when they came. At times, with his theories about this and that, he definitely bored her, she repeated, and she rejoiced in a middle age which could face facts, but, on the other hand, she never lost her interest in the man, and she decided that one of the causes of success or failure in marriage was the immense difficulty each man and woman found in seeing the other as a separate individual. For Edward, the difficulty did not exist: he was sentimental, and he liked to think of Margaret and himself as one, but for her, who had to see for both of them, the difficulty had brought its own success, and she believed that the marriages which drifted into a dull unhappiness were those in which neither of the parties to it troubled to disentangle their own reactions from the character of the other. If she had been unable to make Edward realize this truth of their essential separation, she had left him in no doubt about her own opinion and she had supplied herself with an occupation as enthralling as Edward's probings of the Scriptures were to him. Without it, how could she have endured the sameness of these years in Old Framling? How could she have met the present situation with what she considered her laudable detachment? And yet, she admonished herself, there was nothing praiseworthy in her attitude: it was merely the result of a nature which had never been mastered by other people's conceptions of morality, and though her tolerance might be broad it was rivalled by her conceit. She went about the world in admiration of her quick wit and power to charm, yet she antagonized Maurice, she had not enough sense to prevent herself from turning giddy in Mrs. Blunt's drawing-room, and she could not even manage her own luncheon table! 'If I'm not very careful,' she murmured, 'my presumptuousness will be the undoing of us all.'

A low, booming sound broke into these meditations. It puzzled her for a few moments. She looked for a bluebottle or a bee and could not find one; she hoped the boiler was not going to burst, and then she traced the origin of the noise to Maurice's room. Was he praying, in anguish of spirit, or was this the moaning of physical pain? Ah, if she could put him to bed and keep him there, what a comfort it would be!

She went quietly towards his door and the sound resolved itself into distinguishable words. He was rehearsing his sermon and, resisting a strong temptation to applaud, she stole softly away, thankful that her vigilance could be temporarily relaxed. Life was full of surprises. She had never expected to be grateful for a sermon and she made up her mind to express her thanks warmly when it had been publicly delivered.

She took a book and went into the garden and sat behind the privet hedge where she hoped no one would find her. The hedge blocked out the view of the Blunts' chimneys, she turned her back to the church, and shielded from both these reminders of her circumstances, with the green path stretching in front of her and green walls about her, she opened her book at one of Gibbon's famous chapters and gave herself up to the charm of his sonorous sentences. As though she were afloat on a gently swelling sea, they lifted her to the crest of a wave and let her down again, and so, rising and falling, secure and happy, she read on, caring less for the matter than for the magnificent competence of the manner which, in its testimony to man's power, was like a promise of ultimate order out of chaos. Now and then, she paused and laughed, a little chuckle of admiration, of gratitude for a good thing. It was with laughter that she always expressed her delight and even her reverence: it was her nearest approach to prayer: and with that tribute to what was enduringly fine, she disdained her late preoccupations.

It was in this dangerously high-spirited moment that she discerned a black figure blocking the farther end of her green tunnel. 'Ah,' she thought, 'here comes one of the early Christians,' and as he approached in obedience to her gesture, walking with his professional tread, she felt no indignation for the tortures suffered by his predecessors, for nothing is more enraging than the meekness of spiritual pride.

'I'm afraid I'm disturbing you,' he said.

'No, rescuing me from the lure of pernicious literature,' she said and she tapped her book.

He peered towards it. 'What is it? Gibbon?' He fingered his watch chain. 'Prejudiced, I'm afraid.'

'Perhaps. Get a chair, Maurice. But prejudice is one of those vague useful words, really meaning that you don't agree with the other person. But don't you think life would be very dull without it?'

'I don't know,' he said, hardly troubling about his answer for, as she could not control her spirit of mischief when he was near her, so he was disturbed, more than ever uncertain of himself, in her presence.

'I thought you would be able to tell me,' she said very gently.

He made no reply. He deserved the rebuke and the fact that Edward deserved much more did not affect his effort to be humble, but he saw, patiently, despairingly, that at every turn he was to be frustrated. He had prayed before he ventured into the garden. He knew it was merely silly to ask that he might not be led into temptation, for he was already in the midst of it, and whether he went into the garden where he expected to find her or stayed in the house was all one. He was beset by his own envy, malice and uncharitableness and his petition was for strength to drive them from him. He prayed less for the sake of righteousness than for that of personal peace and he had not tried to deceive himself: he knew God could not be deceived and at Margaret's last words he began to doubt whether such a prayer would be answered. He hung his head, but his thoughts went upwards, to the sky, which from force of habit and a lack of humour, he always pictured as God's home, and they cried piteously that he ought to be given his chance, he ought to have a little help. Childishly he felt that his good resolutions were being scorned, that God should have prevented Margaret from jeering at him, for it was as easy for Him to set things right as for a man to press the button of a bell: and then he remembered how often he had warned other people that God only helped those who helped themselves.

'If you can't tell me that, tell me something else,' Margaret said. 'If you had been an early Christian, would you, could you have allowed yourself to be torn to bits or skinned alive, or used as a candle, for your faith?'

He looked at her steadily and said, 'No, I could not.'

'Good!' she sighed and turning to him quickly, she said, 'Not good because you wouldn't, but because you say so. That's my test question. I ask it of every clergyman who comes to the house. Sometimes it's rather hard to drag the subject in and Edward tries to stop me, but sooner or later, I always manage it. Most of them say they hope they would have been given strength, and some of them try to look as if they're sorry they've missed the chance, but you get full marks, Maurice.'

Her glance was frank and kind, but he could not believe she was keeping nothing back, and he said gloomily, 'You mean you believe I'm a coward.'

'I mean that you said what you really think.'

'It's so difficult to know what one really thinks.'

'Yes, isn't it?' she said brightly. 'But don't change your mind about that!'

'Oh,' he cried, 'it's hopeless, hopeless! You can never give anything without taking it back!'

'Yes, there seems to be a sort of fatality about it,' she murmured, and the detachment of her manner suggested that this was a purely theoretical case, interesting as a problem. 'But with me,' she said, stressing the words a little, 'this lack of generosity is not premeditated.'

'No, you can't help it,' he retorted with surprising quickness and, relapsing into his misery, he added, 'you seem to enjoy making me unhappy.'

'Not exactly,' Margaret said. 'Not that exactly, though you deserve that I should, for didn't you enjoy making me unhappy this morning?'

'No,' he said. 'No, I did not.'

'It hurt you more than it hurt me, I suppose? What would you moralists do without that fiction? Don't deceive yourself, Maurice.'

His past pain, his present helplessness, his anxiety for the future, made a thick, evil fog all round him: back-

wards and forwards, he could not see his way. Behind
him was the accumulation of his grievances, in front
was the increased loneliness he had created for himself, with the shame of an enmity not strong enough
to face danger and of a repentance too weak to sustain
him, and he seemed to be standing, bewildered, in the
gloom, until he descried a wavering light for the guidance of his next step.

'But you didn't believe me!' he cried triumphantly.
'How could I hurt you if you didn't believe me?'

'But suppose I had believed you?' she asked softly.

She was smiling now as she looked at the hands
folded on her book, and in the curve of her lips he saw a
complacent avowal of her inviolable faith in Edward: in
the droop of her eyelids, the cool sureness of her pose, he
thought he saw the essential sweetness of the woman who
could spare none of it for him. What might he not have
been and done, supported by such beautiful surrender?

'Oh, this is more than I can bear,' he muttered, and
he got up and slipped through one of the gaps in the
privet hedge.

He had meant to make amends for an offence he
could not justify with noble motives; he had sadly
realized that in announcing his departure on Monday
morning he would be doing what she would like best,
but he could not bring himself to please her or to lose
his sense of power held in abeyance, and he returned
to the house no more advanced than when he had left it.

It might have comforted him to know that she, too,
had failed in her purpose. The clash of their per-
sonalities had spoilt her plan of adopting those methods
which would have postponed the fulfilment of his
intentions. She half yawned, half sighed. She was
rather tired of entertaining clergymen in the garden
and seeing them retreat in anger, but she was glad she
had not been deliberately feminine with Maurice. He
must do his worst, for she found there were some kinds
of prostitution at which she drew the line.

Chapter 22: *Hilary and James*

HILARY was late for tea. Edward was always late, and Margaret concluded that their united enthusiasm for one of the Biblical authors had deprived them both of any consciousness of time. This was annoying, for it was a little awkward to share the meal with a man who still showed signs of his late distress and, as she looked at him now and then, she wondered, with a sudden flowering of sympathy, whether this expression was the one he wore when he was alone. Not once were his thin, flexible lips stretched in his nervous smile and she felt what was almost a physical chill at this dropping of the comic mask.

As he made no effort to talk, she made none either, and she became absorbed in speculations about a character which she had practically disregarded hitherto. It had been easy, amusing, but remarkably superficial, to accept him as the person he appeared to be, and, for the first time, she seriously considered the possible truth of Edward's assertion that Maurice had always loved her. Remote from likelihood though this seemed, and almost ludicrous in contrast with her own feelings, it accounted for his behaviour as satisfactorily as the bitterness he had revealed, and the two together made a powerful combination. She laughed at her vulnerability, but she could not suppress a new interest in him, for while the impossible lover becomes, in declaring himself, an object of mirth, his silence gives him the dignity which is of no practical use to him. Even silent, however, he was a slightly humorous example of a man nursing a hopeless passion – and no doubt he would have shrunk from such a description of his feelings – but at least she was able to see him as a man who was unhappy, with few chances of meeting happiness on his road, and she wanted to comfort him with that motherliness which, ultimately, was the strongest strain in her character. But how was she to adopt the maternal attitude with the crumpled clergyman sunk in his chair, his watch-chain with the pendant cross lost in the folds of his waistcoat? The silence was thickening under its own increase and becoming another person in the room, and it was a relief when Edward entered, though he flourished a manuscript and offered it to Maurice, explaining that it was the essay he had promised.

'Essay?' Maurice said vaguely, and he blinked as though he were coming out of sleep.

'The one on sacrifice.' He caught Margaret's imploring eye and actually understood it. 'But you needn't read it, you needn't read it.'

'I don't think I shall get any harm from reading it,' Maurice said, and he glanced at the opening lines and refolded the paper.

'Typewritten, I see,' he said.

'Yes. Hilary does that for me.'

'And what is she doing now?' Margaret asked.

'Taking the dog for a walk. That dog's going to be a nuisance. First she insists on letting him sit beside her and strokes him instead of attending to me, and then she says he must have exercise, and I can't resist her eyes any more than she can resist his. And she used to be willing to work as long as I'd let her.'

'Ah, she's growing up,' Margaret said. 'It's the dog's turn. But I wish he wasn't a dog. I wish he was a nice young man.'

'What a horrible idea!' Edward exclaimed sincerely. 'What a perfectly horrible, heartless idea! And she's your own daughter!'

'I know what's good for her,'' Margaret said. 'Maurice, do you know of any young man, with good references, who could be imported to Old Framling with a view to marriage?'

'I shall refuse to have any young men in the house for at least the next dozen years!'

'And then they would have to be old ones. No, there must be import of young men or export of Hilary. I'm not going to have her turned into your curate or a nun.'

'I think I might be allowed to have a daughter,' Edward complained, disregarding his theories about the home. He looked really worried. 'You shan't dispose of her like that. She's as much mine as yours.'

Margaret expected Maurice to cough again, and when she saw that his lips were tightly closed, she feared this firmness was the preliminary to saying that there was a daughter in whom Margaret had no share at Edward's disposal on the other side of the road, but Hilary, blessedly timely, as she might have been trusted to be, came into the room before he could speak.

'I've been for a walk,' she said, 'right along the cliff. There's almost a breeze at the edge. And then I came back by the road.'

Margaret was a little puzzled by the immediate offering of these details. Hilary went her own way, claiming and wanting no one's interest in it. She had never been plied with questions about her doings, she had escaped the only child's conviction of her immense importance, she hardly realized how quick her mother was to notice the slightest changes in her voice or manner, and Margaret was now looking at her with perfect concealment of her knowledge that the little changes were there; but perhaps it was only the uncomfortable presence of Maurice – and she glanced at him almost fondly – which had caused them.

'Any adventures?' she inquired.

'Well,' Hilary said, 'I saw the butcher's wife's new baby.'

'Thrilling!' Edward ejaculated.

'Horrid!' Margaret exclaimed.

Hilary looked disappointed. 'But I thought you adored babies, and it's quite a nice one.'

'Yes, I know, but I don't think butchers ought to have them. It's such a confusion of ideas. People should be taught to live artistically, and if a man chooses to be a butcher, he should renounce all prospect of encouraging life. And the words they use! Family butcher! Home-killed! What thoughts they conjure up!'

'Well, don't conjure them until we've had our dinner,' Edward begged.

'It's all right. Chiefly salad, because of the heat.'

'I think there is a distinct feeling of thunder in the air,' Maurice said with a resumption of the tact he had latterly forgotten. He, too, disliked Margaret's choice of subject; the question of a butcher's rights to fatherhood had made him nervous and he was pleasantly surprised when Hilary did not pursue the argument and agreed with his own remark.

'Yes, there's thunder in the air,' she said. 'Oh, and I saw John Blunt, having a walk,' she added in a little rush. 'But I didn't speak to him.'

'A half-holiday is a new thing for John,' Edward said.

'Yes, isn't it funny?' Hilary replied blandly.

What was funnier still was that he had not been alone, but for this Hilary was prepared before she saw the two figures standing at the edge of the cliff, John in his hard felt hat, an unromantic escort for the young woman at his side, yet romantic enough to Hilary's loyal eyes and, in some odd way, comforting. He had told her there was no need to worry; but everybody was worried except her father, who seemed ignorant of the simultaneous protection and attack of which he was the object, and of which the unknown housekeeper seemed to be the cause; and though she had a delicacy about probing into matters which were evidently being kept from her, that secrecy made her suspense more difficult to bear and, suddenly, she had decided that she must see the girl. She would go for a walk, too, but she must see the girl first, and, accompanied by the dog, she went across the road, feeling happier in an act which she hoped no one would observe, because it took place in full view of the Vicarage windows.

It was James who opened the door to her and he glared at the dog.

'It's all right, Mr. James,' she said quickly, 'I'll keep hold of his collar. Is Miss Mather at home?'

'No, she's not,' James said; 'and the cat's out, too, so you can come in if you like. Yes, you'd better come in and I'll shut the windows.' He pointed at the dining-room door. 'Go in there and I'll be back in a minute.'

She went into the dining-room and half regretted the venture which had led her into this house and the sole company of James. As a small child, she had thought of the house as an ogre's den or a fairy palace: it changed its character with the time of day. From seven o'clock in the evening until half-past eight in the morning it was a fearful place, occupied by the stern man who now lay under the gleaming angel in the churchyard; but with his departure to New Framling the house frowned less threateningly on the street, and inside was the gentle, unearthly lady who moved as though she had no feet under her Quakerish attire and allowed Hilary to play with a work-box of intricate design. Sometimes Hilary used to cross the road, reach the bell with difficulty and hope Mrs. Blunt was not too busy to receive her, and Mrs. Blunt was never too busy. Smiling faintly, she would take Hilary by the hand and lead her upstairs to the most beautiful drawing-room in the world. The work-box would be taken from the top of the lovely piano with the green silk front and Hilary would sit on the floor, pulling out the little drawers, lifting lids with ivory handles, arranging and re-arranging the bobbins of pale silks, while Mrs. Blunt sat knitting socks for the poor and saying nothing at all. It was a hushed, charmed place: in the mysteries of the work-box she found adventure; in the curly-legged chairs, the flowered carpet, the gilt clock, she found beauty; and Mrs. Blunt, quietly leaving the room, to return with half an apple cut into small pieces on a rosy plate, was a being who had nothing to do with that ordinary life which met Hilary again when she had eaten the apple, put the work-box tidy and been conducted to the door. Adventure and mystery in the midst of beauty, the desires of childhood and maturity alike, were what Mrs. Blunt had given her, and now she lay beside the ogre whose strangeness, without his fierceness, was reflected and distorted for Hilary in the person of James, busy, at the moment, in securing the windows against the cat.

'You woke me up,' he said when he came back. 'I was having a nap.'

'I'm very sorry,' Hilary said meekly. 'I never thought you would be at home.'

'And why not?' James demanded. 'If John likes to take a holiday, I suppose I can take one, too, can't I? He gave me the slip last Saturday – just walked out of the office without a word – but I was too quick for him to-day. When he took his hat off the peg, I took mine off, too, and here I am.'

'But where's Mr. John?' Hilary asked. 'Has he gone to see Sarah?'

With indescribable scorn for her simplicity, James repeated her words. 'Gone to see Sarah! Don't be silly! He's taking a walk – with the servant. What d'you think of that, eh? And d'you know, Hilary, they never so much as asked me to go with them. That wasn't kind, was it? Not that I would have gone, mind – not me. You wouldn't get me to go up the village street with the servant. I don't know how John has the face. For one thing, it's bad for business;

you can see that for yourself. And then I don't like the girl; I don't like her at all.'

'Why not?' Hilary asked.

'Never you mind,' he said slyly. 'Because I don't. If I knew where her father lived, I'd write and ask him to take her home; but that's what she won't tell me. She's very close, and when a person's close there's something wrong, isn't there?' A deeper shadow fell over his face. 'I mean when it's a woman. A man's different. Business secrets and all that. And, if you ask me, she hasn't got a drunken father. I don't believe she's got a father at all.'

'Then it wouldn't be any use to write to him.'

'Now don't you try to be clever,' James said slowly. 'What do you know about it?' And looking at her anxiously, he repeated, 'What do you know about it?'

'Only what you're telling me, Mr. James,' she replied sweetly.

'It's not a thing I would talk about to a young girl like you!' James exclaimed indignantly. 'I'm simply saying that I don't believe a word of what she says. Now, look here,' he said reasonably, and he pointed an impressive index finger on the table, 'If she's telling the truth, wouldn't the Vicar have come across to see her? Of course he would! But he's ignored her, and quite right, too. I'll tell you what it is, Hilary. Your mother's a very knowing lady and she's not to be taken in any more than I am, and if we don't get rid of that girl there's going to be trouble. For you see,' he said wistfully, 'there's no telling what other stories she may set about. It's not safe. You might just drop a hint to remind your mother of what I say. You might do that for me, Hilary, and mind, it's as much in your interest as it is in mine. I'm not the man to be thinking only of myself. And don't you come calling on Caroline again. Lucky she was out. You don't want to make a friend of a girl like that. A good cook, mind you, but not,' he shook his head sadly, 'not a good girl. Drunk or not, she shouldn't have left her father. It's a girl's place to look after her father.'

'Yes, if she knows how to,' Hilary said and her voice was pitched a little higher than usual.

'Well, that Caroline knows everything she wants to. Clever! I should think so! You should see how she manages John. She knows everything she wants to,' he repeated, 'and a good deal she shouldn't.' He nodded emphatically. 'That's just what Caroline knows.'

Hilary was in the opposite position. She was in ignorance of the things she desired, and half feared to know, but she was in complete agreement with James about a daughter's duty. She thought tenderly of the parents who, to her young seriousness, so often seemed like children, clever children, even wise sometimes, but wilful and impulsive. She did not know how to help them or what their need was, but she could not believe in the evil nature of a girl with whom John Blunt went out walking and who stood, as though she feared nothing, at the cliff's edge, clearly, heroically, outlined against a pale sky.

Chapter 23: *Saturday Night*

SUNDAY dawned with the peculiar sanctity of expression which village Sundays wear and, like the warningly placid face of a parent who means to see justice done, it reminded waking children of the torture of clean clothes and mothers of the extra burdens imposed on them by the day of rest.

The street could hardly be quieter than usual, but the blinds and curtains shrouded the windows till a later hour and the houses, with these closed eyelids, resembled people who were trying to persuade themselves they were still asleep, in their wish to postpone the realities of another day, and this resistance was touching in its humanity, saddening in its suggestion of man's lot, yet exciting with the unknown thoughts and fears behind it. The Blunts' house had the face of a tired old man, patient under the prospect of more fatigues, but the Vicarage kept its air of possessing a superiority for which it took no credit but which could never be denied, like a person of good lineage who, honestly believing he is unconscious of it, contrives to impress other men with its importance and his own difference from themselves. 'Here I am,' the Vicarage seemed to say, 'secure in my generations of beauty and assurance, unassailable and set apart' – yet within its walls it harboured the emotions it would never betray, for Maurice opened his eyes and turned over with a groan, at first the mere protest of an ill-oiled machine which is driven to work again, but prolonged into the more pathetic and more controlled murmur of an indefinite mental distress, and slowly the details of his trouble cleared themselves from the mass. He had to preach a sermon and he was not sure which it was to be, he had to speak of his departure and he did not know how to do it or whether he wanted to go, and these indecisions had the same cause, for the last evening had been pleasant, the kind of evening he had pictured in his more optimistic moments before the Stacks' return. No argument was started and certainly none would have been pursued, and the desultory conversation marvellously escaped provoking anybody into a dangerous word. Perhaps this lassitude came of the thunder in the air, perhaps Maurice, in giving up the effort to be bright or feebly menacing, had unwittingly discovered the way to avoid appearing funny, but this was an idea which, naturally, did not occur to him and it was only now that he began to suspect Margaret's quietness and to see in it the possibility that, after all, her belief in Edward had been shaken. He turned hot. He was not fit for these anxieties, he mourned, and why could he never get a thing when he wanted it or like it when he had it? And well might Margaret applaud his estimate of his own courage, for he dreaded the anger of the sinner he had righteously accused. Righteously? His mind slipped over the word, and he set himself to calculate the actions of an incalculable person.

She had been to see that girl and she had returned with no loss of the poise, the gaiety, which he found so irritating and so attractive; it was only after their second interview in the garden that the serious mood had fallen on her and unless she were bracing herself to put her faith to the test he could not understand the change. Once he had seen her put down her sewing and look consideringly, tenderly, at Edward who insensitively continued to read and smoke, and Maurice, dropping his head over the chessboard he shared with Hilary, had been surprised at his own indifference. He felt no jealousy. Was it because while there was so much for which he envied Edward he gladly exchanged

it all for his own blameless past, or was it because he so
strangely found her less attractive when he felt himself
in no danger from her eyes and tongue, when she was
behaving as a woman should and approached the ideal
he had always vainly sought in her? He did not understand it, he did not understand anything, he told himself petulantly, fidgeting under the bed-clothes, but
his memory lingered on last night's oasis, reached after
what seemed an illimitable desert of time. He had
played chess with Hilary and beaten her, in spite of his
inability to concentrate exclusively on the game, and
this sure proof of his superior skill made him feel
kindly towards her, for there was no doubt she had
been doing her best. Not once did she look up, as he
did, and see Margaret sitting by the open window, the
flame of the lamp perfectly steady in the motionless
air, her embroidery making a brilliant splash on the
pale lace of her dress. He knew when she picked up
her scissors or put them down and when she went to
the hearth to stir the unnecessary fire which was only
lighted, as she had told him, to make the room look
prettier. Fortunately, it gave out very little heat, or he
would not have been able to keep what remained of his
attention on a game which Hilary played with a somewhat exaggerated seriousness.

'Perhaps we had better stop,' he suggested once.
'You mustn't tire yourself.'

'But that's just what I want to do,' she said with her
candid look, and she added quickly, 'if you go to bed
really tired, you wake up really fresh.'

'I'm afraid that's only true of the young,' he said,
wagging his head paternally. This was her one contri-
bution to his knowledge about the care of the health
and she let him have the last word. They were getting
on very well and when they parted it was with amia-
bility on both sides.

And indeed, Hilary was grateful to her cousin
Maurice for the game which had successfully occupied

her for a whole evening. She had plenty of good sense and she saw that it was folly to attempt the solving of a problem when its nature was unknown to her and its existence a possible fancy of her own, but she did not understand Maurice's side hits at her father or his secrecy about Caroline: John Blunt's question kept recurring to her and the only way to evade it was to put it out of her mind. This she had done with Maurice's help and at the same time she had prevented the family conversation which had hitherto been a little unfortunate. She admitted her own fault: she had meant to be kind to the guest, she had even asked her mother to be kind to him, and then her anger had over-ridden her courtesy, and though he deserved to get what he had given, she was ashamed of the bad manners she had shown with what she knew was so irritatingly good a grace. Moreover, and here the practical side of her character appeared again, it was stupid to goad the person who seemed anxious to gore. She went to bed happier than she had been, though not without a sense of guilt for concealing her interview with James under a show of frankness and she was relieved when her mother did not come and offer herself for the confidences she never seemed to want.

Margaret would have been glad to have them. What she feared and what turned her back from the door of her daughter's room, was the temptation of giving her own, or, at least, of showing the anxiety which pressed on her more heavily with the decision to leave Maurice to act as he chose. Her pride refused to appeal to him frankly; another kind of pride, surprisingly strong and mixed with a little pity, scorned the kind of influence which, at a distance, had seemed a worthy enough weapon for her antagonist, and which she now recognized as outside the rules. She was going to play fair, even if he liked to cheat, she told herself as she went down the stairs, and she found she was adopting a noble mien to suit her noble statement, going slowly, with her head in the air, and no doubt her face expressed her consciousness of resignation and virtue. She stopped and shrugged her hypocrisy away. This scrupulousness was nothing more exalted than her desire for a morning bath; she would have felt uncomfortable without it; this pity was only the vanity of a power she was not sure she possessed, and all this scheming and worry was unnecessary. The right thing to do was to tell Edward everything and she reached the bottom of the stairs in that determination.

Then she paused again. She wished she had seen the letter Caroline had destroyed: it seemed unchivalrous to neglect the desires of the woman who, being dead, was dependent on the generosity of the living, yet it was possible, it was even likely, that she had maintained her silence on the crucial point and had asked for no more than friendly help for Caroline. If this were so, what right had Margaret to betray her? And Caroline had destroyed the letter and with it some knowledge she wished to keep, and what right had Margaret to betray Caroline? Why should the dead receive more consideration than the living? She thought of Caroline, sitting in the room which was so odd a setting for her, the big, capable hands idle on her knee, her face childlike above the mature body, meekly taking instruction which at this moment she might be using to bring John to a surrender more complete than the one she had planned.

Slowly Margaret went down the passage to the dining-room. She would do nothing. She would not tell Edward. He would think only of his own obvious obligations and with his blundering goodness he would make himself and every one else unhappy, for he kept all his subtlety for Biblical exegesis and the worst of his intolerance for his own sins.

She sailed into the room under the fair wind of these resolutions, buoyant, and almost ready to tease the silent lover – but he was not there. The room was like a person thinking, in the way rooms have when they are left alone, for though Edward still sat there reading, he was far away, in Babylon, in Palestine, in Greece, anywhere but in Old Framling, and the room could ignore him and devote itself to the impressions left by the others, by Hilary who wanted to be really tired before she went to bed, and Maurice whose emotions were probably a confusion to himself. And now Margaret entered and the room lost its alertness and became a receptacle for more impressions: she could feel it retiring into itself, pretending to be four walls and furniture, and encouraging this pretence, forcing the room into its place, she said clearly. 'Where's Maurice?'

'Maurice,' said Edward. 'Maurice? I don't know.' He put down his book but he kept a finger between the pages. 'Isn't he here? Oh, I think he went out directly after you did. Yes, he did.'

'I never heard him. He walks like a cat. Did he say good night?'

'I expect so, I expect so. He doesn't omit the courtesies. Can't remember. Doesn't matter.' He began to read again. 'Don't talk. I want to finish this chapter.'

She took no notice of this request. 'Perhaps he hasn't gone to bed. Perhaps he's gone out.'

'Why not? But where to?' Edward growled.

'He might be paying a call. He might have had a sudden longing to see the Blunts,' Margaret said softly.

Edward flung down his book. 'There now! You've spoilt it! You have a perfectly damnable gift for spoiling things. I can't finish this chapter now that you've reminded me of the Blunts.'

'Reminded you!' she cried, not in the least abashed. 'I can't forget them. I wonder you can.'

'And you're determined that I shan't. Here I was, having a happy evening and you've ruined it.'

'It's the fault of my frankness,' she said, and she knelt in front of his chair and put her hands on his knees. 'My admirable frankness,' she repeated. 'The quality you like so much.' She lifted a hand and laid it against her heart. 'My touching inability to keep anything from you.'

'I never said you mustn't choose your times and seasons.'

'You'll let me do that? Thank you, Edward. I shall remember. And if I'd only realized it, you could have finished your precious chapter. But all the same,' she murmured, 'I wonder where Maurice is. Didn't you think he seemed rather glum this evening?'

'I thought he was playing chess.'

'Oh, my poor dull dear!' she cried. 'And I suppose it's no use asking you how long you think he's going to stay?'

'He told me he needn't be back till Friday.'

'How nice! And of course that will give him plenty of time. I expect he really has gone to bed, after all.'

'Plenty of time? What for?'

She would never, never, be able to control her tongue, she told herself, but with Edward, it did not matter: he was more guileless than a child and without a child's instinct for detecting fraud. 'To feel more comfortable in his inside,' she replied.

'Oh, it's his inside, is it? It would be! But you don't mean to say he was immodest enough to tell you!'

'No, I guessed.'

'He always was an unhealthy little beggar,' Edward said, 'dabbing his nose or having a stomach ache, and now he's getting fat.'

'But he doesn't like to have his health discussed,' she said warningly.

'And I don't want to talk about it. A very uninteresting subject. And you'd better persuade him to stay till Friday. It will do him good and he's no trouble, is he?'

Margaret went to the window, shut it and drew the curtains.

'Edward,' she said, when she came back. 'I've been thinking.'

'That means you're going to say something I shan't like.'

'I'm afraid I am. I don't want you to go and see John Blunt. I have a feeling that he'll put things right himself.'

'Your affection for the Blunts is becoming rather a nuisance,' he said. 'You know what I think about it. You know I've promised Sarah. I must go and see John to-morrow night, so don't worry me any more, dearest.'

'I'm always worrying you or teasing you,' she said remorsefully. 'Anyone who heard our conversations would think that I disliked you and it's really my unfortunate way of showing my affection. Do as you think right. I won't say another word, and I'll have the bandages and the ointment ready for your black eye.'

'But it may be John who gets one,' he said.

'That's what I'm afraid of. For who,' she asked daringly, 'would anoint his?'

'I don't know,' Edward said, ruffling his hair. 'The new housekeeper, I suppose.'

Chapter 24: *An Apple of Discord*

THE Vicarage party walked through the garden together and Margaret was careful not to remark on the wastefulness of spending such a morning in a church, and this restraint added to the irritability incident to most of her Sunday mornings, for she had never become used to seeing Edward dressed for his part and going through his performance, and she thought it must be almost impossible for the most orthodox wife to take seriously such a service conducted by a husband. It was not, in her case, because of the contrast between the known frailties of the man and the words he spoke, but she suffered from the kind of embarrassment which descends on a drawing-room when a member of a party stands up and recites. There was something artificial, forced, something which made her want to look anywhere except at him, in this sudden transition from husband to priest. She felt as if he were acting in a rather dull charade, as people will, for their own enjoyment and without considering their audience, and her painful experiences had made her a strong advocate for a celibate clergy: in fact, she thought, they would be better without any relatives at all, for here was Maurice, who was only her cousin by marriage, adding a new, though less intense, embarrassment to the old one, and again she agreed with Edward about the destruction of the family. The service, for her, was nothing more than an ancient rite designed to hide, rather than to reveal, the truth, but if she had found it as sacred as she supposed it was to many people, she knew she could have felt none of the suitable emotions in this little village church, with Edward near enough for her to see how well or badly he had shaved that morning. Only in some vast building, in which the ministrants dwindled to tiny replicas of men, could she get near the feeling of exaltation she had always missed in organized religion and found so naturally among the hills. Yet she had not known the same embarrassment in the church there, nor disliked her Uncle Alec in his vestments, and perhaps this was because he went about his duties in a thoroughly business-like way and was as glad as anybody else when they were done, and this, for which she had once been grateful, she now regretted, for if he had inspired her with this abominable self-consciousness, she might have persuaded Edward to pursue some other calling. As she went into the church and took her seat, forgetting the silent prayer which she tried to remember for Edward's sake, she felt quite angry with her uncle, but she realized that being and doing right must be considered as ends in themselves, for there was no telling what harm they were going to do, and she applied this to her own affairs, in profound doubt about the wisdom of her attitude and with no intention of changing it.

The organ, another reminder of the Blunts for Edward, was alternately squeaking and howling, or breathing stertorously in the hope of producing a note, and Margaret, glancing at the Blunts' pew, and wondering that their ears had not succeeded where their consciences failed, saw that James sat there alone, his thin neck rising from a collar much too wide for it, his features piously composed for the service, his eyes perennially anxious, and the droop of his head apparently expressing his grief or shame for the empty place at his side.

For Hilary, this absence was explained by her memory of John and Caroline standing together on the cliff, but she was disappointed to miss a nearer view of the face she had only seen in the shadow of the Blunts' house and wished to study closely: Margaret, knowing that face by heart, would have been satisfied with Hilary's explanation if she had not suspected another in an indignant loyalty which made it impossible for John to appear in Edward's church, but then, Caroline would surely not have burnt the letter and frustrated her own purposes with unguarded speech.

It was no good puzzling about it. She must try to extend her passive attitude to her thoughts, and she looked at other familiar faces and saw in them a patient resignation to receiving little of that satisfaction which they had been taught to expect. What did they come for, Sunday after Sunday? The girls came to display their finery, the boys came to see the girls: for the middle-aged, the church was at least a place where they could rest and have peace from the importunities of their children. Here and there, an old fisherman sat in a patience of another kind, taught by a hard life which had not been altogether unfruitful of material benefits and in which he saw some dim analogy to the religion wherein he sought what he might find at last. There were not many people in the church, for the more ardent spirits attended the chapel at the end of the village street, and the fishing population, as a whole, preferred to lean against the boats hauled up on the beach, smoke their pipes and look, in a mixture of friendliness and enmity, at the sea. Here were the more genteel inhabitants of Old Framling, a few farmers and their families, impoverished ladies living in neat cottages, the dressmaker, the village schoolmaster and mistress, a teacher of music to the tradespeople's children and the tradespeople themselves. In the choir, now filing into place, there were more well-known faces, the baker's boy, the plumber who sang bass, and the butcher who, persistently inartistic, had a weak tenor voice and a burly frame, and finding them all ridiculous in what she called their fancy dress, Margaret lowered her eyes. She not only felt uncomfortable herself, but she could never rid herself of the consciously erroneous belief that Edward felt uncomfortable too, and it seemed considerate not to look at him.

Edward's own eyes were as keen as those of a shepherd for his sheep and he had the same tolerance for their habits of straying: he was nevertheless surprised that the faithful John was not there. Maurice was both surprised and relieved, for here was proof that Edward's attraction for his parishioners was not irresistible, a suggestion that his own personality had not offended and that there was some other cause for the churchwarden's absence. Like Margaret, he wondered what that girl had told him, but Maurice's thoughts wandered only for an instant. The church was the one place in which he lost his consciousness of himself and as he prayed and preached he forgot Margaret and Edward and John Blunt; he did not hear, through the open door, the occasional voice of a cow or sheep in the meadow where the chestnut tree stood; he detected no signs of inattention in his hearers and, indeed, there were few of these, for he preached well, simply, and to-day without trying to force a moral. In despair of finding a subject congenial to his own uncertain feelings, discarding that of Jonah as one which Margaret might find amusing, in fear of provoking argument with one of his successful sermons about the home, he told a story from the Gospels and left the lesson to be found by those who looked for it, and even Margaret listened as though it were a stranger speaking.

She left the church in a state of some humility. She could not despise the mind of a man who could preach like that, nor could she ignore the signs of character behind it; it was impossible that Maurice was merely weak, comic, resentful, prudish and mean. His defects, she thought, must have been imposed on something really sound until they almost buried it, and in a rare and temporary mood of penitence, she saw that her flippant dealings with him had been wasteful of him and of herself. She would try, yes, this time, she would really try to find the man beneath the body, the heart behind the unhappiness, the heart of the man who had the excellent good sense, if Edward was right, to love her!

These thoughts were dissipated by the sight of James Blunt hovering in the sunny churchyard. His face brightened when he saw her, clouded again with the approach of Maurice and Edward, and twitched when Edward immediately asked for John.

'John?' he repeated, as though the name surprised him. He gazed at the humble grave near his feet. 'John isn't very well, Vicar.'

'What's the matter? Half-holiday upset him?'

'Eh?' said James loudly, cocking up his head. 'What's that?' He looked at each of the four faces attentively turned to him and relapsed into his usual meekness. 'No, but he isn't well. Nothing much. Just out of sorts.'

'Well, tell him he missed a very good sermon.'

'Yes, a very good sermon,' Margaret said, and smiled at Maurice. 'I liked it, Maurice. Why can't you teach Edward to preach like that?'

James looked shocked. 'Oh, but the Vicar preaches a very good sermon, too – a very good sermon,' he said anxiously. 'And I'll tell John what you say, Vicar, and I'll tell him about the sermon. It'll cheer him up. He hasn't been well for some time. I'm a bit worried about him.' He turned to Maurice. 'My only brother,' he said sadly.

'I saw him yesterday,' Hilary said, 'and he was having a walk, so he can't be so very bad, Mr. James.'

He cast a sly, malevolent look at her. 'A walk? That's nothing. It's his head.'

'The weather, perhaps.' Maurice suggested, and he took off his spectacles and wiped them.

'I wish it might be,' James said, without much hope.

'We shall all get sunstroke if we stay here,' Margaret said. There was not a breath of air; the heat shimmered over the graves, and the Blunts' marble angel, pointing tirelessly at the open book, received the full shafts of the sunlight on its bare head. 'Mr. James,' she said, wondering at his courage in telling lies within the angel's hearing, 'will you walk through the garden with us? It's shady there, and you mustn't be ill, too.'

She could not keep a little sternness out of her voice and he glanced at her nervously as he walked beside her in a shambling trot. He looked behind him at the three who followed slowly.

'Mrs. Stack,' he said, 'how did the Vicar find Sarah? Better was she? Talking sense?'

'Oh, yes, I think she talked sense,' Margaret answered cheerfully.

'That's more than she was doing a few days back,' he muttered. 'Very upsetting. I've not been to see her since. John goes. John's not sensitive. Nothing would satisfy her but seeing the Vicar.'

'And now she's seen him.'

'Yes. And she's talking sense?'

'I know nothing to the contrary.'

'Then that's all right. Poor old woman! I'm glad of that. And you're not forgetting about Caroline, Mrs. Stack? I gave Hilary a message for you. We'll have to get rid of her. I suppose, now, Mrs. Stack, you couldn't find some work for her in your own house? But no, what would be the good of that?' he asked mournfully of himself. Again he glanced behind him and then leaned towards Margaret. 'John's taking her for a walk, now!' he whispered. 'And yesterday! What do you think of that?'

Margaret stood still for a minute. 'I thought you said he was too ill to come to church.'

'Hush, Mrs. Stack, please!' he begged. 'I said it was his head and so it is. What else could it be?' he demanded. 'There's no place for me in that house any longer,' he said. He was telling the truth now, she thought. There had never been much of a place for poor James. 'And what'll I do when she marries him?' he went on.

'Perhaps she won't,' Margaret said.

'But that's what she means to do!' he cried in the squeaky voice of his agitation. 'And if she doesn't,' he dropped his voice, 'and if she doesn't, she'll make trouble for us both, for how do I know what John's been fool enough to say to her?'

'But how,' Margaret asked innocently, 'could she make trouble for Mr. John and you? Aren't you getting rather fanciful, Mr. James?' She paused beside an apple tree and examined the fruit, giving him time to plan his answer.

'There are things a lady like you doesn't think of,' she heard him say. 'What about a breach of promise case? That wouldn't be a pleasant thing to happen, would it?'

Again she thought of Caroline and of Caroline's mother. What James pretended to fear was neither in the face nor in the blood, and she turned vivaciously to him and cried, 'I give you my word of honour, Mr. James, if you think that's a good security, I'll make the biggest bet you can think of, that your brother will never figure in a case like that. Now, are you satisfied? Go home and eat a good dinner and be thankful you've nothing more serious to worry you.'

She knew he had a good deal more than that. He feared John's confidences to Caroline as Margaret was trying not to fear Caroline's to John, he was afraid of what Sarah might say to Edward or have said and, at the best, he saw himself ousted from his home. Her pity overcame her natural shrinking from him, she gave him a little nod which she meant for comfort, and let him out of a door in the front wall of the garden.

Then she strolled back to meet the others. Edward was munching an apple he had picked and making a noise like that of a horse eating oats. Maurice was walking with the jauntiness more in evidence than the flat-footedness, smiling and talking to Hilary, spreading himself happily under the remembered praise of his sermon. How annoying they both were in their black clothes and absurd collars! She had told Edward a hundred times that she could not endure him while he ate an apple, yet here he was, crunching close to her ear and trying to talk to her while he crunched. And Maurice, who lost his dignity under praise and blame alike, was ruining her good resolutions. She could not look for the heart of a man who talked so pleasantly to Hilary, while he was planning what must mean unhappiness for her. Hilary herself was not satisfactory this morning, for she had kept back the message from James, and Margaret found that she disliked all three of them.

'And what has James being saying to you?' Edward asked with his mouth full.

She shut her eyes and put her hands over her ears. 'Go away,' she said. 'I can't bear you!' And when she dropped her hands and opened her eyes she heard Edward laughing impenitently and saw Maurice staring at them both with a wavering smile which could be developed or repressed as seemed most fitting.

Chapter 25: *An Unpleasant Meal*

THIS readiness to meet the occasion suitably, to join in a joke or divert a quarrel, was forgotten in a startling thought. 'What has James been saying to you?' Edward had asked. 'Go away, I can't bear you,' was Margaret's reply, a rude answer and one she should not have made in Hilary's presence, but excusable under shock, the sudden conviction of a truth she had been resisting. Maurice saw it all clearly. John had stayed away from church and James, walking confidentially close to Margaret, as Maurice had observed, had given her the explanation he had discreetly withheld from the family group in the churchyard. That girl, and he remembered that he had never trusted her, must have spoken, after all. Maurice was dismayed. This was not what he wanted, but then, when did he get what he wanted? And, indeed, what did he really want? For already he was losing his sense of triumph over Margaret who had not believed him, and over Edward who was to suffer through the revelations of some one else. He had held his own hand; no one could blame him. He had established Caroline with the Blunts because he did not know what else to do with her; at the same time, he had accommodated them and her, and if she chose to unmask Edward, he could not be considered accountable for that. If only he had not spoken to Margaret, if he had left the matter to the girl and to the Blunts, there would have remained his settlement with God, who was so patient, so long-suffering, but Margaret, who was neither, would have known nothing to his discredit. But, since she despised him already, and thought him funny, how was he the loser? Inevitably, he began to recall his wrongs, bracing himself with counter accusations for those which might be brought against him, and he entered the house with all the jauntiness gone from his gait.

By the time he had washed his hands and brushed his hair for luncheon and adjusted his mental attitude to these new conditions, preparing his defence by the hardening of his heart against these people who, to-day, at least, had been kind to him, he found he must adjust it all over again, for had not Margaret shown quite clearly, in the garden; that her anger was to fall in the right place? Stubborn to convince as she had been, she would be angrier with Edward in the end, and now Maurice did not know whether to feel more for her or him. This was very bewildering, everything was bewildering and he felt vaguely that there was something odd in the nature of his love. It ought to have made him passionately loyal to her, careless of himself, still more careless of Edward, and for both he felt a strange mixture of spite and pity. They were being punished as they deserved, yet he half wished they could be spared. The only thing about which he had no doubt was the immediate prospect of an unpleasant meal.

He arranged his face mechanically, out of habit. The smile for social occasions, the manly cheerfulness for his young men, the playful, yet authoritative manner for his boys and girls, none of these would do. The expression of gravity with competence, befitting a parish meeting at which there would probably be trouble, was the one he assumed, and it was like a blow in that ordered face to see Margaret sitting on the arm of Edward's chair and overlooking the paper he was reading.

'If you're only looking at the cricket or the football,' Hilary was saying, 'you might let me have the literary page.'

'Wait!' Margaret said, holding up a hand. 'Don't disturb him. This is most important. The family serenity for the next week depends on this. And it's his paper, Hilary. He pays for it. You must let him have it.'

Was this sarcasm, callousness or hypocrisy? Whatever it was, Maurice took it as a rebuff: it seemed as though she was deliberately flouting his pity, mocking his seriousness. She looked radiant, extraordinarily young, as she sat on her perch with one foot swinging free, and the arm on the back of the chair practically round Edward's neck.

She looked gaily at Maurice. 'Are you like Edward?' she asked. 'I mean in this way,' she added with a smile and an accent of apology. 'Affairs of state, art, literature, even the Church – would you believe it ? – all these are nothing until we know who won the match.'

Why did he like her best when he most disapproved of her? Last night, when she sat sewing in the lamplight, she had not troubled him: there had been peace and content in the room and he had lost the desire to give her pain because she would give him nothing, but now the desire returned.

'I try to take an interest in everything,' he said precisely. 'I was going to say an intelligent interest, but you would hardly believe that.'

She lifted her eyebrows and parted her lips in deprecation of this remark. 'Then,' she said, 'that is more than Edward does. His interest isn't intelligent. It's primitive. Tribal. His native team is always the best there ever has been, even when it loses all its matches.'

'Faithful to the affections of his youth? I see,' Maurice said slowly, toying with his watch-chain, but his fingers closed on it at the sound of Hilary's voice, with a little catch of indignation in it.

'I wish you wouldn't talk over Father's head, like

that,' she said. 'It's not fair. You know he isn't listening.'

'Bless you, he doesn't mind,' Margaret said, and Maurice, who thought he knew all her smiles, found she had a special one for Hilary. Reassuring and intimate, it made a pact of humorous understanding between the two and thrust Maurice's laboured insinuations aside. Was she without all sense of danger, or was she provoking him now because he had been forestalled by Caroline and could do no more harm? He did not know how to express or how to control his impotent anger, and what did it matter, since nothing he did could affect the callousness of these people?

'And if we only talked when he was listening,' Margaret went on, 'when should we speak?' and Maurice played with the bold idea of forcing him to listen, and very attentively, for once.

'Yes, it's all right,' Edward said, but he was referring exclusively to the news. 'We're doing very well. Now let's have some food.' He got up and put a hand on Maurice's shoulder, heavily, so that he sagged a little. 'Come along. Preaching's hungry work,' he said, propelling Maurice towards the dining-room. 'I wish you could stay over next Sunday. I can't preach and now the whole parish must know it. I oughtn't to have asked you to come here. Next Sunday I shall hear them sucking sweets all over the church. They always do. It keeps them awake, I suppose. But you must stay as long as you can. Stay till Friday.'

'No, no,' Maurice said faintly. He was touched, yet he was reluctant to give way to this friendliness which presently would throw him off with a careless word. 'It's time I was getting back.' He adopted a brisker tone. 'There's a lot to arrange, a lot to arrange for the winter, you know. It's time it was all set going.'

In his fancy, he saw it all; strenuous, worth while, certainly, but it was – he waited for a word and found it – but it was dingy; not the church, for that was sacred and beautiful to him, but his own house, the streets, the people, and hating his disloyalty to the good, the earnest, he thought of his women workers in their drab clothes, hurrying, always hurrying, and here, ahead of him in the passage, Margaret walked, as though she had the whole of time to use with beauty. Was it beauty he sought in her and nothing else? It was all she gave him and she only gave that because she could not help it: it was all she had to give him, not virtue, sympathy or appreciation, but the swiftly changing aspects of a beauty he found in no other woman.

'I don't know what I ought to do,' he murmured, and Edward called in a loud voice, pathetic, even to Maurice, in its ignorance of trouble.

'Margaret, you must persuade Maurice to stay as long as he can.'

She turned and smiled with a certain reticence.

'Surely he doesn't need any persuasion,' she said. 'That's not very flattering to us.'

'It's only his sense of duty.'

'What, keeping him here?' Margaret asked innocently.

'Telling him to go. A great mistake, a sense of duty. Hullo!' He stopped as he passed the window. 'There's John. He's been for a walk. Is that what James calls being out of sorts? And who's the lady? Come and look at her, Margaret. Who's the lady?' he repeated slowly.

'It's the new housekeeper,' Margaret said briskly. 'He must have been taking her to see the sights. But really, he ought to get a new hat.'

'Oh, that's one of the sights,' Hilary said with a quick laugh.

'Well, I've stayed away from church, myself, for a

worse cause,' Edward said, taking his place at the table.

'And now, Maurice,' Margaret said charmingly, as though she were merely continuing the interrupted conversation and apologized for the diversion, 'you don't need any more persuasion, do you?'

'No, thank you, I do not,' he said, and if he had been wearing his eye-glasses they would have been shaken in their place with the convulsive, stubborn setting of his head, though neither to himself nor to Margaret was his intention clear. He could have wept behind the smile he at once assumed. She was defying him, bringing out all that was worst in him, spurring him on to the revenge she knew he could no longer take, and he saw her beauty as a snare and the drab women of his parish shone for him with the light of their inner goodness. He was profoundly puzzled by her behaviour, and it seemed as though Edward were puzzled by something too, for presently he looked up and said to Hilary:

'Was John alone when you saw him yesterday?' Hilary shook her head. 'With that girl?' This time Hilary nodded. He looked at Margaret. 'That would be a strange thing,' he said.

Maurice gulped. 'Strange!' he cried. 'Impossible! Impossible!' He was horrified by this suggestion. He stared at Margaret who surely must be as much aghast as he, but nothing seemed to move that woman who had no heart, no conscience, not even the desire to protect her husband.

'Why impossible?' she asked coolly. 'Love laughs at more than locksmiths.'

'Yes, it would have to,' Edward said grimly.

Now what did he mean by that? Maurice wondered wildly, and he hastened to protect himself from the inconvenience of knowing as much as anybody else. He had washed his hands, in private, of this affair, and now he would do it in public, for it was Margaret's responsibility, her business to instruct Edward, if she had not done so already, and he said:

'I was thinking of the apparent disparity in their ages.'

'I shouldn't think there's much in that. How old do you think she is?' Edward asked the question of Margaret, but she passed it on.

'How old is she, Maurice?'

'Really,' he said playfully, while he hated her for her skill, 'I'm not a judge of ladies' ages.' He met Hilary's grave eyes which seemed to measure him: he knew that they saw him puny, even in duplicity, and unable to bear their scrutiny meekly, he said deliberately. 'But I should think she is about twenty-one.'

'Only twenty-one?' said Edward. 'Oh, surely not.' His face was clouded: he did not try to disguise his preoccupation and even Margaret's adroitness and Hilary's cheerful loyalty seemed to have failed them. It was a very unpleasant meal, as Maurice had expected.

Chapter 26: *The Garden at Night*

THE Vicarage was a house with solid walls, inside as
well as out, and it was possible to move about a room
and to be free of the stealthy consideration for the
person next door, or innocent of the careless indifference inevitable with dwellers in flimsy buildings.
In the Vicarage, a sneeze or a cough sometimes
escaped notice, and the whereabouts of its inhabitants
could not be ascertained by aural evidence alone.
The rooms were large and everywhere there was a
sense of space; but only an enormous palace would
have satisfied Margaret that Sunday night, for if
she could not be heard, she could easily be found, and
what she wanted was to be lost to her family for an
indefinite time. Nowhere in the house was she safe
from intrusion: if Edward missed her for longer than
he liked, he would come and find her and look aggrieved at having been put to the necessity, and
though he had seen her leave the study without a
protest, there was no telling when his need for her
would arise.

He had returned from his visit to John Blunt and
she had seen at once that no questions must be asked.
What would have pleased him best would have been
for her to sit there until he chose to speak but, used
as she was to it, she always resented this expectation
of her quiescence until the chosen moment, and to-
night, sitting still was more than she could manage.
She had sat through two church services and several
meals and now she wanted solitude and movement,
yet that sense of responsibility, of which she pretended
to be ignorant, kept her near the house, and the vege-
table garden offered all she could safely take.

Very quietly, she went out of the house and cast back a look at it. Maurice had gone early to bed and she hoped he was now unsuccessfully wooing sleep: a light was burning in Hilary's room and that admirable child could be trusted to stay there, though what her thoughts might be Margaret could not guess and she was determined not to try. She was going to walk on the cobbled paths and imagine she was on the rocky ground of the country where peace went hand in hand with beauty, and if she could not magnify the trees, the tool-house and the church tower into mountains, she could change the cabbages into heather and strain her ears for the sound of falling water.

It was a dark, starless night, fit for such fancies, and Margaret crossed the lawn, feeling sorry for all the people who had no such games to play. There were faults to be found with many of God's arrangements – or was it only with what men made of them – but this gift of imagination weighed down the other balance. Dreams, too, even nightmares, she counted among her blessings, for she had only to sleep to have adventures and only to open her eyes to lose the terror. It was a wonderful invention, she thought, congratulating the Creator, and she wished she could get rid of this waking, sordid little nightmare as easily. It was unnecessary and stupid, but she was well aware of stupidity's power and she had to reckon with it, and not with it alone. The root of her trouble grew in the earth of a traditional morality, the branches were spreading in the bright light of Maurice's jealousy and spite, of John Blunt's power to accuse his accuser, of her fears for Hilary's and Edward's happiness and the whole growth was a monstrosity, unnatural: that thick earth was fed with nonsense which was mocked by an old phrase. A natural daughter! Here was an ironical comment on the married state and a sane acceptance of facts! Kings had had natural daughters –

why was not Edward a king, instead of the Vicar of a little parish in which his sin was constantly repeated? Edward was no hypocrite; he could condone other people's faults, and no doubt, she thought, with a little curl of her lip, his own experience had helped him to this tolerance. And at least Hilary was a natural daughter, too. She had not been wronged in that sense: she was the product of a frank love which obedience to that traditional morality had made fearless. And now her thoughts were turning her own arguments against her! It was all very confusing and she had promised herself not to think. She was going to play her little game of transforming the cabbages, their homely roundness into spikes of heather, and their stale smell into the warm dusty one roused by her passage. Through her thin slippers, her feet moulded themselves to the cobbles, but these refused to play their part. They were too smooth, too regular, and looking up, she saw the tower of the church and she could not pretend it was something else. It was so black that it changed the colour of the sky to blue and in its solidity, unimpaired by time, it seemed to tell her sadly that she was young and foolish, that rebellion did not bring freedom, that the fetters returned.

'Yes, if the rebellion is selfish,' she said aloud, arguing with the church in a reasonable tone, and it was silent with the deaf dignity of the old. She made a little face at it. Edward's rebellion had been selfish, certainly, but rebellion in itself was good and selfishness was the right of youth. She was not going to allow that church to preach at her, yet how much easier it would be to have fixed values and an infallible code of conduct. And if sin was really sin, there was something diabolical in its purifying effects; they were an encouragement to the virtuous to fall, that their virtue might be increased: there was evidence that the sinners made the saints and it looked as though God and the Devil had compromised in the matter, each getting his due share.

'Yes, diabolical,' she murmured standing still. Perhaps Edward would not have been so good a man if his youth had been blameless and now he was going to suffer as only the good can. He did not need punishment, but perhaps – the thought came and held her rigid – perhaps she did! She had never suffered at all, and her turn might be near, but surely there was no sense in that, or was there so much that she could not understand it?

'Oh, I give it up!' she exclaimed.

She heard a cough startling in the darkness, but only for an instant. She recognized the sound as Maurice's tactful warning of his presence and his hat, appearing above the currant bushes, was the signal of his approach.

'I hope I didn't frighten you,' he said. 'Are you alone? I thought I heard voices.'

'You heard a voice. Mine. One must talk to somebody.'

'I've been walking up and down here for some time,' he said.

'Ah, those rubber soles!' she cried. 'I didn't hear you and I thought you were in bed. But no, you didn't frighten me. I'm used to wandering about in the dark, and there's nothing fearful in a garden. I used to dare myself to walk about the country, at night, in very lonely places.' She was speaking quietly for, without effort she was now where she wished to be and under that wide sky, in the solitude of great spaces, her voice became lower and almost toneless. 'So heavenly cold and still and dark,' she said, 'and nothing moves – until you move yourself, and then the rocks seem to march alongside, but a long way off, quietly, like scouts watching an enemy. And when you stop, they stop, too, and you can't get away from them unless you run, and of course you're afraid to run. And if you listen, you hear a voice, not human, very beautiful, babbling or crying, and you don't know where it is, or where it comes from, but walking on, very carefully, because of the scouts, you find something white and shining and swift at your feet, and it's the voice, part of the voice! Water! A stream – chuckling because you didn't know what it was, but wailing as soon as you pass on. Not for you – it doesn't care whether you go or stay. I think it must be crying because it has to go to the sea. As I have. But it's comforting to think part of it is in the sea.'

She lifted her head and saw the pale eclipse of Maurice's face, nearer to her than it had ever been before, motionless, the features stiff with attention. She heard him draw a long breath.

'What's the matter?' she asked sharply. She had returned to Maurice and the garden, but he had been with her in the place she loved, she had let him share what was more sacred to her than bread and salt, and the sharpness of her voice marked her regret for the new claim she had given him.

He turned away from her.

'Nothing,' he said, on a sigh, 'nothing. Could we – could we sit down somewhere?'

'If you're not afraid of the dew.'

'No, I'm not afraid,' he said mournfully, 'not of that,' he muttered.

She did not move. She had a feeling that this darkness was going to reveal a Maurice whom daylight had always hidden, and she was sure of it when almost angrily, he cried, as he swung round again, 'Why did you talk to me like that?'

'I was talking to myself,' she replied.

'That's what I mean,' he said. 'You shouldn't! You shouldn't! It isn't fair!'

'But why not?'

He chose one of his many reasons and said:

'Because you'll make me suffer for it, somehow.'

It was the worst reason he could have offered her, the one which best fitted her conception of him, but she knew she deserved the reproach, and quietly she said.

'I won't. I'll try not to, at least. You're right. It wouldn't be fair. If I've let you in, I mustn't push you out, but you'll suffer more.'

'Oh, I know that,' he muttered.

'Because,' she said gently, 'you'll have one thing less to pity yourself for.'

'Less! One thing more!' he shouted.

This was a new voice for Maurice, but it had a note she recognized: it was the male blare of fury at his own weakness and of rage at its cause, and for his sake, she was grateful to the darkness. There would have been cruelty in seeing him too clearly when he spoke to her, for the first time, with some likeness to a man, yet how inevitable it was that he should choose this place, among the cabbages and the gooseberry bushes, for the expression of this anger, and that he should further spoil it and lose some of her interest, with a renewed request to be allowed to sit down.

'I must have been walking up and down these paths for hours,' he complained.

'Well, come and sit down,' she said. 'Here, in this corner of pleasant memories, where we sat the other day. But I think you would be wiser to go to bed.'

'No good. I couldn't sleep.'

'I'm not surprised,' she said crisply, restraining her desire to make him shout again. It would be easy, he deserved it, and she might do it yet, but for the moment she sat, straight and reserved, at her end of the seat, while he bent forward in the huddled posture of his misery.

He had one more reason for sleeplessness than she guessed and he could not speak of it. He had passed the open door of the study on his way to bed and it was not his fault if Edward and Margaret discussed their affairs in loud tones. They had the clear voices of their self-assurance and though he had not stood still to listen, he had certainly gone extremely slowly up the stairs. It was natural to go slowly, for he was tired and downhearted, but such a painful lifting of his feet had not been necessary and he was ashamed. His excuse was an anxiety which was not entirely for himself. It had been a day of strain. Even the nerves of these buoyant Stacks had not withstood it and Edward's face had not cleared since its first clouding. Something was going to happen, and he knew what it was when he heard Margaret telling Edward that she admired his courage though she thought he was acting foolishly.

'You promised not to say another word!' Edward said angrily.

'But I can always break a promise in a good cause,' she replied in the light way of which Maurice so much disapproved.

'Well, I can't break mine,' Edward said, 'and what is your good cause?'

During the ensuing silence, Maurice held a foot in the air and he did not put it down until Margaret answered.

'Saving you an unpleasant task – and a wasted one. Nothing you say will make any difference to John – not now, and it will make me, perhaps all of us, unhappy. Never mind. Go and do your duty, but I wish you had been born without a conscience. And I've no patience with the exorbitance of the dying. If I make demands of you on my deathbed, I shan't expect you to take the slightest notice of them!'

'Ah, don't! You know that's the one thing I can't bear to think about,' Edward said, and Margaret gave the kind of laugh which no one but Edward was meant to hear.

Maurice had hastened up the stairs in a confusion of

213

jealousy, shame, fear, admiration and remorse. The loyalty of the little boy who longed for the friendship of a cousin who was strong and gay and fearless, who, perhaps, had not meant to be unkind, after all, struggled with the desire to see the discomfiture of the man who could make a woman laugh like that, though she was a woman who would break a promise, who had no conscience and no sense of duty, who had nothing to make her lovable except her charm, and only the charm of a fair body and a sweet voice. She was a temptress, he told himself, growing dramatic in his distress: she had made him sin in spirit and she was trying to lure Edward from a duty which Maurice heartily wished he would not do, of which he would have been in ignorance if Margaret had had the self-control to hold her tongue, and Edward was resisting with a fortitude which was astonishing in the circumstances. And this was the man he had tried to despise!

The whole weight of his sympathy was with Edward now and he crossed his dark bedroom and stood at the window in temporary forgetfulness of himself. He heard the front door opened and shut, then heavy footsteps below, and he saw Edward standing on the Blunts' threshold. There was no light above the door of that frugal household and Maurice could not distinguish the figure of the person who let Edward in; nor could he stay trembling at the window to watch for his cousin's return. He hid himself in the garden, and some of his thoughts in the consideration of Margaret's sadly unsuccessful wickedness.

Chapter 27: *Edward Sees a Ghost*

THE variability of his emotions was exhausting. He was perpetually swaying from one side to the other and a crash was imminent, but he had lived for so long on infirm foundations that he never gave them a thought and, in any case, it was too late to strengthen them. He was leaning heavily towards Edward, who was doing what he would not have dared to do himself, and it was with a wrenching jerk that Margaret had dragged him into an upright, though insecure, position. He kept it, tottering, while she spoke in that deadened, secret voice. She was talking to herself, but it was in his presence; he was getting close to something withdrawn and precious which he could not name, the quality which underlay her beauty and made it potent, and this approach justified, but unfortunately, at the same time, it increased the attraction for which he had been blaming himself. He was not the victim of an entirely evil spell, but he was the less likely to escape his enslavement. She had as good as said so herself, and such was the enfeebling effect of his general agitation, that he never thought of resenting the statement. He had resented the fact, and her share in it, in his shout; he had not yet criticized her cool acceptance of his condition. And, now that he was calmer, his thoughts returned to Edward.

'Is everybody else in bed?' he asked skilfully.

She bent sideways to avoid the screen made by the branches.

'Hilary's light is still burning. But then, it always will be,' she said softly. 'Even on a night like this.'

'It's very dark,' he agreed.

'Not a star – except hers. And the lawn's like a lake. If we stretch our feet out, they'll get wet – wetter than they are already. Really, Maurice, I don't know why we're sitting here, like tramps in a public park.'

'No one could mistake you for a tramp,' he said mournfully. He could see her profile against the darkness into which her hair and dress were merged: he could see the fine line running from her chin into her neck, and he thought her hands were like flowers dropped on her knee. 'Water lilies,' he said suddenly, and smiled deprecatingly, though she was not looking at him.

'Yes, they grow in public parks, too,' she said. 'I don't like them much. They look as if some one had put them on the water to see if they would float.'

He was thankful that, for once, she had missed his meaning but he was hurt. It was a pretty fancy and she had rejected it, and he decided, almost dispassionately, that he would never be able to say anything to please her.

'Association of ideas, I suppose,' he murmured.

'Ye-es,' she conceded indifferently, across a yawn. 'I wonder what Edward's doing.'

He started violently. Had he not come back? Dismayed by her callousness, he asked anxiously, 'Haven't you seen him?'

'Seen him? Of course. When do I see anybody else? The point is whether he's seen me!'

'You mean – sitting here?' he ventured tremulously.

'I hope not. It would make him angry,' she said gravely.

Never afterwards did he dare to remember his callow pride at those words and the succeeding shock as she said with amusement and, as he thought, with malice, 'He would be afraid of my catching cold. And I never do. It's you who will do that, Maurice, after this – this alfresco entertainment. As I said before, why are we sitting here? Because you're afraid you won't sleep? Are you always subject to insomnia, or is there something on your mind?'

'I have many things on my mind,' he said, 'and you know what they are.'

'Not all of them.'

'Not all of them,' he repeated firmly, while he doubted whether either of them spoke the truth. Purposely or accidentally, he was not sure which, she had prevented him from committing a terrible indiscretion and his gratitude was mixed with disappointment. There would have been an immense relief in speech and it might have set him free for ever.

'But I know quite enough,' Margaret went on. Her self-restraint was taking its revenge. If she could not allow him to tell her what he thought of her – and she would have liked to hear it – she would have the satisfaction of giving him some information about himself. 'What you want, Maurice, is a mental purging. You ought to turn your mind out and have a look at it. You're not a bad man. You're well-meaning – and that's always so dangerous, isn't it? It's your well-meaningness that's your trouble now. You started on a nasty job and then you were afraid to finish it. And I was afraid you would, but now I don't care what you do. That's over, thank God. Fear is the only thing one need be afraid of.' She turned to him confidentially and he found the courage to look at her. 'I'll tell you something,' she said. 'I might have appealed to your pity, and you would have liked that – but no, I couldn't. And I might have appealed to your vanity, and that would have been easier still, but that, too, was more than my pride could bear. I suppose my pride is stronger than my love.'

'Love!' he cried fiercely, taking the first chance she had given him. 'You don't know what it means! The only thing you understand is making people

217

unhappy – for your own amusement! You haven't spared me, when you wanted to laugh – not once!'

'Oh yes,' she interposed quietly, 'many times. I shouldn't like to tell you how often! And when I saved my pride, I saved yours, too. You didn't deserve it, I know, but I did it.'

'And what are you doing now? What are you doing to Edward, all the time? Teasing him, making fun of him, just as you do with me! I don't know how he stands it! You're cruel, you're heartless. You're not worthy of his love or of – you're not worthy of his love! Why aren't you with him now?'

'You're very loyal to Edward, all of a sudden,' she remarked.

'Yes, I'm sorry for him. I used to envy him. Oh yes, you know that well enough – but at last I can see what I've been saved.'

'Saved?' she said quietly. 'Saved? What do you mean by that?'

It was impossible to tell her. He could not risk more of her scorn or face his own presumption, and he mumbled miserably, 'I might have married somebody, too.'

'I wish you had. I wish you would,' she said calmly. 'Marriage is one of those institutions which, on the whole, do more good than harm. You mustn't judge them all by Edward's! If you had somebody to look after, you wouldn't think so much about yourself. I know I'm making you angry, but I don't mind.'

'No, you don't mind – now,' he said.

'Because you'll forgive me, sooner or later. Sooner, I think. Perhaps to-night. In a few minutes! Now!'

'No, no,' he shook his head. 'I can never forget what you've said to me.'

'I don't want you to. I want you to remember and still forgive me. A quarrel's the best foundation for a friendship. Maurice,' she leaned towards him, 'if it wasn't quite so dark, you'd forgive me now!'

He started back. 'Oh, don't say things like that,' he pleaded.

She straightened herself at once. 'Well, it's the only one I've said – and I could say so many! But I won't. What a child you are! You've been mean and spiteful, like a nasty little boy, and now you're sorry, but you won't admit it. Why don't you? Look here,' she put out her hand. 'I've been rude to you, and – well, what I haven't done has been more for my sake than for yours. I've had great temptations, but I've had provocation, too. We'll both apologize.'

He took her hand and he did not let it go. 'Words are no good,' he said.

'Oh yes, they are, especially when they're beautiful, and forgive is a beautiful word. All the beautiful things have beautiful names. Forgive us our trespasses as we forgive them that trespass against us. Do we? Must I teach you your own business? Come along! He gives twice who gives quickly. Don't be stubborn. You're a bit of a fraud, you know, but not so much of one as you seem. I decided that when you were preaching this morning.'

'Did you?' he said sadly. 'But there's nothing I can do for you – except go away.' His grasp tightened. 'I'll go to-morrow.'

'Don't do that. Edward would be sorry. He's fond of you, you know.'

'Fond of me!' In his amazement, he almost lost her hand, almost forgot to keep her attention from it, but she was not thinking about it. She let it lie in his warm, damp one, and felt no repugnance for his touch. She was thinking that truth was much more powerful than the evasions in which she had been indulging. The truth, uttered uncalculatingly, was going to do what she wanted. Maurice would be loyal to anyone who cared for him, and she remembered that one of the few precepts her uncle had given for her guidance was to tell the truth when she could.

It was not, he said, because other people had the right to know it or that truth was often as simple as it seemed, but because she owed it to herself.

'He doesn't treat me as though he liked me,' Maurice said gloomily.

'He argues with you. That's a sure sign of his affection. I've tried to crush him, because I knew you didn't like it –'

'Oh, but you shouldn't!' Maurice cried. 'I didn't mind it, I didn't mind it in the least!'

She laughed, throwing back her head and, for the first time, he heard no cruelty in the sound. 'Then I won't interfere – with any of you,' she said. 'I'm tired of it. I'll let you all have a free hand. I'll even,' she gave his hand a parting pressure, 'I'll even have my own.'

'Yes, yes, but what are you going to do?' he asked in agitation.

'Nothing. I'm going to bed.' She stood up and, oddly enough, he found he could look at her and enjoy the sight and look forward to the morning when he would see her more clearly, without a sense of guilt and the enmity it engendered. 'And you'd better go, too,' she said. Her voice, a lovely instrument which she knew how to play, softened and deepened. 'And go to sleep,' she said, as though he were a child.

'Yes. Yes, I will,' he said with a ready obedience which had its pathos. 'But not just yet. I'll stay here for a little while. I think' – he stood up, too, and took a step towards her – 'I think I shall have a walk. I feel restless. Will you leave me to bolt the front door? Be sure not to lock me out.'

'Well,' she said doubtfully, 'don't go stumbling about in the dark and getting into trouble.'

'I shan't do that,' he said quietly. 'I think I shall get rid of the – the remains of my trouble. Good night.' He made her a little formal bow and she saw it not only as his acceptance of everything she had said, but as something in the nature of a compact, or a promise.

'Good night,' she answered gently and she turned back to wave to him as she went towards the house.

She opened the study door and peeped in, ready to look contrite. 'Have you been wanting me?' she asked.

Edward shook his head. He was stretched out in his chair, looking tired and unhappy, and she went swiftly and knelt beside him.

'What's the matter?' she said tenderly. 'Was it as bad as all that?' Her heart began to beat a little faster. 'What did John say?'

'Nothing. You were quite right. He didn't say a word.'

'Or look angry?'

'No.'

'Or hurt? Or surprised?'

'He listened and looked grave and said nothing. What was there for him to say?'

'That's what I should like to know,' she murmured. 'But he didn't say it, so that's all right, I suppose. And you parted with a remark about the weather? You agreed that it was hot, or something of that sort?'

'Something of that sort.'

'Then I think you can begin to make inquiries about the cost of organs. I've been sitting in the garden, with Maurice. We've made friends.'

'Weren't you friends already?'

'Not inseparable ones, but we are now.'

'Poor wretch!'

'Not at all. He's happier than he's ever been.' She held up a hand. 'But all the perfumes of Arabia – No. I mustn't say that. We've expressed our inmost thoughts about each other –'

'Not Maurice!'

'Yes he did. Partly by implication. And this is the dawn of a new era. I shall ask him to come and stay with us whenever he likes.'

'Well, I hope he will, but this is rather an unget-at-able place.'

'One would have thought so, certainly,' Margaret said slowly, and she remembered that truth had served her well this evening and she might be wise in trusting it again. 'Why do you look so tired, to-night?' she asked. 'Why weren't you reading?'

He passed his hand across his eyes. 'I've been seeing ghosts,' he said. 'No, don't ask me to talk about them, but don't go away. Stay here and exorcise them. You're the only one who can.'

'But you know,' she said persuasively, taking his hands and pretending he was a little boy, 'you know there are no such things. And if there were, I wouldn't let them hurt you. I'll take care of you, my dear, until you're old enough to do it for yourself.'

'Then that's for ever,' he said contentedly.

Chapter 28: *Hilary is Puzzled*

THERE was a pile of letters for Edward on the break-fast table and Margaret eyed them with satisfaction. He would have no time to see another ghost if she should appear again on the pavement and though, perhaps, that ghost could not be laid for ever, it might be persuaded to walk elsewhere, in some other part of the country with John Blunt. John Blunt ought to realize the necessity for a change of air and, in an optimistic mood, she began to make plans for him and Caroline, when a loud groan from Edward startled her into a glance at the window.

There was no one in sight: it was not quite half-past eight, when the Blunts would leave their house and, knowing their punctuality, she turned with unusual solicitude to Edward.

'Returned with thanks!' he exclaimed, holding a sheet of paper between a finger and thumb. 'With thanks! I don't suppose they've even read it!'

'Oh dear, what a nuisance! I do wish editors would show a little consideration for authors' wives. And you must cost them quite a lot in those printed slips! But, really and truly, darling, I'm very sorry. Very sorry. But we all know what stupid people they are, and you see, if they took your articles, it would be almost like saying you were stupid, too. So of course it's a compliment. Every writer knows that.'

'You don't care a bit,' he said solemnly. 'You don't care a bit for the most important part of my life. You haven't looked to see which article it is! And why,' he demanded, working himself up, 'do returned manuscripts always arrive at breakfast and upset one for the whole day?'

'Yes, I've noticed that,' she said.

'Luckily to-day's lost anyhow. I'm going to the hospital directly after lunch and then I've got three committee meetings in New Framling. Three committee meetings in one day!'

'Martyrdom!' she sighed.

'And I warn you I shall be in a very bad temper when I come back.'

She shook her head, smiling her supreme faith in him. 'You can't make me believe that, Edward dear.'

'Oh, you're intolerable, intolerable!' he cried. He looked towards the door. 'But give me a kiss, quickly, before Maurice comes in.'

'It's only Hilary,' she said, 'Hilary, I'm comforting the baby. Another article returned.'

'Which one?' Hilary asked in a business-like manner.

'It's no good asking your mother,' Edward said.

'Well, I know it's not Sacrifice, because Maurice is enjoying that.'

'Oh, it's Hosea,' Hilary said. 'Well, I don't think it's one of your best.'

'Don't say that!' Margaret cried. 'I've been telling him they're all too good to be printed. And it's so silly of you because now you'll have to help him to do it again. Praise is the golden rule. It's what they want, it saves trouble, and it explains failure. Therefore let us all praise him.'

Edward looked at Hilary with a whimsical expression. 'She's not so bad as she makes out,' he said.

Hilary's answering look was one of wisdom and of tenderness for his simplicity. It was not necessary to explain her mother to her: she thought she knew why Margaret stood between Edward's chair and the window and continued to talk nonsense while he opened his letters: she knew why Maurice entering with a surprisingly bright greeting, stood still for a moment and then smiled reassuringly, for the Blunts had just marched out of sight and Caroline Mather was standing on the pavement, looking after them. Again she was in shadow and again she disappeared with a quickness which, quite evidently, was a relief to Maurice.

He resumed his smile at Hilary and asked her how she had slept.

'I always sleep well, thank you,' she replied. She distrusted his smile: she did not distrust her mother's motives but Maurice and she shared some knowledge which was being kept from her and from her father, and she felt aggrieved as well as anxious.

'And did you sleep well, too?' Margaret asked cheerfully.

'Yes. Yes, I did,' he admitted bashfully.

'I knew you would! I feel gay this morning. Let's have a nice day. Edward can't, because the poor thing has some work to do – isn't it unreasonable? – but couldn't we – couldn't we have a picnic?'

'What a dreadful idea!' Hilary exclaimed.

'Dreadful? Delightful! We could row up the river.'

'I should like to know who would row,' Hilary said glumly.

'Are you cross, too, darling?' Margaret inquired sweetly. 'Well, really, I don't know who would.'

'Ridiculous!' said Edward. 'It's far too hot and you'd be sure to stick on the mud. For goodness' sake, don't add to my worries.'

'And flies would stick on the food,' Hilary said.

'Very well. I retire. I was only trying to be pleasant. It's always a mistake.'

'Three people isn't enough for a picnic,' Hilary said.

'And really,' Maurice interposed, 'I think the garden is the shadiest place.'

Hilary looked at him thoughtfully. 'I know lots of shadier places,' she said. 'I don't suppose you've ever seen our woods. Mother, if you hired the old cab, you could drive Cousin Maurice there this afternoon.'

'The old cab is smelly,' Margaret said. 'It smells of all the people who have ever sat in it and all the horses that have pulled it and all the drivers who have had their afternoon naps in it. And it goes to funerals, behind all the other vehicles, with the poorest relations. I won't go driving in the old cab.'

'I don't know why any of you want to do anything,' Edward said. 'You ought to be thankful you needn't. Besides, it's going to rain.'

'I certainly think it is likely to thunder,' Maurice said. He was determined to have his thunder.

'Well, that's a good thing,' Margaret said. 'Then we can all enjoy ourselves.'

Maurice marvelled at her high spirits, but he knew from hearsay, that women were always at their best in times of difficulty. She was smiling valiantly, keeping up appearances for Hilary's sake, while Edward made no attempt to hide his ill-humour, and Maurice was amazed to hear him ask abruptly, 'Have the Blunts started yet?' And he decided that this extra-ordinary directness, this inability to behave with dis-cretion or tact, was the chief cause of those offences for which Maurice had forgiven him, the cause, too – Maurice was doing his best to be lenient – of the present trouble.

It was pleasant to have forgiven Edward, pleasanter still to feel that the strong man owed something to the weak one who was ready to give all he had to anyone who cared for him, even though that one was the hus-band of the woman whose hand he had held last night. He could still feel it, firm and cool and trustful, content to lie in his. He would never forget it. With his boundless capacity for response to kindness, Maurice was wonderfully happy. His personal fears had vanished as soon as he attacked them; his love was no longer a thing of which he need be ashamed; and this thought was so welcome in its delivery from a sense of sin that he hardly suffered from the memory of the truths she had told him. He could not have accepted them without her friendship, but she had offered him, with that hand, the only love she had the right or, he admitted sadly, the desire to give him. He was like a child, sweetened by a fit of naughtiness which had been forgiven and he had complete trust in the generosity of the forgiver. There would be no after-reproaches and no reminders, except his own. He had not yet made that submission to God which he believed to be necessary for spiritual health, but God's patience had changed its quality: it was no longer stern and awful: it had the human qualities which man, according to his own necessity, alternately sees and rejects in God. Moreover, Maurice had already given an instalment on account of his final repentance.

Rapidly, his fingers played on the tablecloth: he was in danger of spiritual pride and, in his new security, he was forgetting the material dangers to which Edward's question so boldly referred, and now Margaret was repeating it with what, yesterday, he would have called a callous defiance.

'Have the Blunts started?' she asked of anyone who cared to answer.

Hilary was silent. She was not going to tell her mother what she already knew, and it was Maurice who said lightly, 'Oh yes, they've started – as usual.'

Edward's face wore its puzzled, rather childish, frown. 'I thought John might have had something to say to me.' He looked at Margaret. 'I think he may call to-night, but I don't know what time I shall get back. I've got three committee meetings,' he told Maurice, glaring at him as though they were his fault. 'Hospital Committee, and of course it doesn't fit in with the visit I have to make there – I've got to see Sarah Scutt again – and the Education Committee, and then there's another about united services on Sunday evenings. You know what that means – coffee and cakes and a little jolly Christianity thrown in!'

'It's a very good idea,' Margaret said. 'And try not to lose your temper over it. It's so undignified.'

'I don't lose my temper. You're always warning me about it, and when do I do it? Did I lose it last night? Where's my black eye?' he demanded.

Margaret laughed. It was the only thing she could do. 'You'll make Maurice think we've been quarrelling,' she said.

'No, no!' Maurice protested explosively, and wished he had not spoken, for Hilary was looking at him with the thoughtful, candid gaze he found so disconcerting; nevertheless, strong in his determined good fellowship, he smiled at her with the exaggerated kindliness offered to babies by the inexperienced, and found the effort wasted, for Hilary's attention was attracted by her father.

'Well, you're a muscular woman,' he said, 'but I don't think Maurice would imagine that I was afraid of getting a black eye from you.'

'Of course he knows I'm too much of a lady,' she said genteelly, and again she longed to shake him. What he said to Maurice was no longer a matter of any concern to her, but there was still Hilary to be considered, though, indeed, he did not know it. And Hilary's manner had subtly changed. She had lost her way in these stupid labyrinths of her elders' making and Margaret did not know how to give her a clue without betraying the Blunts' secret and her own.

Hilary sat on at the breakfast table, absently fondling the dog's head, after Maurice and Edward had left the room, and presently she said, with an alien sharpness, 'How long is Cousin Maurice going to stay?'

'Till Friday, I think.'

'But why?'

'I suppose he likes it.'

'But we don't.'

'Well, d'you know, Hilary, I rather do.'

'Not enough to take him for a drive.'

'No. I thought that was rather mean of you. What made you suggest it? Did you want to get rid of us?'

228

'I don't like the way he prowls about,' Hilary answered evasively. 'And if you enjoy having him, it's only because you like making fun of him.'

'Hilary, Hilary, did I say a single thing to annoy him this morning? You were right. We have to be kind to him. He responds. That's the mistake I made. And the queer thing is that he's not so funny to-day. Have you noticed that?'

'I don't think he's ever funny. I think he's horrid. He smiles at me as though he thinks I'm half-witted.'

'He's afraid of you. You may remember telling me he was afraid of me, and asking me to be kind to him. I now turn the tables. Try to be nice to him.'

'He's not nice to Father.'

Margaret went to the window and gave the curtains a fastidious tweak. 'Well,' she said, 'I'll tell you a secret. It's rather mean of me, but I will. Father thinks the poor, dear, old flat-footed donkey was inclined to be in love with me!'

'Oh, I knew that,' Hilary said calmly. 'At least,' she added, 'in the way one knows things one isn't told.'

Margaret took this remark as something in the nature of a challenge, but she ignored it. 'I'm disappointed,' she said. 'I thought I was going to give you a surprise.'

'It was the way he talked about you, the night before you came home. I suppose he thinks I'm as stupid as he is.'

'He's certainly rather stupid,' Margaret agreed.

'And Father's stupid, too, in a different way.'

'But then I'm clever enough for both of us!' Margaret said.

'But nothing,' Hilary said, through trembling lips, 'will ever make me believe he isn't good.'

'My darling!' Margaret exclaimed. 'Who wants to? He's as good as gold.'

'And people can do wrong things and still be good.'

'They do, and are, every day. My precious child, you're crying. There's nothing to cry about.'

'I'm not crying,' Hilary said angrily, brushing her tears aside. 'And when John Blunt asked me if it would be a shock to find out something nasty about some one I loved, I told him it wouldn't make any difference. And it's quite true. It doesn't make any difference.'

'And what have you found out?'

Hilary steadied herself. 'Nothing. But there's something wrong. It's another of the things one knows without being told. It's something – something that beastly Maurice knows, and John Blunt knows, and Father doesn't. And you know they know.'

Margaret went slowly round the table and sat down, facing Hilary. 'When did John Blunt say that to you?'

'On Saturday – no, on Friday, before you came back.'

'Poor John,' Margaret said softly. 'Poor John!' she lifted her hands and dropped them. 'Poor John!' she said again. 'He wasn't thinking of you, Hilary. He was thinking of that girl – and of himself. I hope her answer was the same as yours. Oh, I hope it was.'

'He wasn't thinking of me at all?' Hilary asked slowly.

Margaret shook her head. 'I wish I could tell you about it, but I can't. Not yet. Some day, perhaps.'

'But if Cousin Maurice knows, why shouldn't I?'

'Maurice! He hasn't the faintest suspicion of it.'

'Then why –' Hilary began, but Margaret cut her short.

'Don't ask me anything,' she said, a little sharply.

Hilary stooped down to the attentive, puzzled dog. 'Come along, Bob, we'll go for a walk,' she said, and Margaret was left with the feeling that she had been reproved. She had not satisfied the child, but how was it possible to satisfy her? What she wanted was the truth and it was not Margaret's to give her.

Chapter 29: *The Storm Begins*

THERE was no doubt that Maurice was going to have his thunder. The wholesome heat of the past week, with blazing sunshine and blue sky, turned stagnant during the morning and the world lay very still under a saffron-coloured pall. The weather was behaving with perfect appropriateness, Margaret thought. There was menace in the air and presently there would be a storm and no one could foretell what damage would be done. She felt stifled and exhausted, but she was restless while she waited for the storm to break and she busied herself about the house, turning out her linen cupboard, counting sheets and towels, getting hot to the roots of her hair and more and more bad-tempered, though not a pillow-case was missing. She was an excellent housekeeper, her linen was in good order and she missed the satisfaction of venting her accumulated irritation on her own carelessness or an inefficient laundry. Even her virtues, she thought viciously, were of no use to her, and she turned to the examination of her less satisfactory wardrobe, but now and then, as she went to and fro, she looked out of her bedroom window and saw the real cause of her ill-humour, sitting in the garden, his hands folded across his waistcoat and when he moved, it was to flap his handkerchief languidly at the flies. She hoped they were worrying him a good deal. They were, in a manner, doing her work for her, and she was glad to leave them to it. Maurice and she were both safer when they were apart and she did not venture into the garden. She looked down at the drooping leaves of the trees and the heavily hanging roses and felt their discomfort and anxiety. They wanted the rain as she

231

did, but they knew the storm would hurt them and under it some of them would die. Margaret did not fear the bodily death of any of her family under the other storm she dreaded, but there was no knowing what delicate things of the spirit might be killed, in Hilary, in Edward, even in herself. It behoved her to go very carefully, restraining her temper and her tongue, showing the patience of the roses, the resilience of the trees. She had a comforting feeling of kinship with these growing things, she wished she shared their sane acceptance of trouble; the thought of that trouble, lost while she wrestled with the linen, drew her to a window whence she could see the Blunts' house, and she almost expected to find its aspect responsive to the weather like that of the flowers and the trees.

It looked as it had always done, dark, a little sinister, indifferent to sun or cloud. The windows were all shut. Caroline, too, was expectant of a storm and had taken timely precautions, but the rain, heralded by thunder, did not begin to fall until late in the afternoon, and the sudden cold it brought was a relief to Margaret's body, though none to her mind, for the storm and its consequences had yet to be lived through, and she watched and listened with the intentness of one who believed in omens and could find a meaning in every increase or lessening of the thunder and the rain.

In her own part of the country, rain delighted her: it was more congenial to her than sunshine, and the dry earth of her garden always made her long for the spongy wetness of the hills. There, rain was not a cause for complaint or a subject for resigned humour: it was a part of the landscape, and lovely as that country was under the sun, when thrilling shafts of warmth pierced the hard winds of spring and the hills looked as if they had just been made; when summer brought rare days of heat and the air was light and aromatic and the hills were like queens, securely poised, gracious, a little careless in their security; though the country was lovelier still when the earth swept its offerings of purple and gold and copper, sharply patched with green, in a rush of colour up the slopes, it was through rain it showed itself most clearly, as a voice reveals its quality when the speaker is unseen. Behind soft, drifting mist, or fine rain blown in horizontal streaks or heavy rain falling in bars of metal, the hills withdrew into themselves, grew taller, stronger, in their reserve, and when the rain stopped and great white cloud drifts curled up the valleys, and wound themselves lovingly, ingratiatingly, round the summits, the brighter green of grass and the denser blackness of rocks were like eyebrows raised in surprise at the attempted taking of a liberty. The hills were vulnerable neither to assaults nor fondling: they remained themselves, as though they were in possession of something inviolable as a faith, sustaining as a purpose, while the rain had many varieties of human mood – anger, cruelty, indifference, malice and tenderness, and its appearance also changed. It was blue, grey, gilded, shot with colour, but here in Old Framling, it was only water falling because the clouds could no longer hold it: it had no character: it was useful when the earth needed it and it did its work: it was a nuisance when it was not wanted, and still it fell because it must, at the will of the heavens, under no impulse of its own. And rain falling on the sea was senseless, like watering a pond: it was ugly, too, in Margaret's eyes, and she was glad she could not see it. She looked out at the garden where the flowers were being treated less cruelly than they had feared, or at the street which was very grey and dreary. The air had grown cold, the day was dark, the thunder muttered in the distance and she did not like to think of Caroline Mather in the cold, dark house over the way; she knew that if the girl had been some one else, a stranger in Old Framling, living in the Blunts' house, she would have tried to show her kindness instead of allowing herself to be hampered by considerations she despised. Yet, when she came to analyse them, she found them less unworthy than she had feared. She was giving Caroline a free hand; she seemed to want it and it was fairer to leave the girl alone than to prejudice her with attentions. It was certainly fairer to restrain a natural desire to lead her into revealing those facts which had been left unexplained, about which Margaret had hardly troubled and which now began to puzzle her. Who was this father from whom Caroline was supposed to have run away? What was his attitude towards Caroline? What did he know about Edward? And what would Caroline's action have been if the Blunts had not been conveniently in need of her? She became impatient with her own passivity. She was trusting that girl with a chivalry which might be turned against her. She knew she was far too ready to judge by appearances. Caroline had satisfied her eye and Margaret, touched by the idea of John's romance, had played deliberately into Caroline's hands, without knowing anything of her character. This noble aloofness was no more than folly, based on her trust in a broad brow, clear eyes and a remarkable facility for sitting still. But Edward had seen a ghost, Hilary was gathering hints and piecing them into suspicions, and as Margaret stood at the study window and gazed at the opposite house, dark, lifeless, grilled by rain, it took on a malignant aspect. She wondered if Maurice knew more than he had told her and, much as she disliked appealing to him, she thought she was justified in making use of him. She had been avoiding him all day: he was as absurdly sensitive to kindness as to neglect, his gratitude had the exaggeration of his resentment, and again she had to liken him to a child who has been forgiven and is too simple to disguise his happiness. The sudden change to his extreme cheerfulness, his readiness to please, might have seemed suspicious if his methods had been more subtle. There remained the possibility that this simplicity was subtlety itself; perhaps it was she who was simple, and Maurice's geniality might be the expression of his amusement. This was a humiliating thought. She had been consistently adored by Hilary and Edward, she had always managed them successfully, and she was ready to believe that a naturally good opinion of her powers, thus encouraged, had resulted in an over-estimation of her quick wits. No one was more easily beguiled than a person who was occupied in beguiling others, and she wished she had not let Maurice hold her hand. Characteristically, her first reaction to these meditations was the desire to prove them wrong; the second was the humorous acknowledgment of a vanity which could put a personal triumph before the welfare of her family, and so poor a triumph, after all, for Maurice, entering at that moment, a little paunchy with his smile ready, one soft white hand on the door handle and the other fingering his watch-chain, seemed, at his best, hardly worth the trouble of a conquest.

'I came for a book,' he said at once.

'Which one do you want?'

'Oh, just a book,' he said, stepping towards the shelves.

He stood in front of them, the lift of his head making a crease at the back of his neck, and Margaret could see that his eyes were not moving to and fro.

'Where's Hilary?' she asked.

'In the drawing-room. I found I was getting very sleepy in there by the fire.'

'It's cold enough here,' she murmured. 'Cold and wet outside, and Edward has gone into New Framling without a mackintosh or an umbrella.'

'Oh dear! how foolish! And he said, himself, it was going to rain.'

'Yes, he's like that,' said Margaret, 'but it's my fault. I hate a man with an umbrella.'

'Oh! Do you?' He looked thoughtful and troubled. 'I'm afraid I often carry one myself.'

235

'Why not?' she said indifferently. She knew he would not be able to answer that.

'Would you like me to go after him with his mackintosh?' he asked eagerly.

'Oh no, certainly not. You wouldn't know where to find him and if he gets wet through he can go to bed.'

'But isn't he – I thought he was expecting John Blunt to call.'

'There's no reason why you should run all over New Framling in the rain, so that Edward can be dry for John.'

'You'd rather he didn't see him, perhaps,' Maurice suggested.

'No, we're always glad to see John Blunt. You're looking at all the stodgy books, Maurice. If you want a novel, you'll find one lower down.'

'Is he a narrow-minded man?' he asked, obediently stooping.

'I should have thought his books would have told you.'

'Now, would I have asked a question like that about Edward – and of you?' he said playfully. 'I meant John Blunt.'

'John? I don't know. Everybody is narrow-minded about something, I suppose. One might have lax views about property, for instance, and severe ones about something else. And then, there are moods to be reckoned with, too, aren't there?'

She smiled annoyingly and, with his occasional capacity for surprising her, he straightened himself and looked at her frankly.

'Yes, or misunderstandings,' he said.

'Plenty of those,' she agreed.

'But they can be put right,' he said firmly.

'Not always,' she sighed. 'Maurice,' she turned to him with sudden vivacity, 'I wish you'd tell me about your interview with that girl.'

'There's no need to talk about it,' he said soothingly.

'Is it possible that you've been mistaken?'

'I wish it were,' he said sadly, 'The only thing to do is not to believe her. Unfortunately,' he lowered his voice, 'she had that letter from her mother. She wouldn't show it to me –'

'You don't mean to say you asked to see it?'

He looked astonished and hurt. 'Of course I did. How else was I to know she was telling the truth?'

'And when did you decide to believe she was? And why are you deciding not to now?'

'I've – I've had time to think things over,' he said feebly.

'I wish you had thought them over first.'

'It wouldn't have made any difference, in the end.'

'The end is not yet,' Margaret said.

'I think you had better put the whole thing out of your mind,' he advised her gently. 'There's nothing you can do.'

'I can at least satisfy my curiosity,' she said. 'You were easily convinced.'

'I know! I know! But don't, I beg you, say anything unkind.' .

'You expect a good deal of me,' she said. 'I've seen the girl and she's not in the least like Edward. She might be taken for my daughter more easily than for his.'

'But you didn't see Edward – at the time,' he said painfully. 'And the girl was obviously embarrassed.'

'Was she? I'm surprised. What embarrassed her?'

'Well, she had to explain her mission, somehow.'

'You think she didn't do it properly? What about this father of hers? I mean the one she gets her name from.'

'Oh, don't talk like that, don't talk like that,' he pleaded.

'You're so modest,' she said, 'but I had to make my meaning clear.'

Maurice swallowed hard. His eyes looked watery and anxious.

'She said she had to leave him because he was unbearable. Drink. The usual trouble, with the usual complications. It appears,' he said awkwardly, 'that he was bringing undesirable women to the house.'

'Was that the part that embarrassed her?'

'No, but – well, she blushed when she told me her age, I felt sorry for her.'

'Oh!' Margaret said eloquently.

'You see, rather foolishly, perhaps, I told her I remembered her mother.'

'Ah, you're so impulsive,' Margaret said sweetly. 'And was she pleased?'

'She could hardly be pleased at that,' Maurice said reproachfully. 'She showed a very proper feeling, but all the same, I never trusted her.'

'Yet you put her into a position of trust,' Margaret said softly, and, to her great surprise, he turned away, swinging on his heel with an oddly smooth movement, and went quietly out of the room.

The very gentle shutting of the door seemed to her ominous: she had offended him again: she had made friends, then distrusted him, and changed him into an enemy. It was the fault of her wretched tongue, or rather of her ungenerous mind. She had not been able to resist giving him a little stab, though he had begged her not to be unkind, as if he feared the consequences.

She suddenly felt tired and sad. His face had changed rather horribly as he turned. The geniality which had been so evident all day had given place to a thin, stricken look, and she did not like to remember it. Whatever he had done, or might do, it was she who had caused that look: it was a bad thing to have made, a sin against her love of beauty, her essential gaiety, her unacknowledged creed, and impetuously she opened the door and called his name.

She saw him going very slowly up the stairs, holding to the balustrade, a black, shapeless figure, with the back of an old man, and she ran up the stairs until she stood beside him.

'Maurice, I'm sorry,' she said, on the tenderest notes of her voice, and then, with a little irresistible trip of laughter, she added, 'I don't know why I should be, but I am!'

It was dark on the stairs and she could not clearly see his face, but very plainly she heard the rain falling heavily outside, and gurgling in the gutters.

'Poor Edward,' she murmured.

'Yes,' Maurice said, 'but don't be troubled,' He paused. 'I didn't really want a book,' he said hesitatingly. 'I came to find you. I think you ought to get that letter. She'll give it to you if you ask her.'

'But why should she?'

He let out a kind of groan. 'Because she couldn't help herself,' he replied. 'Go now, and get it before John Blunt comes home. If you have that, what proof is there?'

She did not answer for a moment. She was actually a little shocked and somehow she could not tell him that the danger he feared lay in Edward's character and that she was glad of it, but, treating him openly for once, she said quietly, 'There is no letter. She burnt it. She told me so herself.'

She heard him draw a quick breath. 'Why didn't you tell me?' he whispered.

She left that question unanswered, too, and he said mournfully, "But, of course, you wouldn't. When did she tell you that?'

'On Saturday, when I saw her.'

"On Saturday! What else did she tell you?'

'Nothing else.'

'On Saturday!' he said again, and after a long pause he sighed. 'Well, I've done my best. Useless, of course. I wanted,' he said bashfully, 'to show you that I cared for you – for you and Edward. I'm not very successful in anything I try to do.' He made a weak, fluttering motion with his hands and continued his way up the stairs.

Chapter 30: *Margaret Crosses the Road Again*

It was just like Maurice, she thought, to do a best which was of no value, to concentrate his anxiety on a letter which did not exist, to feel a personal grievance, rather than relief, when his advice was shown to be superfluous: moreover, she resented such advice, not only because it came from him, but because, in his neighbourhood, her spirit of pride and independence was in renewed revolt against this scheming. It was paltry, it was vulgar, and with her usual doubt of the fineness of her impulses, she added ironically that it was unnecessary. Caroline had burnt her boat, perhaps because she thought it would merely sink her; perhaps, it was pleasanter to think, because she disliked the use of such a craft.

Margaret could not share Maurice's distrust of her. She had tried to distrust her own belief in a good face and she had failed, and as she stood on the stairs and listened to the rain, she remembered that Caroline, by this time, might have a trouble greater than her own, and she was alone in that dark house, with her faith in John shattered or enduring painfully in the midst of anxiety and suspense.

The thunder, coming a little nearer, growled a comment, but whether of denial or acquiescence she did not know.

'I thought we should have a lot of thunder,' she heard Maurice say in a satisfied tone, and then he went to his room, with the peculiarly flat, soft tread begotten of moving reverentially in sacred buildings.

Margaret sat down on the stairs and leaned her head

against the banisters. She felt tired, incapable of emotion, and her mind, detached from agitating considerations, could deal reflectively with the double drama of John's dishonesty and Edward's youthful sin, known to each other, unless Caroline had been silent, and both depending for proof on assertions alone; both hasty sins, if Margaret judged John aright, and both, in their complications of fear, repentance, jealousy, revenge and love, liable to change the currents of many lives. This might be well, or it might be ill: the problem of good and evil, in intention and in result, could not be settled until the end of time, for, as the cause of sin might lie in some good intention generations back, so what seemed evil might be productive of future good. There was nothing to be done with the past or the future except what seemed good in the present, and even that was doubtful.

Below her, in the hall, the clock remorselessly ticked away the seconds, making time into a real and rather terrifying thing, like a man's consciousness of his own heart-beats. There was no way of getting back the time and the power that had gone, and Margaret, to whom life was precious, had a sudden feeling of panic because so much of hers was behind her, a sudden desire to grasp each second and each impulse as it came, and make the most of them.

And meanwhile the thunder, a sound impersonal, yet applicable to many states of mind, to fear, triumph, despair, suspense, was gradually coming nearer and the rain slackened a little, as though to listen. Margaret listened, too, without trying to interpret the growls and mutters, enjoying the sound of a great power held in leash, but she wondered if Caroline were afraid of thunder and heard a menace in it. 'The right thing at the moment,' she said to herself, and, with less than her usual buoyancy, she rose and went down the stairs.

Mentally, she had crossed the road so many times

during the last few days that there was relief in taking her body with her, and the rain gave the street a refreshingly different aspect. On each side, a little stream was running between the pavement and the cobbles; the road was like the bed of a shallow river and the fresh water through which she passed had washed the salt out of the air. She had thrown a coat over her shoulders, but her head was bare, and in her short transit there was time for sharp drops to strike through her hair with an emphasis which seemed to mark her as their special target. She turned up her face to receive them there and what might have been tears were on her cheeks when Caroline opened the door, but Caroline's own set face looked as though real tears had stained it.

'You'd better come in,' she said dully, when she had glanced at the swaying grey curtain behind her visitor's back.

Margaret cheerfully accepted this invitation, for which, apparently, she was solely indebted to the weather. 'I thought you might be afraid of the thunder,' she said.

'I don't like it,' Caroline admitted, 'but it wasn't thundering early this afternoon nor yet last night.'

Margaret took this remark at its face value. 'No, we don't often get thunder here,' she said. 'May I hang up my coat?'

Caroline took it from her and hung it on the hatstand where there were no hats. The only ones in the Blunts' possession were on their heads or the office pegs, but two overcoats, one bulky, the other limp, were suspended there, like skins the brothers had sloughed.

'You'd better come into the kitchen, by the fire, and dry your feet,' she said.

'Thank you,' Margaret said with pleasant obtuseness. It was disappointing to go on an errand of mercy and receive so grudging and enigmatic a reception; but she had been prepared for proof of her theory

242

about the ill-success of the well-intentioned and, accepting it meekly, she followed Caroline down the dim passage to the kitchen.

Caroline pulled a wooden arm-chair near the fire and stood with her hand on the back of it, playing the hostess dutifully, if ungraciously. Margaret, however, remained on the threshold.

'But what have you done to it?' she cried in genuine pleasure, and Caroline, her lips softening a little, said impassively, 'I've cleaned it up.'

'Cleaned it! You must have scraped it! It's not the same place.'

'That's what – that's what they say. Well, I couldn't be expected to live in a pig-sty, could I?' Folding her hands in front of her, she looked round modestly. 'It was a job getting the old paper off, but I did it, and then I put up fresh. I know a flower paper isn't proper for a kitchen, but I liked it.'

'It's very pretty. And you did it all alone?'

'I wasn't going to put them to any expense,' Caroline said.

'No, that would never have done,' Margaret agreed in a tone which made Caroline exclaim at once, 'Mr. John would have given me anything I asked for, but I knew there'd be trouble with Mr. James,' and it seemed to Margaret that these words described the effect of Caroline's presence in the house. It seemed, too, that Caroline, hearing them uttered, applied them in the same sense, for she looked at Margaret with that attempted frankness, not innocent of appeal, with which the young challenge the quickness of the experienced.

'Ah, yes, Mr. James is very difficult, I know,' Margaret murmured, moving towards the window. The thunder had made a feint of retiring, but the rain fell heavily on the untidy patch of garden and dispersed the smoke from the fishermen's cottages below. On the right, the extreme point of the white cliff was like a dazzlingly white pennon hung out for a signal to those at sea. The sea itself was invisible and the breaking of the waves, audible from the house at times, was lost in the noise of the rain. Margaret detached her thoughts from Edward who, in the irritability brought on by his committee meetings, was probably refusing to take shelter from the storm, and turned to Caroline again.

'And you've got new curtains,' she said.

'Not new ones. I found those with the linen – put away dirty, too! There's no knowing what you'll find in a house like this. I was half afraid to open the cupboards.'

'Skeletons in the cupboards,' Margaret said carelessly, from the mere association of ideas, but Caroline took her up with an angry cry.

'Oh, you needn't come here saying things like that! There's more than Mr. John have things they want to hide, and he doesn't go poking into other people's secrets! And if it comes to that, he doesn't care what anybody does with his; but I do, and I won't have it! Mr. John knows what's right. There's no need for people to come hinting at him. I've had job enough to get him reasonable. First one and then the other! And Mr. James listening at the doors! Why can't you leave us alone?' she demanded.

Margaret advanced a step. She wondered if John had seen Caroline in this aspect. Her eyes were sombre, but colour had flown into her cheeks; she had lost her brooding look, yet remained magnificently maternal, and when she turned from Margaret and flung up her head, the sweep of her hair lifted her to an increased height of passionate indignation.

'I was thinking of mice,' Margaret said, speaking very slowly. 'Dead ones. Did you find any? I was thinking of all the messy things Sarah might have left behind her. Nothing else. And I didn't come to hint, or to spy. I came because I thought you might

244

be frightened and lonely. You're not much older than my own daughter. You see, I was imagining this kitchen, dark, as it used to be, not bright and pretty as you've made it, and the rain and the thunder outside, and I shouldn't have liked Hilary to be here. That's why I came.'

'But why did she come?' Caroline asked. She was pale again, and she was not convinced. Her hands, still folded, grasped each other tightly.

'Hilary? I didn't know she'd been. Did you mean Hilary?'

'Yes. Early this afternoon. She said she thought I might like to see her dog. Well, I've seen plenty of dogs.'

'Did you tell her so?'

'No,' Caroline said thoughtfully; 'you couldn't be rude to a girl like that.'

'No, I don't think you could,' Margaret said, and, remembering that suggestion of taking Maurice to the woods, she had to admit that she did not know exactly what kind of girl Hilary was.

'All the same,' Caroline went on, 'it didn't seem a good enough reason to me, and then you, about the thunder, after all the others. I felt I couldn't bear it and I didn't see why I should. I think I'll draw the curtains. I don't like these flashes.'

'They're not very near.'

'I know it's silly, but I don't like them.'

'Then I was right to come,' Margaret said, and she sat down.

Caroline approached the fire and put a foot, large but not unshapely, on the fender, as if she knew what attitude best displayed the line of her body from toe to shoulder, and again Margaret was reminded of a statue, though the face of this one had an expression not fit for the permanence of stone. Little flecks of emotion crossed it before she said, 'And if I've said anything I shouldn't, you'll be kind enough to forget it. I've got the right to ask you that. Mr. John said I was too young, and you see I am.'

'So you took my advice. You made him tell you about his trouble.'

Caroline lifted her foot from the fender and brought it to the ground with a stamp. 'I've asked you to forget it!' she cried.

'I know. I can't.'

'Oh yes, I suppose the Vicar had to tell everybody!' Caroline said bitterly.

'Of course not! As a matter of fact, I've known about it for years,' Margaret said, and she heard a faint echo like a sigh: 'For years?'

She glanced up and saw that her statement, meant for comfort, had produced the opposite effect. Caroline's mouth was quivering and her words were a little distorted when they came.

'But he gave it to me – to me – his secret. It was mine, and now you've taken it away!'

This was the true cry of the woman jealous of possession, ready to receive his sins as well as his virtues, and hold them greedily, because they were his.

'He has told it to no one else,' Margaret said quietly.

'And he told me first,' Caroline said. 'He said he had to tell me before he gave himself up. He said nobody else would understand.'

Margaret stood up and asked sharply: 'What nonsense is that?' She took Caroline by the arms. 'Sit down. Sit down in that chair. I'll get another. What did Mr. John say?'

'He said nobody else would understand,' Caroline replied, looking with simple pride at Margaret, who suppressed a smile. It was natural for Caroline to insist on that ancient and eternally new pronouncement, but it was not what Margaret wished to hear. 'And it's quite true,' Caroline said. 'It seems to me the world's full of bad fathers, if you only knew. I could understand about that. We've both been un-

happy children, me with drink, and Mr. John with –
well, I'd rather have had my trouble.'

'I remember Mr. John's father,' Margaret said.
'He was a hard man.'

'And it isn't hard men that ought to have children,'
Caroline cried. 'Or weak ones, either, if it comes to
that. But Mr. John was worse off than me. He said
he never drew a natural breath. It was as if' – she
pressed one hand heavily on the other – 'as if he was
corked down.'

'And then the cork flew off.'

Caroline nodded. 'He did it in a temper. And then
he stuck to it out of a – out of a kind of spite. He
didn't care.'

'I know. It pleased him to think he was paying his
father back. I know all about that.'

'But he didn't tell you!' Caroline begged, and when
Margaret shook her head she asked, 'Then how did
you know?'

Margaret leaned towards her. 'In exactly the same
way as I know Mr. John is a good man.'

At that, Caroline began to cry, slowly and quietly
at first, and then with choking sobs, and Margaret
waited patiently until the sobs were punctuated with
words.

'And – he will have it – he's a thief!'

'So he is. We've got to face that.'

'And he's all for giving himself up to the police!'

'Oh yes! Of course. Very noble and satisfactory for
him, but what about you? They're all like that, Caroline. Great babies! Thinking of themselves! They
imagine they can put things right as easily as that.
They can't. They can't. People who do what we call
wrong must go on bearing their burden for other
people's sake. That's their punishment.'

'And so I told him,' Caroline said, wiping her eyes.
'He can give back the money – and more. He can give
all he's got, but he hasn't the right to give me too. I

247

made him promise, last night, and then Mr. Stack came across.' She paused before she said slowly, 'I didn't think he would be like that. I don't think he'll tell the police about Mr. John. Well, he'd have more sense! I don't like parsons. I thought he'd be more like that other one with the glasses, sort of pretending to be good and smiling. I can't do with a man who's too quick to smile. My mother thought a lot of Mr. Stack. She was always talking about him lately, and now I've seen him I can't make out why she married my father, when she'd had a friend like that. But she said I was to be sure not to marry in a hurry – like she did herself.'

Margaret kept perfectly still, waiting for what was to come next, but she could not control a start when Caroline said, with sudden vivacity, 'And there's another thing.'

'Well, what is it?' Margaret asked, and Caroline answered solemnly:

'I can't think how a woman who left a house like this one could have the face to do another such dirty trick.'

'No, no,' Margaret said, 'she meant it kindly.'

'And Mr. John took it that way, too,' Caroline said. 'It was when the other one came that he got all upset. And I'd had enough to do, keeping Mr. James quiet while Mr. Stack was here. Mr. John didn't seem to mind the Vicar, but what business was it of Mr. Roper's, I should like to know? He was all upset. I couldn't get any sense out of him. And then this afternoon your daughter came, and then you. I'd had enough of it, I'd had enough! We were happy till Mr. Roper came, and then Mr. John – froze up. He wouldn't talk. You don't think Sarah told Mr. Roper, too?' She put her hands to her forehead. 'And, you see, we've had to keep things from Mr. James. I've been nearly worried to death,' she said.

It was getting dark in the kitchen and Margaret,

standing up, rather shakily, was glad the fire gave the only light. 'What time did Mr. Roper call?' she asked.

'It was just after we'd managed to get Mr. James to bed,' Caroline answered ingenuously.

'I don't think he'll trouble you again,' Margaret said.

'Ah, but I'm afraid he's said something to make Mr. John change his mind. I wish he'd come home! I do wish he'd come home! I don't feel safe about him when he's not here.'

Chapter 31: *Maurice Puts Things Right*

WHEN Margaret reached home, half an hour later, with dripping garments and her hair plastered to her head, she was met in the lamp-lit hall by Hilary, who hastened forward, looking anxiously reproachful, then shocked by her mother's state.

'You'll have to have a bath at once,' she said, as she helped to remove Margaret's coat. 'Another, I mean, and very hot. I didn't know where you were, and Cousin Maurice said you must have gone into New Framling with an umbrella for Father, but you wouldn't do that without a hat.'

'I wouldn't do it with one! Hasn't he come back? The good Maurice misunderstands my character – at present. We shall have to have an explanation. What fun!' She bent down to take off her shoes and stockings. 'In the meantime, you can tell him I've been doing nothing so dutiful. I've been for a walk, down to the bridge and along the river road and home through the churchyard.'

Hilary made a little sound of vexation. 'I do wish you wouldn't do such silly things. You might have been struck by lightning.'

'Ah, but I wasn't. And I might have fallen into the river or met a mad bull, but I didn't. The only adventures I had were inside myself, and, after all, those are the best. In imagination, I fought with beasts at Ephesus; in reality, my encounter will probably be with a purely domestic animal. Would you mind wringing out these stockings for me? No! Don't let them drip on my precious table!'

Moving from its neighbourhood and making a basin

of her hands, Hilary asked quietly, almost reprovingly, 'Are you vexed about something?'

'Vexed?' She gave Hilary an odd look. She might have reproached her for that secret visit to Caroline, but she remained loyal to her conception of family freedom. 'No, I'm not vexed. I'm in very high spirits.'

'I know,' Hilary answered enigmatically.

'I'm afraid I'm rather a trouble to you,' Margaret said pleasantly.

'No, but you're really not like a grown-up person at all.' Hilary sighed. 'I wish you'd go and have your bath.'

'I will. It must be nearly dinner-time. But I feel talkative.' She stood at the foot of the stairs, holding up her skirt, her eyes sparkling and, as Hilary saw with admiration, her beauty undiminished by her flattened hair. She put her hands to her head and removed them, showing Hilary her glistening palms. 'Drenched! But it doesn't matter. But suppose I'd met that bull. You would have been a demi-orphan, Hilary, for no better reason than my naturally wavy hair, because if I hadn't known it would look all the better for the rain I should never have gone for a walk without a hat. Such a little thing as that! It's really a terrifying thought.'

'And Cousin Maurice would say it was the Hand of God.'

'So, having arranged for my hair to curl, He had to make sure there wasn't a bull about this evening. What detail! Maurice gives God a tremendous lot to do. Go and ask him about it.'

'You said we had to be kind, and I don't think I'll tease him, because he seemed so worried about you.'

'Oh, did he? Well, go and reassure him.'

She thought it very likely that he had seen her passage of the street and she could understand his anxiety, yet she could not understand his actions: he had gone to John Blunt immediately after the recon-

251

ciliation in the garden and it galled her to think he had been deceiving her throughout, that she had misinterpreted his cheerfulness, and she tore off her clothes with the energy of her anger and splashed vehemently in her bath. She found it exhilarating to be so gloriously, justifiably angry, sparkling on the surface and deadly cold within, and sitting up and rubbing her head vigorously, she planned what she was going to say to him, continuing that flood of eloquence which had swept her down the village street and along the road by the river which, swollen by the rain, rushed tumultuously to the sea. And everything, except the sea, dull and grey and curiously submissive, had seemed to share her anger. The river roared, the rain fell, like spears darted with precision by the hosts of Heaven, and shone, for a bright instant, before the thunder came with the sound of iron doors rolled back. New Framling was almost blotted out, as it deserved to be, and she was the only survivor of the flood. Lights in the houses, here and there, intensified her sense of triumphant loneliness, and only when she turned aside and reached the churchyard could she feel that the world was peopled. Hundreds of men and women were lying under the sodden earth and she thought they were all awake, imprisoned, listening to the storm and resenting, in their consciousness of themselves, the indignity of the tombstones which marked their places and gave them a name and date lest they should be altogether forgotten. And Margaret wanted to set them free, all except Andrew Blunt, who must endure the kind of suffering he had inflicted on his son. He must stay there, weighted by the marble angel who was still pointing, still imperturbable, under the rain, and as she hurried on through the garden she wondered if Andrew would have erected so costly a monument if he had not expected to lie under it himself. She felt very bitter towards Andrew Blunt who had indirectly complicated her own affairs, but perhaps he had served his son better than either of them knew. John would have loved Caroline in any case, but her honesty, which had shamed him, and his fear of losing her must have trebled her value in his eyes. And so, she thought, it was foolish to be angry with people for what they did or left undone, yet she continued to be angry with Maurice, for he had lessened her confidence in herself; and while she might have forgiven him if he had been witty, or even handsome, finding excuses for herself in his disarming charms, the remembrance of him, plump, soft, spectacled and nervous, made her as ridiculous and revengeful as himself. And how meanly revengeful he had been! Yet he had told her to secure the letter, and then, oddly enough, he had seemed disappointed to learn of its destruction. She did not know how to account for that – but she would know soon, she told herself, as she left the steaming bathroom and issued on to the landing, which was cool and dim, with the voice of the clock, quiet but sonorous, still uttering its warning about time; but now the nature of the warning had changed. It did not urge her to action, to the grasping of what life could give her: it was like the voice of the house itself, mellow, wise and old, cautioning her against any violence of emotion.

She stood and listened to it for a moment before she passed on to her room, and she might have been soothed out of her anger if she had not seen a pale disk apparently floating towards her up the stairs. She recognized this as the head of Maurice before she distinguished the black body below, and she knew that the Lord had delivered him into her hands.

'Ah,' she said, 'I wanted to see you. You're just in time.' She stood at the head of the stairs in her gay dressing-gown, a towel slung over her shoulder, her hair disordered and damp, but she had that fineness of structure, of face and figure, which made her independent of aids; moreover, she had the lack of self-consciousness which is one of the best results of beauty, and when Maurice lowered his eyes and tried to edge past her modestly, she said firmly, 'No. I want to talk to you. Come into my room.'

He hesitated, murmuring that what she had to say might be postponed.

'But it can't be, and I'm not going to say it on the landing.'

'Has something happened?' he whispered.

'Yes, a great deal.'

'Then, in that case –' he said, and followed her delicately.

Candles in tall holders were burning on the dressing-table, and in one furtive glance he saw them and their reflection, an arm-chair with some garment thrown over it, the bright curtains covering the windows, before he cast down his eyes.

'Now,' she began, and she sat down on the bed. 'No, shut the door.'

'But really –' he protested.

'Shut the door,' she repeated, and he obeyed, but he stood near it. His feet, in their felt slippers, sank into the carpet, giving him the sensation of being bogged as well as trapped, and he was vexed and em-barrassed by her indiscretion. If Edward should return and discover him in this situation, he would not know how to explain it, and Hilary or one of the ser-vants might appear at any moment. 'It's nearly dinner-time,' he said.

To that hint she made no response, but after a moment's pause, she said, in an even voice, 'I've had a shock,' and raising his head, he saw that she was looking at him, but the candle-light was behind her and he could not see whether she showed the signs of agitation which she so successfully kept out of her voice.

'A shock?'

'Yes – about you. I've been trying so hard to like you, and I did last night, when we'd made friends. I thought I understood you. I thought you were resentful and narrow-minded and self-absorbed and lonely and rather stupid, but fundamentally kind and honest. Yes, I liked you, and I thought you would be faithful to a friend. And I'm annoyed at having misjudged you and allowed you to deceive me. It was I who was stupid. Why did you go and see John Blunt last night?'

He did not answer; he stared at her, open-mouthed, horrified by these accusations, conscious of nothing but pain, and he heard her say slowly, 'Why are you so startled? You must have known I should find out.'

'But who told you? Who told you?' he managed to stammer. 'I didn't mean you to know. I was trying to pay back – and get no credit for it. What else could I do? I did the best I could. I don't know why you should say such cruel things to me. I told John Blunt he wasn't to believe the story. I told him I knew that girl's mother and she wasn't to be trusted. I told him Edward was a young man, easily deceived. I made the best I could of it. I told him,' his voice sank, 'that there must have been others before him, and the girl and her mother had put their heads together to get what they could out of him. I don't know what Edward said to him last night, but I – I gathered something of his intention. As a matter of fact, I overheard you talking before I went and I – I couldn't bear it. It was a thing,' he murmured, 'I couldn't have done myself. And I thought I must do what I could for him – and for you. And if I told lies, they were lies that might very well be true.'

Margaret, bowed forward, had buried her face in her hands. Her shoulders shook a little and he took a step forward, anxious to console. His hand hovered above her head and then fell to his side.

'You mustn't – you mustn't!' he begged. 'I shall forget what you said.' He paused hopefully, but fruitlessly. 'And you were justified,' he confessed. 'And you see, if John Blunt comes to-night, as Edward seems to expect, it will be all right. Perhaps by this time he has made the girl own up, and, anyhow, there's no proof, no proof at all.' He breathed deeply and seemed to wait for something; but still she did not speak, and very quietly he went out of the room. He thought he understood the overwhelming nature of her feelings.

With the shutting of the door, she flung herself backwards, laughing weakly, tearfully. In all her calculations she had missed this possibility. How could it have occurred to her? It was grotesque, fantastic, it could not be true! But it must be true, for Maurice could not have invented anything so ingeniously complicated, and misunderstandings so natural. And she could not feel an adequate anger. The very enormity of his blunder was impressive: it numbed her feelings, but she saw most of the links in this chain of circumstances which was being twisted round their feet, and she dried her eyes and began to dress with quick, nervous movements, foreign to her, and every now and then she laughed. The situation might be dangerous, for Maurice, in attacking Caroline, had hit on the surest method of rousing John Blunt's rage, but there was no denying it was funny. And she had not even thanked him for his kindness, for being so artistically true to type! There would have been too much cruelty in letting him see her laughter. He must never know that she had laughed, even if she had to lose the pleasure of enlightening him. But she was determined, now, to tell Edward everything as soon as he came home.

It was not a pleasant task, for she knew his anger would be formidable, to say nothing of his distress, and though she might retort that his own confidences had been reluctant and incomplete, there would not be time to quarrel with him, still less to let him quarrel with her. She had to prepare him for the next move, which was John's, unless Edward insisted on forestalling him, and that impulse she must frustrate if she could. She must try to make him see that Caroline's wishes should be considered, yet she knew that John's knowledge now made that argument useless. She must remind him that Caroline's mother had never broken her silence; but the destruction of the letter was almost a proof that, at last, she had, and once more she was forced to reflect that what seemed like good fortune was often the reverse, that the ultimate effects of action being incalculable, all human efforts seemed to be in vain, and she would have felt something like despair if she had not believed, in spite of all she said, in the value of intention. It had seemed good that the letter should be burnt, and now she longed to get it back and have her doubts set at rest: she felt she had a duty towards that dead woman, who had married in a hurry, but she could not name it when she tried, for if she served the mother, she might be injuring the daughter. She had an honest wish to deal righteously by Caroline and just as honest a conviction that they were all conspiring against her interests. She had made her own wishes clear enough, and, indeed, why should she want to lay claim to Edward? She might justly say that the connection was no honour. She had got what she wanted in John Blunt and there was neither sense nor delicacy in forcing her into a situation she had chosen to avoid. And again her decision wavered. But if John Blunt did come, how could she allow Edward to meet him without warning?

She was sure that whatever she did would be wrong in its results and her helplessness made her almost light-hearted. She was able to reward Maurice with the kind of smile she thought he would like best, and with another to defy Hilary's grave distrust of this gaiety.

'Father hasn't come home yet,' Hilary said. 'I've never hated thunder before. I think it must be because the dog's frightened. I do hope he's safe.'

'Oh, he's safe enough,' Maurice assured her. 'Perfectly safe, isn't he?' he added, looking at Margaret with bright significance.

Chapter 32: *The Bell Rings*

AT dinner, the dog lay under Hilary's chair, stiff with fright, and her few remarks were of a soothing nature, addressed to him. Maurice's efforts were valorous, but unassisted, and the chief voice was the thunder's, and that was growing fainter again, as if it were tired, or perhaps trundling off in search of other prey. Margaret did not trouble to talk. She suffered from a sense of unreality and, as Maurice had once seen her standing by the drawing-room window, like a character in a play, at the rising of the curtain, she saw this room, the dinner-table with its pretty china and bright glass and silver as the setting of a scene in a comedy. She supposed she was the traditional woman who never spoke the truth when it would save the situation, Hilary was the necessary young girl, and Maurice, of course, was the comic man. There was a temporary suspension in the action of the piece, but presently there would be a peal of the bell and the audience would know that the great moment had arrived. She looked at the comic man and she had a primitive desire to throw things at his bland face, to break the spectacles glistening in the candle-light and change his satisfied expression into one of dismay. It was a pity she could only like him when he was unhappy, but she foresaw grimly that her affection had every prospect of increase.

And still the pealing of the bell was delayed. It was a badly constructed play and the author had missed the perfect moment for his crisis.

'But I really do wish Edward would come home,' she said, as they all went down the passage to the drawing-room.

It was then that the bell was heard and Margaret stopped and looked behind her. She saw Maurice shaking a finger at her in playful reproach for her unnecessary anxiety.

'You see!' he said, smiling.

She disregarded him. She stood taut and much more like a character in a play than she was aware of, and Hilary, catching her alarm, said nervously, 'But, of course, Father wouldn't ring the bell.'

Maurice dropped his finger. 'No, no, of course not,' he said meekly and looked at Margaret.

She walked on slowly, with a little added indolence in her movements, to assure herself of her control. She knew who was at the door and before she reached the drawing-room, Alice had overtaken her, to say that Mr. Blunt would like to speak to her. He had refused to come in; he would not keep Mrs. Stack for more than a minute.

'Perhaps I could take the message,' Maurice said helpfully, but Margaret swept past him and went quickly into the hall.

She saw John Blunt, wrapped in the coat which had lately been hanging in his house. The collar was turned up and if it had not been for the hat, she would have thought the coat had taken a fancy to make a trip across the road, for John's head was lowered and he was no more than a bunch of clothes. Behind him, the rain, thinner than it had been, was slightly silvered by the lamplight, and it had the caressing sound of a shower in spring.

John raised his head and at once he was the man for whom she always wished to be at her best, and instinctively her last steps towards him became slower and more gracious, and her voice was welcoming as she said, 'Come in, Mr. John, you mustn't stand out there.'

He took off his hat and she felt her usual surprise that it could be so easily removed. 'No, I'd rather not come in,' he said. 'I hear the Vicar's out.' He looked at her steadily. 'I thought you would be able to tell me where I can find him.'

'He's somewhere in New Framling.'

'And do you know when he will be back?'

She shook her head. 'I haven't the least idea.'

'Then I'll just stroll down the road and see if I can meet him.'

'It's hardly the night for a stroll.'

He glanced at the dark sky. 'The storm's nearly over,' he said.

'Is it?' she asked and she did not trouble to keep a hint of wistfulness out of her voice. 'Well, I'll take your word for it. You'll remember you once told me I could do that. But why not wait till to-morrow?'

'I'm very anxious to see him,' John murmured, lowering his head again.

'And there's Caroline to think of,' she went on.

'Caroline?' he said in a strong voice and he looked at her keenly. 'Yes, I know that.'

'I mean,' she said smoothly, 'that she's rather afraid of thunder. Go and take care of her, Mr. John, or, at least, come inside. Won't you even come over the door-step?'

'No,' he said stubbornly, 'I must see the Vicar. As for Caroline, I don't believe she's afraid of anything.'

'She's lucky,' Margaret said curtly.

'No, she's brave,' he replied.

'It's the same thing.'

'Is it? For her? I don't know about that. And any-how, James is there.'

'If you think Mr. James is reassuring! Well, go and find Edward, if you can.'

'Yes, I oughtn't to be keeping you here, in the cold.' Again he took off his hat and held it while he gravely bade her good night, and she thought there was some-thing final, irrevocable, in his expression. He was not to be moved, but he paid her his tribute of appreciation and made her an offering of his regret, and only afterwards it occurred to her that he might have been thinking more of himself than of her, and sadly accepted what he believed must be her view of him.

She leaned into the street to watch him as he went, with his head down, like a dog on the trail, and before he had taken many steps, she called after him. She did not know how to keep him, but it was impossible to let him go so easily, and again she imagined him and Edward, shouting at each other, gesticulating fiercely, with the rain insufficient to quench their anger.

'Yes, Mrs. Stack?' he said politely. 'But please go in. I'm afraid you're getting very wet.'

'You force me into this position,' she said. 'You're an extraordinarily impatient man. Can't this errand to Edward wait?'

'No, it can not. When I've made up my mind to do a thing, I like to do it at once.'

'Ah yes,' she said quietly, 'and sometimes you regret it.'

She was as much startled by those words as he was and they stood and looked at each other in a silence which held many dangerous emotions in suspension: it seemed as though neither of them could break it and it was John who, at last, moved stiffly and spoke in a dull voice.

'But I shan't regret this,' he said, and he set off without another salutation.

She waited until she could hear his footsteps no longer and then she went in and shut the door and leant against it for a moment, and in likening herself to Maurice for adroitness, she found the only way of expressing her contempt for this new example of her folly.

It was unfortunate for Maurice that she caught sight of him, cautiously peeping round the corner of the passage.

'What's the matter?' she asked sharply.

She was his fellow-conspirator, and he came forward

with an air of secrecy. 'I was getting anxious. I thought you might need me.'

'No,' she said, 'one of us at a time is quite enough – more than enough. If anyone else comes to the door, you'd better have your turn.'

'Certainly I will.'

'In fact, we might have a little competition – competitive exercises in tact. But then, who would be the judge?'

She sat down on the chair with the curved legs and her dress, the dusky blue one threaded with gold, fell in opulent folds on each side of her. She clasped her hands behind her head and smiled at him.

'Of course, you'd have an unfair advantage, with all your practice in your parish. You're an expert and I'm only an amateur!'

Meticulously, he straightened his spectacles. He was afraid she was laughing at him: he was still more afraid of a sort of pleasant torture her mirth always roused in him and at once he renewed his disapproval of that dress; he was shocked by her attitude and the slim legs of which she appeared to be unconscious. They were remarkably slim for a woman of her age, and her feet were fine and slender, but then, what was her age? She had none. She would be like that when she was seventy, taking her charm for granted and expecting it to be recognized in the form of unlimited indulgence.

'I don't pretend to be an expert,' he said with dignity, 'I hope I haven't given you that impression.'

'Certainly not. I was laughing at myself. You're not nearly so funny as I am.'

'Not nearly so funny,' he murmured reminiscently. He would never be able to hear those words without a pang.

'Or so conceited,' she added, and before he had time to make a protest, on his behalf or hers, she said slowly, 'John Blunt has gone down the road to see if he can meet Edward.'

'Well, I hope Edward will have a pleasanter interview than he expected,' Maurice said with satisfaction.

'It will be quite different, I'm sure,' she said.

His lips twitched: he was trying not to show his consciousness of success, but she thought she had never seen a man who displayed his thoughts so readily: they took physical form in the colour and quality of his skin, which glowed damply, and even his body looked more lively in a limp fashion.

A quiver of rage ran through her, so exquisitely painful that it had to find relief. She was as bad as he was, but at least, she was getting her punishment, and he must take his, too.

'You fool!' she said in a low vibrating voice, and immediately the uncontrollable pain of her anger gave place to another. She felt a horrible remorse, as though she had struck a happy child. Maurice's rosy cheeks had turned a sickly white, tears had started into his eyes which were blurred and distorted behind his spectacles, and his figure, curiously crumpled, looked exactly like that of a Jack-in-the-box when it is pressed down in preparation for its spring, but Maurice did not spring: he looked helpless, broken: she had shattered his self-esteem and now she longed to give it back to him. It was a shame to have robbed him of anything so precious. There were tears in her own eyes and, acting as impulsively as she had spoken, she got up, with her hands out, and put them on his shoulders.

'Oh, my poor dear,' she said, and rested her forehead on the back of her own hand. She felt a limp arm round her waist and before it could tighten, while she was wondering if it would, the bell jangled again, urgently, as though it was determined to stop this strange embrace.

'I must go,' she whispered unnecessarily, for already

263

Maurice's arm had dropped and without looking at him she went to the door.

This time it was Caroline who stood there, bare-headed, and speaking breathlessly, as though she had been running for a long time.

'I've lost Mr. John,' she said. 'I don't know what he's doing. He wouldn't tell me. I believe he's gone to – to do what I told you. Mrs. Stack, how am I to get him back? You said you'd help me. I've got to get him back.'

'Yes, yes, I'll help you,' Margaret said soothingly. She glanced behind her and saw that Maurice was still standing where she had left him and that Hilary had appeared in the hall. She waved them away and turned back to Caroline.

'Of course I'll help you, but Mr. John has only gone down the road to meet my husband. They'll come back together.'

'And what would he do a silly thing like that for?' Caroline cried. 'He hadn't the face of a man who was going to do that. No, no, he's been different ever since that other one came to see him. I don't know what to do, and I'm alone in the house. I don't know where Mr. James has got to, either.'

'Hush, I hear footsteps now,' Margaret said.

Caroline turned and looked down the street. 'Yes,' she said, 'but it's not him. I think it's Mr. Stack,' and running out into the rain, Margaret saw Edward walking slowly and not quite steadily up the street.

Chapter 33: *Blind Man's Buff*

SHE had once told Edward that she had never felt a physical repugnance for him, but she experienced that sensation when she saw him in the light, and she found it intolerable that Hilary and Maurice, who had disobeyed her command and remained in the hall, should see him, too, with this silly expression on his face. And this, she supposed, was what the wives of drunken husbands constantly had to endure, but Edward could not be drunk, and she was horrified by the detachment with which she watched him as, very wet, smiling feebly, he sat down on her best chair.

For a moment nobody spoke and then Maurice said briskly, 'I think I had better shut the door,' and went to do it, lightly, quickly, with an air of being equal to anything.

'Where's Caroline?' Margaret asked anxiously.

Edward's look sharpened momentarily. 'What did you say?' he said, and he leaned forward, covering his face with his hands. 'I've had a terrible time,' he muttered.

'Let me take your boots off,' Hilary said, moving for the first time, it seemed to Margaret, since Caroline appeared at the door.

'No, I'll do that,' she said. 'Go and turn on the bath water and put a hot water bottle in the bed.'

Hilary went slowly, with backward glances, and Margaret knelt in front of Edward. She was rough with the sodden laces and when she spoke to him it was in a loud voice, as though he were deaf.

'Did you meet John Blunt?'

Edward dropped his hands to his knees and looked at her earnestly. 'I didn't meet a soul,' he said solemnly. 'Not a soul.'

'Did you come by the old bridge?'

He gave this question his serious consideration. 'Yes, I think it was the old bridge. I think so.'

'Then I don't know how you missed John.'

'You could miss anybody on a night like this. You can't blame me for that. And I got my black eye all right – or very nearly. Just here.' He touched his forehead. 'I'm a bit dazed still. Can you see anything?'

'No, I can't.'

'It will show more to-morrow. It will be black and blue in the morning.'

'Edward,' she begged, 'do talk sense. Did you come over the old bridge?'

'I don't know. I'm not going to commit myself – to anything. Don't worry me. I'm not fit. I tell you, I walked into a lamp-post and I've felt queer ever since. Those gas lamps aren't safe. They blow out in a storm. I had my head down and I didn't see it. If you'd let me have a hat like John Blunt's, I shouldn't have these accidents. John Blunt's better equipped. You can't hurt his head in a hat like that. No good trying to hurt his head.' He got up stiffly. 'I'm going to bed. I feel ill. But I did think you'd be amused about the black eye, even if you couldn't be sympathetic!'

Still kneeling, she watched him go towards the stairs and she signed to Maurice to follow him. She did not believe a word he had uttered. It seemed impossible that they could have missed each other. And where was John now? Had Edward tried to hurt him in spite of the hat and was the lamp-post Edward's name for John's fist? But Edward had never told her a lie in his life and, like a bright light, there came to her the idea that, if he told one now, it was

266

for the sake of protecting John. Dazed or not, he had had the sense to keep the truth to himself and he would tell her what had happened when he was with her alone.

Not quite satisfied with this conclusion, but accepting it for practical purposes, as a means of raising her from the floor where she had felt like remaining for ever, she was on her feet when Hilary reappeared, looking, in her pale frock, with her composed air, astonishingly remote from all this welter.

'Father's in the bath,' she said, 'and Cousin Maurice is standing outside the door, looking important. When I spoke to him, he whispered. Why?'

'Why indeed? You may be quite sure that Maurice always acts under some misapprehension. Always. About himself or somebody else.'

'Well, I suppose we all do,' Hilary said.

'Now, isn't that exactly like you! As soon as I attack him, you take his side. Yes, we all do, but not to Maurice's extent. What amazes me is that he's still alive. Forty-five years of hopeless blundering and nobody has killed him! It speaks volumes for the patience of human nature.'

'Do you want to kill him?'

'Oh, no, I feel for him. I'm like that myself, but I hide it better. No,' she said thoughtfully, 'I don't want to kill him. He's too soft. It would be like hitting a cat – no satisfaction in it at all. Dogs get hit but cats don't. There's no resistance in a cat. That must be the reason, and that's why Maurice has escaped.'

'But what is he misapprehending now?' Hilary asked, carelessly.

'His own usefulness, I suppose. He thinks he's taking care of Edward. He's keeping guard, ready for a faint or a fit, but he'd be certain to apply the wrong remedies, so I think I'd better go and relieve him.'

She was half-way up the stairs when Hilary said, 'Father looked very funny.'

'Yes, very. No wonder. He was wet through. And oh, Hilary, do get a cloth and try to dry that chair.'

'D'you think he's going to be ill?'

'No, I don't.'

'Really?'

Margaret smiled down at her. 'Faithfully,' she said, and wished she had been vaguer. It was generally wise to be vague.

'And did he see John Blunt?'

'I don't know.'

'And do you think he's still looking for father?'

'Playing Blind Man's Buff? I should think he has given it up by this time. It's a silly game for a wet night. Don't forget about the chair.'

She found Maurice pacing up and down, outside the bathroom, like a sentry.

'He's all right,' he said. 'I've heard splashing, but also – groans.'

'Edward groans very easily. It only means he has lost the soap. I'll go and find it for him.'

She was glad Edward had not locked the door, for she wanted a refuge in which she could burst out laughing at Maurice's delicate expression.

'Laughing!' Edward said reproachfully. He was sitting on the edge of the bath in his pyjamas and carefully drying his head.

'It's Maurice.'

'Maurice?' he grumbled. 'I don't think he's a very good joke. Not nearly so funny,' he said angrily, 'as my black eye! Does it show yet?'

'Not a sign.'

'That's unfortunate.'

'Is it? Why?'

'Because it may be very serious.'

'Serious?' she repeated. She found a sinister meaning in every word.

'Internal injuries,' he said impressively.

Yes, she thought, that was where they would be and, making another effort to get the truth, she sat down beside him and said persuasively, 'Edward, did you really walk into a lamp-post? People don't do such things. It sounds like a comic paper. Which one was it?'

'If I'd known which it was, I wouldn't have walked into it,' he said slowly, and smiled triumphantly.

She sighed noiselessly. Talking to him was useless. She did not know whether he was a little light-headed or lying cunningly, and she was not in a fit state to judge. Her mind was filled with pictures backed by rain, the ones she had seen and the worse ones she imagined, and she had a strange conviction that this man sitting on the edge of the bath, with Edward's face and his absurd, boyish hair, was somebody she did not know, that there was impropriety in her position and Maurice had been right to appear shocked.

She began gathering the sodden clothes from the floor. 'You'd better go to bed,' she said.

'Yes, I've got an awful headache.' He looked at her as though he felt, but could not believe in, her detachment. 'You don't seem at all worried,' he complained.

'Oh, yes, I'm worried. I'm quite properly worried!' she said.

'And if anybody calls, I'm not to be disturbed.'

'No, certainly not.'

She was at one with him about that and, comforted by this acceptance of his condition, he went obediently to bed, and he did not speak again until she had put out the light.

'There was somebody at the door when I came back. Who was it?'

'The Blunts' housekeeper,' she replied. She waited in the darkness for a comment or another question, but none came and, when she went away, it was like leaving a child to unhappy thoughts she had no power to dissipate.

She could love him when she compared him to a child, even a deceitful one, but as a man, with a foolish smile and pitiful prevarications, she could not bear to think of him. Without the smile and his concern, real or assumed, about his condition, she could have forgiven the prevarications for, after all, the had prevaricated herself and brought him to this pass, but she demanded physical vigour; strength and beauty, if possible, but strength, at least, and though he might have walked into a lamp-post or been assaulted by John Blunt, the cause could not make her lenient towards the result. This was inhuman, but she could not help it: as a man, he was almost negligible while he remained sorry for himself and desirous of sympathy. To a certain extent, he had always wanted that; it was one of his amiable weaknesses, and she wondered if there was a woman in the world who did not long, at times, for the perfect husband, the man who never said too much or did too little, the wise protector, the man who did not exist! And yet, what a dullness he would introduce into their common life. There would be nothing but patronage and gratitude in a marriage like that, the awed gratitude of a dependent female, and it was better to have reasonable cause for complaint, to have some one to fight and, best of all, to laugh at, but to-night her laughter was not joyous and what there was of it was directed against herself. She was to blame for whatever mysterious thing had happened out there in the rain, and she had not the decency to feel as she should towards Edward. She had been kinder to Maurice than to him, yet Maurice was consistently absurd. She had been able to pity him because he did not belong to her, because he did not matter; there was no secret standard to which he must conform; and she found a little consolation in attributing her cruelty to love.

But here she was, with two useless men in the house; across the road, or perhaps wandering in the night. Caroline was looking for another, and of these three men and two women not one was clear about the intentions, or properly understood the actions, of another. Among them all, they had made a pretty mess of things and across this thought there flashed her superficial annoyance at the milder mess in the hall. Edward's boots were where she had left them and his damp tracks remained. Alice, robbed of her duty of answering the door, was proudly pretending ignorance of Edward's return – that was the worst of these efficient servants – and if Hilary had dried the chair at all, she had done it very badly: Margaret could see it glistening from where she stood, half-way down the stairs.

The clock still ticked with its exaggerated indifference and there was another sound, muffled and regular, which she could not define until Maurice came within her field of vision: it was the sound of his pacing, felt-slippered feet.

He offered her a hesitating smile. 'I thought I'd better be on guard.'

'Against what?' she inquired coolly of this blundering man with the thoughtfully bowed head and the plump hands clasped behind him, childishly important in his self-imposed task.

'That's what I don't know,' he confessed, 'but I think you ought to tell me. I might be able to help you.'

'My good soul,' she said, 'do anything else you like, but don't try to do that. You've been helpful enough, and specially to John Blunt.'

'To John Blunt?' he repeated.

'Yes. I wonder where he is now.' She had a vision of him, running on and on, like a mad dog. He had snapped at Edward in passing and then he had gone on, and Caroline would never find him. She and Maurice between them had started something they could not stop. But he had not looked mad; he had simply looked determined, and now, perhaps, he was satisfied. There must be a great satisfaction in a physical assault, she thought, and she longed for the relief of smiting Maurice's slackly puzzled face when she heard him echo her again.

'Where is he now?' he said vaguely, and suddenly it seemed absolutely necessary to find out.

She stared at Maurice, forgetting him and her anger. It was not likely that Edward would take a blow without giving another: he 'had said himself that it was no good trying to hurt John's head: he had said that, but he had refused to commit himself – to anything.

'This is worse than my worst dreams,' she said in a dull voice, and she went into the unlighted dining-room and beckoned Maurice to follow her.

'Shut the door,' she said.

She could hear him breathing heavily and she had a passing pleasure in knowing she had frightened him: she knew his silence was one of dread. He was afraid of what she was going to tell him and of putting questions which would painfully enlighten him, and he remained near the door while she went to the window and drew aside the curtain. She wanted nothing in the world so much as a sight of John Blunt walking up the street, but it was empty and the Blunts' house was dark. The rain had almost stopped and the sky was clearer. She could see the Blunts' windows, like blind eyes, and the Blunts' door: even the knocker so assiduously polished by Caroline was visible but, as she watched, it slowly disappeared and wondering when she would wake from this nightmare, she realized that some one was opening the door.

It was only Caroline who stood on the pavement,

looking up and down the street, and then went back again, and the knocker, as if by some sleight of hand, returned to its place.

'He hasn't come home,' Margaret said.

'And I'm completely in the dark.'

'Yes, and I wish it was darker still outside.'

'Darker still?'

'Oh, don't say everything that I say! Haven't you an idea of your own?' she cried, and he answered ponderously, mournfully:

'Not one.'

Her laughter rang out inappropriately. 'That's a good thing,' she said. 'Don't try to get one. I want you to go down the street and across the bridge, as far as – well, as far as the second lamp-post, and come back quickly.'

'Come back quickly?' He coughed hastily. 'I mean – what am I to look for?'

'Anything you can find. But don't look as if you're looking for anything. You're just having a stroll. Do you think you can remember that?'

'Yes, I can remember that, but I think it would be wiser if you would tell me a little more.'

'I may have to,' she said, 'when you come back.'

She took him to the door, left it ajar, and returned to the dining-room.

Chapter 34: *A Bowler Hat*

IF she kept quite still in the darkness, perhaps nothing
dreadful would happen. She felt that on her immobility the security of the household depended. It was
not only Edward who must be left undisturbed, or
Hilary who must be prevented from asking those
silent questions of hers, but big, inhuman powers
which had to be placated and might reward her by
undoing what had been done. Behind her, as she
stood at the window and made a crack between the
curtains, she felt the cold antagonism of the room.
It was not used to being invaded at this hour. It was
a place where people had their meals and then de-
parted, leaving it to itself, and while she looked into
the street, she was conscious of the critical, unfriendly
room at her back. She wished she need not personify
inanimate things like this, for they could not be
trusted: their attitude changed with their owner's
fortunes. They were not like human friends who
would share trouble; they were not like Maurice,
out there in the dark, looking for something though
he did not know what it was. He could not be trusted,
either, but that was in a different sense, and she was
running the risk of letting him do his dangerous
best because there was no one else to help her. She
had to know whether John Blunt was lying injured
somewhere near the bridge, whether, to use what
she called Edward's paraphrase, the lamp-post had
been overturned. And if he was not there, where was
he? He had missed Edward and gone on to New
Framling, she told herself sensibly, yet it was practically
impossible for either to have missed the other. John

274

must have reached the bridge at much the same time as Edward. The bridge had a low, crumbling parapet and the tide was rushing out to sea. Was John Blunt going with it, his hat still firmly on his head? 'No!' she cried in a loud voice, defying the powers, careless of the inimicable room, and immediately afterwards she saw Maurice pass the window.

She stayed where she was and the door was stealthily opened, in a way which would have aroused suspicion in anyone who happened to be in the hall, but this consideration – and it was wonderful how Maurice always managed to annoy her, even at such a moment – was lost in an equally stealthy whisper.

'I've found a hat.'

If he had spoken loudly, she might have whispered: as he whispered, she said in normal tones, 'Oh, where did you find that?' and went to the mantelpiece to get matches and a candle.

By the light of the single flame, she saw a hard felt hat in Maurice's hand. 'Is there a dent in it?' she asked.

He turned it over. 'I don't think so. It's muddy. It was lying in the road, just this side of the bridge.' Holding it out, he said, 'Would you like to examine it?'

'To see if you've concealed a rabbit? It looks like John Blunt's hat. I don't think a rabbit will come out of that. But what will? What will? And how did it come off?'

'There's no wind,' Maurice said.

'Yet,' she said thoughtfully, 'it comes off much more easily than you'd think.'

'If he walked into a lamp-post, for instance,' Maurice said.

She looked at him with interest. 'So you picked up that idea, as well as the hat?'

'Yes, but it's of no use to me,' he said suggestively.

'So much the better. Give me the hat. "Give me

the daggers"!' Maurice might annoy her, but he
raised her spirits: in the face of his solemnity, she had
to be flippant. 'What shall I do with it? I must hide
it – but negligently, so that it can be produced – if
necessary. Will you go and keep Hilary occupied in
the drawing-room, while I mislay it?'

He set his mouth stubbornly. 'This isn't fair,' he
said. 'You call me – you call me a fool, and you don't
tell me why. You send me out on your errands and
you don't explain them. I did my best. It seems to
have been a mistake.'

She put the hat on the table and quietly took it off
again: a dirty hat, outside and in, and if its owner
had gone floating out to sea, she ought to treat it
with respect, but she laid it, gently, on the floor.

She looked at Maurice again. 'Yes. There's been
too much silence altogether, yet, when you broke it,'
she made a vague gesture, 'all this happened. One
doesn't know. One simply doesn't know. And I
don't know now. And I have to hide the hat. I
can't tell you now.' Her face changed. 'I'm terribly
tired,' she said, very low, and in a voice lower still,
he murmured, 'I can't bear this. Margaret, I can't
bear this.'

She looked up, smiling, not radiantly or mockingly,
but rather childishly. 'How strange to hear you use
my name,' she said. 'You don't often do that. But
everything's strange to-night. Lamp-posts and lost
hats! It isn't natural, is it? I'll put it – no, I won't
tell you where I'll put it. Go and talk to Hilary.'

She would put the hat in the hall cupboard, a
suitable place, not too secret, and with a conveniently
dark corner, and then she must go and comfort
Caroline and that would be a stranger mission than
either of the others she had undertaken. 'Third
time's lucky time,' she quoted, shutting the cupboard
door, but how could it be lucky when the father had
walked into a lamp-post and the lover had lost his

hat? It would have been easier to comfort Caroline if Maurice had not found the hat, and she had known she was wrong in sending him out. No one else would have found it, but he, with his short-sighted eyes, must needs discover it.

And now he came tiptoeing conspiratorially down the passage.

'Hilary isn't in the drawing-room,' he said.

'Then she must be upstairs.'

But she was not in her room or watching over Edward, who slept peacefully: she was nowhere in the house.

'It's worse to lose a daughter than a hat,' Margaret said.

'She must have taken the dog for a walk.'

'Of course!' This reasonable explanation steadied her altogether. Middle-aged men who were, in a manner, friends, did not resort to blows for argument or accusation. John Blunt had heard Edward's story without a word: why should not he tell one, and Edward hear it, with the same dignity? There were reasonable explanations for everything and John might have cast off his hat in the sudden conviction that it was not worthy of the man who was loved by Caroline. And it certainly was not: she could still feel its greasy dampness on her fingers.

She closed her mind to the facts that Edward had a hasty temper and would naturally be startled out of self-control, and that John had been outraged in his deepest feelings about that girl, and she said calmly, 'I'm going across the road.'

'Across the road?' His mouth twitched. 'You must try to be patient with me,' he said, referring to his repetition. 'And while you're there, what am I to do?'

'Pretend you're deaf and blind and dumb,' she said. She was being cruel, she had to be cruel to somebody, and she would make it up to him some day, if she had the time, if she had the heart, though he would never be able to make up for what he had done to her. Yet she herself had done worse to Edward, because she had not spoken in time. 'Silence is golden:' 'Third time's lucky time,' what lies these sayings were! They misled people at the most important moments of their lives. She gave the Blunts' door a push and found it yielding under her hand.

If she rang the bell, Caroline would think the police had arrived, so she stepped into the hall and called clearly, 'May I come in?' She could see a light in the kitchen and she advanced towards it when she heard a chair pushed back, but it was not Caroline's figure that blocked the doorway. She saw her daughter, who was lost or taking out the dog, and she held a basin in one hand and a wooden spoon in the other.

'Oh, come in,' she said hospitably. 'I'm making soup.'

'Making soup?' said Margaret, without realizing that she had caught the trick of Maurice's uncertainty.

'Yes, I said we ought to have some soup ready. I think Caroline has rather lost her head.'

Margaret looked round the kitchen. It was warm, bright and clean. Caroline had not lost her head to the extent of neglecting the house, and Margaret sat down in this cheerful place, for her legs were aching. The dog, lying in front of the hearth, wagged his tail lazily and looked up half guiltily. He was not sure that he ought to be there.

'What a lot of things people can lose,' Margaret said. 'Tempers and heads –' she thought of the dark object in the cupboard –'and hearts.'

'Yes, she's lost her heart, too,' Hilary said, stirring her mixture.

'And who is the soup for?' Margaret inquired. 'And how long have you been here?' She had a blessed, if fond, sense of relief in Hilary's presence. Of all the people she had seen during the last few hours, Hilary alone was in complete possession of herself. Her smooth, shining head, her tilted nose, as optimistic as Edward's, but neater, finer, her clear eyes and skin, were an omen of sanity and order, of light and peace, when they had all struggled through this darkness.

'I hope you don't mind,' she said with a slight embarrassment. 'You see, I heard what she said at the door and it seemed unkind to leave her quite alone. And I've made friends with her and Bob's made friends with the cat, and that ought to please Mr. James. And you said Father was all right –' She broke off. 'Is he really all right?'

'He's asleep. Where's Caroline?'

'Upstairs. Crying, I think. She cried a lot down here, but it was uncomfortable for her, trying not to, so I said I'd make the soup and listen in case anybody came. I've never heard crying like that before. I've never heard anybody cry, really, except children. It made me feel ashamed. I mean of being so happy.'

'I'm glad you've been happy,' Margaret said. Her great desire had been to make and keep Hilary happy and she wished time were elastic so that these minutes could be stretched out for ever.

'And she hasn't been,' Hilary said. 'I suppose it's because you're happy and Caroline's mother wasn't.' She put a saucepan on the fire and knelt down to pet the dog. 'She's been telling me a lot about herself,' she murmured, with her face against his head.

'Has she?' Margaret said, and she got up to stir the soup. 'Is that what made her cry?'

'Oh no. She cried because she's made up her mind that she won't see Mr. John again.'

'And why shouldn't she?'

'Well,' Hilary said slowly, 'I found out rather a lot I wasn't meant to know. D'you think it matters? I mean, I rather led her on. I knew everybody was worried and I was worried myself.'

'And what did you find out?' Margaret said, and she forced herself to stir evenly and slowly.

'But you know. Caroline said you knew.'

'Yes, but I want to know what you know,' Margaret said sharply.

'And it doesn't make a bit of difference. I said that before, didn't I? And Caroline agrees with me. She's had a good deal of experience of life. But I suppose it's easy to be tolerant about a person one loves. Other people wouldn't feel the same but then other people needn't know. Only, Caroline's convinced he's going to tell the police.'

Margaret breathed more easily and behind her the clear voice went on.

'Otherwise, why hasn't he come back? she says. She thinks he was going to see Father first and then he went on to New Framling. But she says he promised he wouldn't and I've told her he would never break a promise, and that's why I've made the soup. He'll come back. I'm sure he will, because I feel quite comfortable inside me. I'm sure I should know if he wasn't coming back. She wouldn't be comforted. She's made up her mind. And then she had to make out Mr. James has hurt him. He's out, too, you know, and she says he's been very odd lately, frightened, and spying on them both. She thinks he must have gone after Mr. John. But of course Mr. James couldn't possibly hurt him. He isn't strong enough. And when I told her that, she said madmen can do anything.' Hilary sighed deeply. 'I couldn't comfort her.'

Margaret pushed the saucepan aside and sat down again. She had forgotten James and, with the remembrance of him, she tried to reconstruct her confused theories which were hardly more than dreadful pictures, but her mind would not work: it was tired out: and it was almost indifferently that she heard Hilary begin to speak again, a little hesitatingly.

'I don't think she's quite sane, herself.'

Margaret opened her eyes for an instant and saw that Hilary, slowly stroking the dog from head to tail, was very carefully watching her own movements. This Margaret took as a warning that there was more to come, and she shut her eyes. She did not care what it was: her limbs were limp, her brain was numb.

'She's got something on her mind,' Hilary said. 'Something she ought to have told Mr. John. He was honest with her and she wasn't honest with him. That's why he liked her so much – because he thought she was honest, and she daren't tell him, in case he stopped loving her, and now she says she'll never have the chance. She seems to think they would put him in a dungeon straight away.'

Hilary paused and Margaret struggled out of her torpor to say, 'Go on,' And, after all, she thought, she need not have been so careful for Hilary's sake. All her efforts had been wasted, worse than wasted, for the child was taking this matter with the reason-ableness she had tried to feel herself, and John Blunt was lost and Edward had walked into a lamp-post and she had left Maurice in the house, free to commit another idiocy beyond her power of imagining, and it was all terrible and unnecessary.

'You'd better tell me at once,' she said. There must be no more of this secrecy.

Hilary gave a little laugh. 'It's really Cousin Maurice's fault. She says everything is his fault. He looked so prim and so suspicious that she told him a lie – about her age.' Hilary's voice rose a little. 'She isn't twenty-one. She's only twenty, but she was sure Cousin Maurice would try to send her back to her father if he knew she wasn't of age and she's never told the truth to Mr. John. At first it didn't matter, and then she was afraid. Don't you think that's a very small thing to make a fuss about?'

Chapter 35: *The Door Ajar*

FOR a few minutes there was not a sound in the kitchen. Margaret's relief was like a pain so great that it went, in some strange way, beyond the limits of experience and only her fear that Hilary would divine her state forced her into what was practically a return to consciousness.

So that was why Caroline had burnt the letter. How simple things became when they were explained!

'But she misjudged Maurice,' Margaret said, after a long silence. 'He would not have sent her back.' She was glad she could speak calmly, covering, with those sharp words, her immense thankfulness, her bitter regret, her sense of her own folly, which she knew she felt yet could hardly feel, and lest Hilary should interpret them correctly, she added that Maurice's intentions were not always bad.

'He manages to give that impression. He is unfortunate.' To herself, she said that he was not so unfortunate as he deserved to be, but, remembering him repentant, and also forgiving, faithfully doing her errands and perhaps happier in his bewildered service than he had ever been, she felt a kind of tenderness for him and she smiled at Hilary who was looking at her, puzzled, a little disappointed at evoking no expression of surprise. She ought to have shown her surprise, but she had concealed it with the rest of her emotions and she would never know how much Hilary had guessed or feared. And, she reminded herself hastily, casting aside her new-found peace, there was still occasion for more guessing and more fear, for where was John and where was James

282

and how could Edward have missed them both? And this new fact, coming so ironically late for her, could not alter what had happened, though it might excuse it. Yes, it excused it! her mind cried joyfully, and she sprang up, startling the dog.

'It's terribly hot in here,' she said. 'I'm going outside for a minute, but I shall come back.'

'Like Mr. John,' Hilary said in a tone which hovered between determination and persuasion. 'Of course he'll come back. Why, they've made all their plans! They're going to get married and go to some new place, and they think Mr. James will be happy enough with the cat. That's all he really cares about and a cat's the kind of thing you can always get another of.'

'Yes,' Margaret murmured, finding this innocent prattle unbearable, and going to the door, 'it's well to fix one's affections on something like that.'

She did not mean what she said. She spoke under the necessity of expressing, somehow, her conviction of her own inadequacy to deal with human beings. She had made every mistake she could. She had accepted Maurice's suspicion and made it her own: she had seen corroboration in everything Caroline said: she had not been frank with Edward and if she had failed to injure Hilary, it was because there was something graciously immune in the spirit of that child. And now, when she might have been rejoicing, she was faced with the dread of having brought a worse trouble on them all.

There was not a sound in the dark passage as she stood there with these dark thoughts: she saw emotions in the shapes of Edward and John and James, running through the night: she pictured Caroline, flung across her bed, giving herself up to grief, and suddenly, surprisingly, the girl's readiness to despair made her feel practical and sane. There had been a happy solution to one problem and she could not believe that Fate would give happiness with one hand and deny it with the other. Why should not John be merely searching for the hat he had impulsively discarded?

'Third time's lucky time,' she sang within herself, and when she stepped on to the pavement she found that the rain had stopped and a pale moon was struggling with the clouds. On the other side of the road, the long front of the Vicarage was all in darkness except for the fan-shaped window above the door. There was a little light in the sky, a little light in her home – she hesitated and then walked into the middle of the road. Yes, there was a light in the Blunts' house, too, shining from the window of the topmost room. A blessed trinity of lights! Now, surely, John Blunt would come marching stoutly up the street, but there was no one in sight and though she stretched her ears she could hear no footsteps from that direction. From the other, some one was approaching and she slipped back into the shelter of the doorway and in the reaction of her disappointment there came the thought that she ought to be with Edward, for to what memories would he wake? And the heart which had hardened against him because he had been evasive and looked foolish, was softened when she remembered that most touching unconsciousness of a grown man asleep. She would go back to him as soon as this wayfarer had passed.

He did not pass. She heard the footsteps stop and, looking out, she saw a man standing at the Vicarage door. It was John Blunt and he was wearing his hat, and with a sound which was half laughter, half sob and wholly thankful, she rushed across the road.

'You've come back!' she cried.

Slowly he removed the hat. 'Yes, I thought the Vicar might be home by now.'

She stared at him for a moment. She longed to put her head on his shoulder and cry. She thought it would be comforting to have his arms round her, but the arms belonged to Caroline and he would not know how to put them round his vicar's wife.

'Mr. John,' she said in a strained, uneven voice, 'will you promise to stay here for thirty seconds. I want to speak to Hilary. Don't move. If you're not here when I come back, it will break my heart.'

'I won't move,' he promised, and when she came back he said quietly, 'I've never seen a lady run like that before.'

'I could run for miles,' she said, 'but what I want is to walk with you to the bridge and we'll sit on the parapet, as we did once before.'

'I'm afraid it will be very wet.'

'Oh, Mr. John,' she cried, 'what does it matter on a night like this! It's a lovely night. And look at all the New Framling lights. Fairy lights! It's a beautiful place – when you can't see it! Hilary's keeping Caroline company, so you can spare me a few minutes. I wanted to tell you something. That story of Mr. Roper's – there was a misunderstanding. It isn't true.'

John stopped. 'But of course it isn't,' he said. 'I knew that. I was going to tell the Vicar about it. He treated me fairly, Mrs. Stack, and I wanted to do the same by him. He told me what Sarah had told him. Well, I wanted to tell him what Mr. Roper had told me. I didn't believe it, but it wouldn't have made any difference if I had.'

'I see,' Margaret said. 'I see. Thank you very much.' How simple things became when they were explained! 'You're a good friend, Mr. John. I was anxious about you, when you didn't come back. I – Mr. Roper went out a little while ago and he found a hat –'

'James's hat,' said John.

James's hat! That was why she had not liked to touch it. And here was another explanation. The world was full of explanations, but poor human

285

beings were blind. She had a moment of intense humility in which, as though a door was opened, she had a glimpse of mysterious things made plain, but John Blunt changed from one foot to the other and the door was gently shut.

'And where is Mr. James now?' she asked.

'Well,' he said, 'to tell you the truth, we had a bit of a scuffle. He followed me. Frightened. He didn't know what I was up to and – well, his hat came off. But I got him quieted. I took him along the river road and calmed him down. No use trying to find the Vicar with James in that state. But he's all right. He's looking for his hat now, I believe, and I came back the other way. I wanted a walk. I've had a lot to think about. You know that, I dare say.'

'Yes, I know that,' she said. 'And I'll tell Edward why you wanted him and, as we understand each other, I needn't take you as far as the bridge.'

'Yes, but I want to see Mr. Roper, too,' John said quickly. 'He said things about Caroline –'

'I know, I know, but you can leave that to me, as well. You've got quite enough to do without that, Mr. John. Do you know that Caroline thought you were never coming back? She's been crying –'

'Crying?' he shouted. 'Crying? And you've kept me talking –'

She had never seen a man run like that before, and she followed him very slowly up the street. She had never seen a lovelier night and, like John Blunt, she had a lot to think about. For this comedy of errors she could only blame herself, but all her emotions found their vent in laughter and she was laughing when she let herself into the house and saw Maurice sitting, crumpled, in his chair, keeping his unnecessary watch.

'All's well!' she said in a ringing voice and, waving a hand as she passed, she ran up the stairs and into Edward's room.

She went swiftly to the bedside and knelt down.

'Are you awake?' she whispered.

His arm went round her. 'Nearly.'

'Head better?'

'Much. I was rather frightened. I really didn't feel quite sane.'

'You didn't look quite sane. And that lamp-post story didn't ring quite true.'

'You should have felt it! I had my head down, against the rain –'

'Yes, I understand, but I want to tell you something. Can you stand it?'

'You've got such a heavenly voice,' he said drowsily, 'that I'll listen to as much of your nonsense as you like.'

Not yet would she tell him all the complications of this affair, but she told him about John and Caroline.

'Your Caroline's daughter, Edward!'

'Yes,' he said, and she felt him shift and stiffen. 'I thought I'd seen a ghost. You ought to have told me,' he said reproachfully. 'You oughtn't to have let me think I was seeing a ghost.'

At this characteristic remark, she smiled against the pillow. 'I know,' she said meekly, 'but I'm telling you now. You said I could choose my times and seasons. And for a little while, Edward, I thought she might be your daughter, too.'

'Mine!' he cried, springing into a sitting posture. 'Mine!'

'You'll make your head worse,' she said with a pleasant touch of malice.

'But how could she be mine?' Edward demanded indignantly. 'You surely didn't imagine –'

'But of course I imagined! Why else should you have been so conscience stricken about it?'

He sank back on the pillows. 'Because I treated her badly. I was morally bound to her and I broke my bonds. Do you think I like the memory of that?

287

Can't you understand anything but a physical betrayal? How do I know that what I did was not worse than that?'

Astonishment kept her silent. Yes, she had made every mistake she could and she did not know whether to feel admiration or impatience for Edward. He had no tolerance for himself and with this humility he clung to his belief in his attraction for that woman. And he was right. She had sent her daughter to him; she sent the best thing she had to the best man she had known, but in all her imaginings Margaret had not imagined such scrupulous delicacy as his. She began to shake with nervous laughter and, as tender-hearted for her as for the dead Caroline, he put his arm round her again.

'You're not crying, are you?' he asked.

'No. Laughing,' she replied.

He sighed. 'I shall never teach you to be serious.'

'Don't try,' she said. 'I don't believe we were meant to be serious. I believe God likes us to be gay.'

'God?' he said, wondering at that name on her lips. 'I thought you always pretended to know nothing about Him.'

'Yes,' She remembered that moment – in the street – when the door had opened. 'But sometimes He leaves the door ajar,' she said.